Acclaim for the author

'Smartly written, extremely readable, and gives us a fascinating and funny glimpse into the dark side of love'
Heat on *The Matchbreaker*

'If it's not a man keeping you up until 3am, it'll be this book . . . it's a diamond-encrusted, guiltily pleasurable romp'
Cosmopolitan on *Marrying For Money*

'Lots and lots of uncomplicated fun'
Heat on *Spa Wars*

'Nothing short of brilliant'
Marie Claire on *Seven Sunny Days*

'Very funny, hugely feel-good'
Fiona Walker on *Lizzie Jordan's Secret Life*

'Funny and inventive – prepare to be won over by an unlikely heroine' *Company* on *The Matchbreaker*

'Devour it in one go'
Company on *Ready Or Not?*

Crazy in Love

CHRISSIE MANBY

HODDER

First published in Great Britain in 2009 by Hodder & Stoughton
An Hachette UK company

First published in paperback in 2009

I

Copyright © Chrissie Manby 2009

A CIP catalogue record for this title is available
from the British Library

A format paperback ISBN 978 0 340 95191 0
B format paperback ISBN 978 0 340 93704 4

Typeset in Plantin Light by Palimpsest Book Production Limited,
Grangemouth, Stirlingshire

Printed and bound by Clays Ltd, St Ives plc

Hodder & Stoughton policy is to use papers that are natural,
renewable and recyclable products and made from wood grown
in sustainable forests. The logging and manufacturing processes
are expected to conform to the environmental regulations of
the country of origin.

Hodder & Stoughton Ltd
338 Euston Road
London NW1 3BH

www.hodder.co.uk

For Koren Shaw

ACKNOWLEDGEMENTS

With thanks to: the unbeatable team at Hodder, my esteemed agents and everyone I've ever flaked on with less than twenty-four hours' notice.

'Sometimes, when you have everything, you can't really tell what matters.'

Christina Onassis

I

Birdie Sederburg, heiress to the Sederburg Golf Resorts fortune, met her boyfriend Dean Stevenson when she bumped into him on Sunset Boulevard in Los Angeles.

'I quite literally bumped into him!' she would tell anyone who cared to listen. 'In my Mercedes!'

What Birdie didn't tell everyone is that she had been stalking Dean Stevenson for weeks, since being briefly introduced to him at the launch party for *PCH*. *PCH* was short for *Pacific Coast Highway*, the hot new Californian soap opera in which Dean played trust-fund surfer dude and loveable bad boy Mitch Macdonald. It wasn't much of a stretch for his acting abilities, trust-fund surfer dude that he was.

Anyway, Birdie was instantly smitten with Dean's beach-bum style. She loved his tousled blond hair, his intense blue eyes and the perfectly muscled flash of stomach above the waistband of his Quicksilver board shorts. She dragged her best friend Chipper Dooley (youngest scion of a family who made their money in medium-density fibreboard) into the ladies' room at the 1960s surf-themed party and – after much '*ohmigod*-ding' – she told Chipper earnestly, 'Dean Stevenson is *my man*. I felt that click. He is *The One*.' Alas, though she pouted and posed in his general vicinity for the rest of the evening, Dean Stevenson did not ask for Birdie Sederburg's number. In fact, he didn't even talk to her. Neither did he try to track her down after the party, as Chipper had assured her he would.

But from the moment she was born with the golden golf tee between her gums, Birdie Sederburg had been used to getting what she wanted. And thus, about three weeks or so later, when she saw Dean driving towards her on Sunset Boulevard in his new Lexus SUV with private plates, Birdie decided to take the initiative. Faint heart never won fair soap star. She made an illegal U-turn and slipped into the lane behind him. And when Dean stopped at the next set of traffic lights, Birdie drove right into his rear end. Three times.

'What the f—?' Dean was understandably furious.

Birdie was prettily contrite.

'Oh my God!' She clutched her head in her hands. 'My foot must have slipped. It's these shoes.' She waggled a narrow ankle and flashed a little red sole. 'They're Christian Louboutin. Wedges are such a nightmare. I'm sorry. I am *so* sorry. Perhaps you should give me your number and I'll take you out to dinner to apologize?'

'What?' spat Dean. 'I don't want dinner. I just want your insurance details. What the hell were you doing driving in those stupid shoes anyway? You've practically written off my car. Do you have any idea how much this SUV is worth?'

Of course Birdie knew how much Dean's car was worth. Every time she got even the tiniest snippet of info about Dean Stevenson's life and habits, she turned to Google. And thus she knew exactly what Dean's silver Lexus with the red-leather trim had cost him. Just as she knew that he always wore a Breitling diving watch (a twenty-first-birthday gift from his father) and his preferred surfing shoes were old skool-style Vans. He had them in twenty-three different colours. His shoe size was a twelve and a half.

Though the impact of driving her car into the back of Dean's Lexus would leave Birdie with back and neck problems that would require months of chiropractic therapy, she was otherwise delighted with the outcome of her daring little plan. He'd certainly had to take notice of her. She recited her cellphone number out loud. And the number of her landline and her fax machine for good measure. Then, while Dean picked his broken bumper off the hot tarmac and loaded it into the trunk for the drive to the nearest body shop, Birdie perched on the bonnet of her bright blue Mercedes and texted Chipper: 'Dean Stevenson has my digits!'

'Ohmigod!' Chipper texted in reply.

'So,' Birdie turned back to Dean, with a flick of her long blonde extensions, 'how about Saturday night?'

'What?'

'This Saturday night? For that dinner I owe you?' She dipped her chin and gave him her best 'Princess Diana' eyes. Vulnerable. Seductive. Ever so slightly mad.

Dean shook his head.

'Or Friday?' she asked instead.

No dice.

'Thursday? I could even manage tonight if that suits you better. Though of course, I'd have to cancel someone else ...' Birdie remembered a little too late that a girl should be seen to have options.

'There's really no need,' said Dean. 'I'm sure our insurance companies will sort it all out between them.'

'But you'll let me make it up to you, won't you? Personally? I mean, it would make me feel so much better. And you and I meeting again like this after the *PCH* party ...'

'You were at the *PCH* party?' Dean narrowed his eyes.

'Yes. We were introduced. But you were pretty occupied, being the star of the show and all that. Wouldn't you say it's fate that's brought us together again?'

'Fate? I'd call it bad luck.'

'Oh, well, the accident. That was bad luck, of course. But ...'

'I've got to get to an interview,' said Dean. 'Goodbye.'

'See you around?' said Birdie hopefully.

'Not if I see you first,' Dean muttered.

He climbed back into his car and drove off.

'He didn't say "no" to a date,' Birdie told herself. Not specifically.

Ignoring the angry drivers in the queue of traffic building behind her, Birdie took another moment to check her make-up before she headed back to the Sederburg mansion in Bel Air.

Later that same day Birdie sent Dean Stevenson a muffin basket via his management agency. Of course, she had already researched his representation. The day after, having heard nothing and figuring he was probably on some kind of diet that precluded wheat, she sent fruit. The following day, thinking that perhaps he had a fruit allergy, she sent flowers. When she still heard nothing in response, she called the agency and accused Dean's manager Justin Springer of keeping the gifts for himself.

'But I'm allergic to wheat and pectin,' said Justin. 'Also, I suffer from hay fever.'

'You have to understand that this is important to me,' Birdie reiterated. 'I caused a terrible accident and I want to make amends. I'd like to speak to Dean in person to confirm what you've been saying.'

'For crying out loud,' said Justin, when he called Dean straight afterwards. 'Will you just call this freakin' girl and put both of us out of our misery?'

'But she's a nut-job. She drove into me and now she wants to take me out for dinner,' said Dean.

'Perhaps you should let her.' Justin surprised him. 'I've had two people ask me whether you're batting for the other side this week alone.'

'You what?'

'At least call to say thank you,' said Justin paternally. 'A gift is a gift and it's not nice to ignore it.'

'I didn't ask for anything.'

'She's the Sederburg heiress. She may send a free golf pass next. I would like that. Do as you're told.'

And so Dean called Birdie to thank her for the gifts, which had been distributed around the assistants in Justin's office.

'They were really great,' he told her. 'Thoughtful.'

'So you liked them?' Birdie bounced on her bed with delight. 'What colour were the flowers?'

'Orange,' Dean improvised. 'Roses. Really lovely. Just right in my dining room.'

'What?' Birdie stopped bouncing. 'Roses? But I told them to send stargazer lilies!' She made a note to call her florist and demand that the person responsible for the roses get the sack.

Perhaps sensing that someone would lose their job if he failed to describe the contents of the fruit and muffin baskets correctly too, Dean moved swiftly to change the subject. 'Er, perhaps we could go out for dinner like you suggested?'

'Dinner? Do you mean that?'

'Of course,' said Dean. 'The only reason I didn't agree right away was, er, shock, I guess.'

'Ohmigod!' said Birdie. 'ohmigod, ohmigod, ohmigod.' She jumped up and down on the spot, flapping her hands and looking a lot like her name.

'It's just dinner,' said Dean, already slightly panicky.

Just dinner? He had *no* idea.

They arranged a date for the following evening. It was short notice but Dean had an unexpected gap in his schedule, thanks to the co-star he was meant to be kissing on a night shoot having developed an enormous cold sore. Birdie would simply have to let down the eight friends she was supposed to be entertaining at home. She'd lose a three-thousand-dollar deposit with the caterers and one of her girlfriends would vow never to talk to her again, but, really, this was so much more important. When he got the news, Dean's manager Justin secured a table at top celeb hang-out The Ivy on Robertson Boulevard. Dean had never particularly liked the food there but, as Justin pointed out, the place was always crawling with paps and this was an opportunity to be seen worth taking.

'Do I really have to do this?' Dean asked Justin the next morning.

'Are you sure you're the only person who has pictures of you dressed as Dorothy from *The Wizard of Oz* eating caviar off the Tin Man's silver-painted abs?'

Dean had to admit that he couldn't be certain.

And so another Hollywood romance was born . . .

2

Julius Sederburg was ready to sink his special silver-plated spade into the ground at the site of his new golf resort. He addressed the crowd.

'The Sederburg Grand Golf Resort Marshlands is the one hundredth resort in the Sederburg chain. I am delighted to be able to welcome you here today to witness the beginning of construction. You've already seen the plans, ladies and gentlemen. I'm sure you'll agree that what we're starting here today is something really special. I cannot wait to invite you all back for a round of golf when those five hundred luxury executive suites are completed and Jimmy here' – he indicated his golf pro – 'has finished designing my new course.'

In a gesture of rare generosity, Julius Sederburg handed the spade over to Jimmy Assise, one-time third reserve for the Ryder Cup team.

'Jimmy,' said Julius, 'I would be honoured if you would make the first cut in the ground today.'

'With pleasure, Mr Sederburg.'

'I look forward to my new eighteen holes . . .'

'Someone ought to rip you a new hole in your ass!' came a sudden cry from the back of the crowd.

There was a collective gasp from the assembled guests as they turned to see who had shouted something so vile. Sederburg's heavies made straight for a young guy standing by the drinks' table. Dressed in a grey suit, clean-shaven and with his dark hair neatly trimmed, he didn't look like the troublemaker he obviously was. Sederburg signalled for his security guards to hold back.

'Let him speak,' he instructed.

'Mr Sederburg,' the young man continued, 'Do you have any idea how valuable this piece of land is?'

Julius Sederburg chuckled. 'Of course I do.' The crowd laughed with him.

'Not just to you and your bankers, Mr Sederburg. To the people of the United States of America. To the people of the entire world!'

Julius Sederburg folded his arms and sat down on the director's chair that had been brought out in case the seventy-something got tired during the course of the ceremony. Jimmy Assise leaned on his spade. The young man took their relaxed postures as a sign that he should continue. He stepped up onto the stage to stand right between them and turned to face the rest of the crowd.

'Ladies and gentlemen.' He opened his arms to include them all. 'This patch of land we're standing on may not look like all that much to you. What can you see here? A bit of scrubby grass? A lot of mud? It would probably be improved by a golf course, right?'

A few members of the crowd nodded their agreement.

'Wrong,' the young man informed them. 'Because in these few acres of land, there exists a variety of wildlife you would not believe. There are species to be found here on this piece of marshland that exist nowhere else in the world. Extinction doesn't just happen in the rainforests of South America or on the plains of Africa. There are unique life-forms at risk right here in California. Mr Sederburg, if you push ahead with your plan to develop this piece of land as a hotel and golf course, their habitat will be destroyed. We will lose whole colonies of sea birds, small mammals, invertebrates and plants. We'll lose an entire ecosystem. The damage may go further than that. Your hotel won't just destroy this piece of land. The energy requirements of your guests will demand the burning of fossil fuels, mined in such areas of outstanding natural beauty as Alaska. The water required to keep your golf course green in this area, which does not naturally support the kind of grass you propose to plant will rob neighbouring areas of their water supply. The decimation will be vast. And for what? So a few privileged people can gain momentary satisfaction from getting a *birdie* where once a far rarer bird nested? Mr Sederburg, I beg you to rethink your plan to develop this area and, instead, mark the huge international success of your worldwide golf hotel chain by making a gift of these few hectares to the American people. That, sir, is a legacy that will truly make a difference.'

The young man ended his speech. There was no applause, but he felt pleased with the reaction of the crowd. Sure, they were silent, but as he looked around, he caught the odd nod. A few shy little smiles. One woman looked as though she was about to clap but paused with her hands in mid-air after catching her husband's eye. Still, the young man was convinced he'd made a positive impact on Sederburg's guests. Perhaps they weren't all heartless capitalists. He felt supported by their silence. He looked towards Julius Sederburg expectantly. The old man's eyes crinkled. The young man would have bet everything he owned that Julius Sederburg was about to give in to his plea.

'Young man,' Sederburg began. 'What's your name?'

'It's Nate. Nate Hathaway, sir.'

'Nate Hathaway,' Sederburg murmured. 'I'll remember that. You made a very pretty speech there. Opening remarks notwithstanding . . .'

The crowd tittered as they remembered how the young man's entreaty had begun.

'I apologise for that, sir. It was an immature way to attract your attention. I should have been more polite.'

'We all make mistakes,' said Julius Sederburg with a smile. 'Well, Nate,' he continued, 'you may think me a cold, hard old man, but my heart is warmed when I meet people like you. So full of youthful passion and verve. It cheers me immensely to know that there are still young men and women out there who are prepared to go to the wall for the things they believe in. Reading the news today, you could be forgiven for thinking that nobody cares about anything any more except what my granddaughter wore to last night's film premiere.'

The crowd laughed again. Gawping at Birdie Sederburg and her ridiculous outfits was practically the national sport. When the laughter died down, Nate Hathaway stood firm and hopeful.

'But the problem is, young man, like all too many of history's idealists, you're passionate about the wrong things. You talk about ecosystems but in reality, dear boy, it's clear you don't have a clue just how the world works. The American people won't benefit if I *don't* develop this wetland. If I do develop it, I will be creating jobs and prosperity. What does it matter to a family man in Torrance that there are rare corncrakes in California if he can't feed his children? What do you think the owner of the local Italian restaurant would choose? A unique species of newt or the opportunity to cater for a construction team two hundred strong? Ecology or economics? It's economics that most affects our lives.'

'But Mr Sederburg, that's such a short-term point of view . . .'

Sederburg silenced the young protester with a raised hand.

'That is the real way of the world. You're an idiot, Nate Hathaway. I could tell that the moment you opened your mouth. Now, since I very much doubt you had an official invitation to this gathering, I think it's time you left.'

Sederburg's eyes flicked in the direction of his security staff. Two enormous bouncers immediately flanked the unfortunate protester.

'Take him away.'

They did. Roughly. So roughly that some of Sederburg's invited guests began to murmur their concern.

But Nate Hathaway's protests and predicament were swiftly forgotten. For just as he was being bundled out of the area, Birdie Sederburg was sweeping in. She brought with her a couple of young starlet friends. The spectacle of so much young Hollywood loveliness soon distracted from the nastiness of the eco-warrior's ejection.

'I'm sorry I'm late, Grandaddy,' Birdie called.

'On the contrary, sweetheart,' said Julius Sederburg. 'For once your timing is spot on.'

The following day, news of the beginning of construction on the Sederburg chain's hundredth property appeared in most of the media. And as Julius Sederburg had predicted, it was his grand-daughter's outfit and not the eco-warrior's outburst that became the headline story. For the first time ever, Julius Sederburg was grateful for his granddaughter's ridiculous dress sense. Who cared about some bird when someone had managed to get a shot of Birdie Sederburg getting out of a limo wearing no knickers beneath her micro-miniskirt?

3

The reason why Birdie had been late for her grandfather's ceremony was, of course, her upcoming date.

Birdie was in ecstasy when Dean finally gave in to her suggestion of dinner, but a date with Dean Stevenson required a great deal of preparation. First there were announcements to be made.

On Facebook, Birdie changed her status message from 'excited about picking up my new Birkin from Hermès' to 'going crazy about tomorrow's top secret date with DS'. Anyone in any doubt about who DS was would only have needed to glance at Birdie's 'wall' where, moments after Birdie changed her status message, eleven of her friends posted variations on 'ohmigod, you're seeing Dean Stevenson!!!!', exactly as she had hoped they would.

It was only a matter of time before the gossip spread to the public domain. Within two hours of Dean putting down the phone, the news that he would be squiring Birdie Sederburg about town the following evening had appeared as a breaking news item on Hollywood's hottest celebrity website, www.Ohmygahd.com. Birdie was delighted when her email inbox pinged with a notification that she had made the top story on the site, even if the idiots at Ohmygahd insisted on including a link from the breaking news to a previous item on young Hollywood's worst dressed, wherein Birdie had made number two, behind Britney Spears. 'At least Britney can blame her condition on a nervous breakdown' the writers at Ohmygahd had sniped.

Like most of the gilded youth of Los Angeles, Birdie had a violent love/hate relationship with Ohmygahd.com. The 'Gahd' of the title was a chap called Adam Gahd (not his real name). A former bit-part actor, he had started the site as a means of venting his spleen against those less talented actors who were getting all the speaking roles that should (in his opinion) have gone to him. Gahd was a far better writer than thespian and he soon found that the popularity of his site kept him busy all day. It wasn't long before celebrity PRs were deliberately dropping him the odd piece of juicy gossip. And then the celebrities themselves joined in, sending Gahd the bad news about the people they hated. Overweight and unpopular in real life, Gahd quickly became an Internet star and soon no one dared cross him. These days he was a permanent fixture at premieres and parties all over town.

After her appearance in Gahd's Hollywood's worst-dressed list, Birdie had wished the evil gossip dead on several occasions, but that day she loved him for putting her name next to Dean Stevenson's in print. She emailed everyone in her address book to draw his or her attention to the site.

'Can you believe this?' she asked in faux outrage. 'Isn't a girl allowed to have a private life any more?'

In truth, Birdie's life in Hollywood was an updated version of that old riddle: if a tree falls in the forest and there's no one there to hear it, does it make a sound? If Birdie was the tree, then if the news about her falling off her wedges as she exited some restaurant or having a tantrum when she got a parking citation didn't appear on the Internet, it was as though it hadn't happened. These days, thanks to her iPhone, Birdie never missed a second of her life (though she had nearly lost her entire life on several occasions by stepping out in front of traffic while checking her status on a website).

Anyway, an hour after she made Ohmygahd, news of the date was breaking on Perez Hilton and Popbitch too. Birdie texted Chipper: 'Secret out. Mission accomplished'.

With the word out, Birdie could spend the rest of the day dressing. She cancelled her personal assistant Clemency's afternoon off because she would need help with various zips and buttons. Clemency reluctantly agreed in return for a hundred dollars in cash. She needed all the money she could get her hands on right then. The name on her birth certificate was Frank and having recently undergone sexual realignment surgery, she was saving for a bigger, better boob job to complete the transformation.

Following her decision to become a woman, Clemency had found it difficult to get even as far as a job interview, but Birdie was delighted when she saw Clemency's CV and read the attached letter. It wasn't that Birdie felt particularly strongly about equal rights for everyone no matter their origins or orientation. She simply liked the idea of having a personal assistant who could offer both a woman's *and* a man's perspective on the traumas of dating in LA. Plus, it was something to talk about over cocktails.

Birdie's best friend Chipper was also summoned. Chipper and Birdie had been bosom buddies since prep school, when they were both teased for their family business-related names. Fifteen years on, they still shared everything including a psychotherapist. Chipper arrived ten minutes after Birdie's call in her new BMW convertible, conveniently forgetting that she had been banned from driving on a DUI charge just a week before. This was an emergency, after all.

While Clemency was run off her feet fetching dresses and shoes that had been 'archived' in the further reaches of Birdie's enormous dressing-room, Chipper issued judgments on prospective date outfits from the comfort of Birdie's vast mahogany *bateau lit*. All the while, Chipper carried on an argument with her mother by text. It was regarding the whereabouts of yet another rare Hermès Birkin (which had not, as Chipper claimed, been stolen at some nightclub. It was covered in vomit in the boot of her car).

'What do you think of this?' Birdie asked of outfit one.

A classic tweedy Chanel suit was deemed too boring. A floaty dress by Alberta Ferretti was 'very last year'. A seventies jumpsuit by Halston smelled 'too vintage'.

'Didn't they have deodorant in the seventies?' Chipper asked. 'And this one?'

Outfit number twenty-seven.

Birdie twirled for her audience in a multi-coloured see-through kaftan with appliqué sunflowers covering her nipples. She accessorized with high-heeled raffia gladiator sandals trimmed in mink and a bag that looked very much like the kind of net you use to protect your lingerie in the washing machine.

'It has echoes of Balenciaga,' said Chipper. 'But . . .'

'How about if I wear my hair up? Like this?'

Birdie twisted her hair into a topknot, which she fastened with a parrot-shaped comb. She turned to her personal assistant.

'What's your opinion, Clemency? As a man?'

There was nothing Clemency hated more than being asked her opinion 'as a man'. She looked her boss up and down while inwardly counting to ten.

'Isn't that the exact outfit you're wearing on Ohmygahd's worst-dressed page?'

When the contents of her vast walk-in wardrobe had all been deemed unsuitable – 'What? Even the kaftan?' 'Especially the kaftan.' – Birdie knew it was time to shop. But shopping for Birdie Sederburg and Chipper Dooley was not a matter of jumping into the Mercedes and heading for the Beverly Center. That's what civilians did. A celeb like Birdie needed a different approach. She called her stylist.

Deanna Delaware, or 'DD' as her favoured clients knew her, was the hottest stylist in Hollywood, having totally eclipsed Rachel Zoe. Except that DD couldn't have actually 'eclipsed' anyone in the traditional sense: she was so thin she could have hidden behind a microphone stand. It's said that at a certain age (and DD was of a certain age) a woman has to choose between her face and her ass. DD had chosen her ass and thus she had the face of Mahatma Gandhi on a wheatgrass detox. Her outfits, likewise, usually had something of the alien about them. Still, enough people in Hollywood relied upon her to make them look good that she was able to afford a six-bedroom house just off Laurel Canyon. With pool.

It was impossible to get an appointment with DD without three months' notice, unless you were Oscar-nominated or richer than God. Birdie Sederburg was richer than God, so she had DD's secret number: the one for the Swarovski-crystal-embossed cellphone that only vibrated to the distress calls of the most VI of the VIPs.

As it happened, DD was expecting Birdie's call.

'I read about your date on Ohmygahd,' she said. 'I still can't believe they put that Balenciaga *homage* kaftan in their worst-dressed section! Those people have no style.'

DD was, at that moment, wearing a not dissimilar outfit herself. In fact, three of her clients had made that year's international 'worst-dressed' lists in pretty much the same look. Still, Birdie believed DD when she promised she would find the ideal dress for Birdie's first date.

'What's Dean's star sign?' DD asked.

'Aquarius,' Birdie responded immediately. 'He was born twenty fifth of January, 1983.'

'Then I'm thinking Age of Aquarius,' said DD, showing the startlingly original creativity her clients paid thousands of dollars an hour for. 'Meet me in Fred Segal.'

4

Fred Segal was *the* place to go in Los Angeles for unreasonably expensive rags that looked weird on the hanger and even weirder on a size-zero heiress. But the girls drew a blank there and so DD, Birdie and Chipper set off on a whistle-stop tour of Rodeo Drive instead. Accompanying her boss in case bags needed to be carried, Clemency tried to look enthusiastic as DD persuaded Birdie to spend the equivalent of a month of her wages on a dress that looked like a piece of BacoFoil. Used BacoFoil at that. It had the peculiar charred patina that comes of smoking crack.

'That dress will resonate with Dean's inner psyche,' DD assured Birdie as she rustled her way out of the changing-room. 'He will love it. It will let him know that you understand his Aquarian need for individuality and creative expression.'

Chipper nodded wisely in agreement.

Clemency nodded because she just had to see how far that mad cow DD would go to justify dressing her client in such a dreadful outfit.

'Now we need to accessorize,' DD announced. 'Purse first.'

DD found the ideal bag in 'Money for Old Rope', a vast vintage store on Melrose that smelled like the inside of a laundry basket.

'This is the one,' said DD as she handed her treasure to Birdie and Birdie tried in vain to find a comfortable way to carry it. The strap was too short to go over her shoulder.

'It's the perfect bridge between retro and modern. It recalls the classic vintage shape of a 1960s chiller bag.'

That was because it *was* a 1960s chiller bag. When Birdie opened the big white poly bag up to see if there was a dedicated space for her iPhone, Clemency and Chipper caught the distinct whiff of sandwiches past. DD pretended not to notice and Birdie continued to struggle to tuck the bag under her arm.

'Like a Birkin,' said DD, taking the bag from Birdie and demonstrating by hooking it over her own forearm in a manner guaranteed to cause tendonitis (as allegedly afflicted the eponymous Ms Birkin herself).

'I love it!' said Birdie, when she saw it hanging from DD's bony elbow. 'It all makes sense to me now.'

Clemency was glad that it made sense to someone.

Birdie handed over three hundred dollars.

After that, shoes were easy. Louboutin had conveniently made a pair of his famous wedges in silver patent for the summer.

'Take a size larger than you normally get,' said DD.

'Is that because Louboutins always come up small?' asked Chipper. Despite her family wealth and generous monthly allowance, she herself had never owned a pair of Louboutins. The new master of shoes simply didn't accommodate her man-sized feet.

'No,' said DD. 'It's because Birdie is going to wear them with these hiking socks . . .'

She pulled a pair in ribbed white wool from her handbag and had Birdie put them on.

'By the end of the summer,' she said, 'everyone will be doing the same.'

Clemency predicted Birdie's rise in the ranks of Hollywood's worst dressed.

Jewellery they found at the *atelier* of Ronan Esposito (a.k.a. a garage beneath a crack den in Venice Beach). At first Birdie wasn't sure about the earrings that DD picked out. They looked like a ping-pong ball cut in two that attached to the ear with a loop of red wool (which is roughly what they were). But DD persisted.

'These earrings complete the outfit. You either go with my

recommendations wholesale or you go with Rachel Zoe,' she said when Birdie pulled a face.

The threat of being excommunicated by LA's most important fashion maven was too much, so Birdie took the ping-pong balls. And DD took the difference between the retail price (five hundred bucks) and the wholesale price she'd agreed with Ronan beforehand (roughly a tenth of that).

With the elements of the outfit assembled, all Birdie had to do was sort out her hair and make-up. Clemency drove Birdie, DD and Chipper to 'Champagne and Set', the most talked-about new salon in Santa Monica (owned by another of DD's friends). There, Birdie, DD and Chipper sipped glasses of Cristal while Birdie had her nails painted a pewter grey (called 'Corpse') and three stylists transformed her straight shoulder-length hair into a helmet straight out of a sixties sci-fi special. DD insisted that Birdie's do be sprayed silver as a finishing touch.

'How do I look?' Birdie asked, as she emerged from her dressing-room in the full ensemble later that evening.

The truth was Birdie looked like she was auditioning for the first series of *Star Trek*.

'You look incredible,' said Chipper.

'You certainly do,' said Clemency. 'In every sense of the word.' She deliberately dropped a hairpin on the floor so that she could pick it up and thus hide the smile on her face.

'Will Dean like it?' Birdie asked.

'Dean will *love* it.' DD was insistent.

When Birdie arrived at The Ivy, Dean was already there, chatting to Justin on his cellphone.

'Holy cow,' said Dean when he saw his date. 'I think she's come as a baked potato.'

5

Unfortunately, Dean Stevenson was not such a good actor that he could disguise his shock at Birdie's outfit. Fortunately, Birdie didn't particularly care. As she walked into the Ivy and took her place opposite the man she'd had a crush on for months, she was far more concerned with who else might be in the celebs' favourite restaurant than how her date reacted to her new look.

'Is that Benicio Del Toro?' was the first thing she said.

'I think so,' said Dean.

'He's shorter than I remember. Did I tell you that I met him at Grandaddy's golf resort in Phoenix?'

The evening proceeded in a veritable flurry of name-dropping and swapping. Neither of the young lovers ate very much. Birdie's BacoFoil wrap was too tight to allow for the passage of anything but a bite of chargrilled chicken. Meanwhile, Dean had developed a horror of eating in public after a pap got a shot of him stuffing down a fajita and the pic appeared in an English gossip mag under the heading 'Who ate all the pies?' He'd lost a lot of weight since then so now, when he did have to take a bite, he did it quickly, making sure his mouth was shut again before anyone saw it open. For the same reason, he had recently become paranoid about scratching his nose (a nose scratch could easily look like a nose *pick* in a photo), which meant that it itched pretty much all of the time.

So, the young lovers didn't eat. Neither did they drink. The most popular club in LA that month was AA. Starry-eyed hopefuls arriving in Tinseltown soon realized that joining Alcoholics Anonymous was equally effective as a way of getting to meet the people in power as hanging out at the right nightspots. It was certainly cheaper than cocktails at the Sky Bar. That didn't mean to say that either Birdie or Dean were teetotal. In fact, Birdie had necked a small bottle of vodka while getting dressed, to help steady her nerves. If not to help her walk in those wedges.

The vodka seemed to be working. Birdie felt very relaxed. She was gratified to see Dean's gorgeous eyes crinkle into a smile on several occasions and not just at the texts he received every couple of minutes, she was sure. When Dean excused himself to go to the men's room, Birdie immediately texted Chipper. 'Date going fabulously. Outfit a big hit. Everyone in the place is checking me out.'

When Dean returned from the rest room, Birdie was still texting, DD this time, to tell her that the crowd was loving her ensemble (Birdie didn't differentiate between admiring looks and the double takes that said, 'Is she really carrying a chiller bag?'). Birdie wasn't apologetic when Dean caught her SMSing. There was no need, since Dean was absorbed in sending his own message to Justin. 'How much longer do I have to stay?' his text asked.

'Have dessert,' was Justin's response. 'I just fielded a call from a magazine asking if you would be willing to talk about your "manorexia".'

So Dean insisted that they order a sticky toffee pudding.

'Two spoons?' Birdie suggested.

Dean agreed. Though less out of romance than concern for his figure. He would have to do an extra fifty crunches the following morning, but it was a necessary evil. People hoping to get a scoop on a celebrity lurked everywhere. Justin was right. You skipped dessert, next thing you knew there was speculation about a tragic eating disorder. But if you finished a whole dessert on your own, you'd soon draw comparisons with Vegas-era Elvis. Dinner in Los Angeles was a minefield for anyone with a famous face.

The sticky toffee pudding was returned to the kitchen minus two bites and finally, not a moment too soon for Dean, the bill was paid and the date was almost over.

'It has been so great getting to know you,' said Birdie. 'But I feel that there's so much more to talk about. Don't you?'

Dean avoided the question of another date by calling the waitress over and asking her if service was included. The waitress was only too happy to hover and chat. She asked Dean to sign her pad. Birdie pursed her lips. Dean shrugged.

'I'll guess I'll have to get used to these nobodies bothering us,' said Birdie, which worried Dean. A lot.

Hearing Birdie's snipe, the waitress asked whether she would like her leftovers to take home.

'I mean,' she said, 'seems a terrible shame not to when you've brought your own chiller bag . . . '

Birdie bristled. But at last the waitress had to get back to work and Birdie and Dean were alone once more.

'Walk me to my car?' she asked.

He couldn't refuse. If only to make sure that she left.

As Birdie got to her feet, she wobbled a little in her wedges, like a newborn deer. Dean had been raised to have impeccable manners and so he stuck his arm out to help Birdie down the steps to the street. She was delighted. The paps let off a volley of shots. On the pretence of taking another stumble in her shoes, Birdie leaned heavily into Dean's side. He had no choice but to put his arm right around her. She beamed up into his face. Both Birdie and the paps got exactly what they wanted.

6

Not everyone had such a fun evening as Birdie Sederburg. After his daring speech at the inauguration of the building works at the new Sederburg Golf Resort, Nate Hathaway spent a night in the cells.

On his release from the police station, Nate made his way back to the house in Santa Monica he shared with his friends Melanie, Tony and Jason, a.k.a. Mother Nature's Avengers. Like Nate, his friends were passionate about the environment. Jason, for example, had spent six months living in the branches of a Giant Redwood to prevent it from being chopped down to make way for a development of executive homes. Melanie had streaked across the pitch at several large sporting events to make her point about pollution. Tony pontificated. A lot.

'Nate, man!' Jason clapped him on the back. 'It's so good to see you. You did it. You got in there. We are all so proud of you, man. You are the fucking bomb!'

Jason led Nate into the lounge where his fellow eco-warriors were assembled around a bong. It was ten in the morning.

'Hey, Nate!' He was greeted warmly. 'We saw you on TV.'

'Awesome,' said Tony, who had dropped out in the sixties and was still falling. 'You really told Sederburg where it's at.'

'I was so proud of you,' said Melanie, planting a kiss on Nate's cheek. Nate reeled slightly from the smell of patchouli oil. It was the one aspect of hippy life that he had never come to appreciate.

'Want a hit?' Tony extended the bong pipe towards him.

'No thanks,' said Nate. 'Not now. I've got things to do.'

'Like what?'

First on the list was a call to his lawyer who was investigating the possibility of Nate pressing charges against Sederburg's heavies.

'Suit yourself,' said Tony, collapsing back into the pillows with a sigh. Melanie followed, giggling. Weed did that to her.

'So,' said Jason, pulling Nate into the kitchen. 'Tell me all about it. I'll fix you some herbal tea.'

Oh God, thought Nate. Not herbal tea.

Nate had never quite understood why being environmentally friendly seemed to equate to being quite so, well, skanky. There were eco-friendly detergents out there. And cutting your hair didn't damage the ozone layer, as far as Nate could tell. He'd tried to raise the subject with Jason once before.

Jason looked the part of a fairly typical eco-warrior. He had long grey-blond dreadlocks and a beard that acted as a handy portable larder. Jason believed that consumerism was evil. Full stop. To the extent that he had not bought anything but life's essentials (food, gas and a subscription to cable TV) for the past seven years. His trousers were a series of holes in search of a shape. He didn't own an intact pair of socks. On the other hand, thought Nate as Jason embraced him at the door, perhaps it was for the best that Jason's clothes were well ventilated. He hadn't washed since he climbed up the tree and 'learned the truth about man's place in nature', which did not include hot running water or soap.

'The thing is,' Nate told his dear old friend, 'if we want to be taken seriously by the establishment, then we've got to approach this as if we were approaching a job interview at one of their corporations. You turn up in those trousers, you're not even going to make it into the lobby. Turn up in a suit, like I do, and they might just give you five minutes.'

'A suit? How does that fit in with my stance of anti-consumerism?'

'You don't have to buy a suit. You can borrow one. You and me, we're about the same size. I could lend you one of mine.'

'You've got more than one?' Jason was incredulous.

'I was studying to be a lawyer, remember? It seemed important then.'

Jason shook his head. 'I see what you're trying to say, but I'm not buying it. Why should I have to change the way I am? I'm on the side of good. I don't need to disguise myself. The way I see it, you look like one of them, you start acting like one of them. You start acting like one of them, you end up thinking like one of them. Before you know it, you *are* one of them. Sometimes I wonder whether you're actually one of us, Nate. I really do.'

Now it was Nate's turn to shake his head. There was no way he was going to persuade Jason to see things his way that day.

The funny thing was, Jason had grown up with a great deal more privilege than the average guy. Jason was the youngest son of a wealthy family who had made their money in plastics. He'd attended the best prep school in America. He followed that with a stint overseas in the UK, at Harrow. His vacations had been spent in all the right places: sailing off the Hamptons, skiing in Gstaad. It was while he was at college in California that Jason chose to abandon the values that his father and mother had paid so much to instill in their only son. He fell in with a crowd that did a lot of drugs and justified it to himself by saying that their lifestyle was about environmental integrity, not just getting wasted.

Nate's beginnings were altogether more humble. He attended the local school. He had a Saturday job at the local video store to raise money for his first car. He had never been outside the United States until he joined his high-school football team on a tour of Australasia. He got a scholarship to college, which was where he'd met Jason when they both minored in Psych.

Likewise, Nate's conversion to a greener way of life had happened very differently to Jason's. There had been no sudden flash of inspiration born of a hit of particularly strong skunk. Nate's moment of clarity came when he was very sober indeed. He had hiked to the top of a mountain to scatter his father's ashes. It was a spot that had special significance for him, being the high point of a hike that he and his father had made together many times. This time, Nate was with his father's younger brother, Marcus.

As they paused for a rest and looked out over one of the most beautiful views in the world, Uncle Marcus turned towards his nephew and said: 'You see how narrow that river's got since we were last up here? That's because they're diverting most of the water into a new development of luxury homes on the other side of the ridge. The local farmers are going crazy but it seems like there's nothing they can do. The river goes through the rich guys' land first.'

Later on that trip, Nate read up about the development and the scandalous way in which the rich developers had taken water from the poorer farmers, forcing some to leave a way of life that had supported their families for generations. In a bar one night, he heard the story from one of the old farmers himself.

'Nobody cares,' the farmer sighed. 'It's all about the short term.'

Well, now Nate cared. He'd studied law because he cared about justice and this was one of the clearest cases of injustice he had ever seen. He decided to get involved in memory of his dad.

It was shortly after that weekend that Nate met up with his old friend Jason again at a party. Jason told him that he was setting up a commune based around green living principles in Los Angeles. It sounded as though he had plenty of good ideas and energy. Nate signed up on the spot.

Sadly, Mother Nature's Avengers hadn't turned out to be the dynamic bunch of truly concerned people that Nate had hoped to meet. But having given up his position as a trainee lawyer, he needed somewhere to live. And he was optimistic that over time and under his influence, the commune would become better organized and more effective as a result.

One thing Nate knew for sure was that the only way to persuade someone to really listen to your point of view was to first convince them that you cared about theirs. And that meant talking their language. Camouflaging yourself in the clothes that made them think you respected their way of life. That was why Nate still sported a short haircut that wouldn't frighten anyone's grandma. It was why he still washed. His were the kind of looks that wouldn't have been out of place in a catalogue for Abercrombie and Fitch. Unlike Jason's Aber*crumb*ie style.

He tried one more time on the morning he got out of custody.

'I'm pretty certain I got treated differently because I didn't look like the average eco-warrior. If I hadn't been wearing a suit, I wouldn't have got anywhere near Sederburg. I certainly wouldn't have been allowed to speak. I wouldn't have made the news. And I would still be in jail.'

Jason nodded distractedly.

'Sure thing, bro. We all appreciate what you put yourself through. And we know that we've got to capitalize on your gains. That's why Tony and me have been putting together a new plan of action for the next three months. There's a new development going up near Calabasas. They're going to have to take down three acres of indigenous California forest. Tony, Melanie and me are going to go up there and chain ourselves to the construction equipment. Melanie found these great adult diapers online. Like the one that astronaut wore when she went to kill her love rival? If we all wear those, I reckon we can last out a week before anyone moves us. Long enough to set that project right back on the drawing-board.'

'What?'

Nate blanched at the thought of adult diapers. So far he had managed to steer clear of any protest that involved sitting in his own excrement. The very idea of it made him want to be sick.

But Jason's eyes sparkled as he described the plan that he and the others had come up with while Nate spent the night in jail with a load of uncomfortably flirtatious drug pushers.

'It's going to be a blast. We'll take the bong, of course. Since we're going to get arrested anyway, it hardly matters if we've got our drugs.'

'Wrong,' said Nate. 'It does matter. You're proposing to chain yourself to a digger wearing a diaper. And you're going to smoke weed while you do it. Jason, do you think that is going to win any sympathy whatsoever with the people of middle America? Do you think any hard-working guy, any church-going grandmother is going to look at news coverage of you monged out of your brain and think 'good for you'? They're not going to make the connection between your actions and your environmental integrity. They're going to think you tied yourself to a bulldozer because you were high on crack.'

Jason stared at Nate.

'You finished laying down the law?' he asked. 'You want to tell me how to talk to the man again?'

'*Talk to the man?* Jason, it's the twenty-first century, not the 1960s. You weren't even born until 1986. Will you please wake up and see that we're not fighting the 'man' any more? That kind of protest is old hat. No more protest. What we need to focus on is persuasion. You can count me out of the diaper thing.'

'You're losing your nerve,' said Jason.

'You need to lose your naivety.' Nate got up and headed for his room.

'You want to get kicked out of the community?' Jason called after him. ''Cause that's the way you're going, bro!'

'Yeah, yeah,' said Nate. 'Whatever.'

In the privacy of his room, Nate turned on his computer and logged in to check his bank account. He was running out of money. Never mind chaining himself to a log. He had to find some work.

*　　*　　*

Predictably, Jason's resolution not to talk to Nate didn't last for long. By six in the evening, he was tapping on Nate's door, asking for help to move the furniture. That night, the house was hosting a party for Melanie's birthday. She thought it was her thirty-first. Nate didn't feel much like partying, but he relented and helped Jason carry the TV into Nate's room, which was the only one with a working lock on the door. Parties at the green house tended to be fairly organic affairs and they had learned the risks of admitting all-comers the hard way, when some previous uninvited guests left with Jason's stereo.

When they had finished humping gear, Jason offered Nate his hand in a gesture of conciliation. They shook and Nate slapped Jason on the back.

'Let's just forget about it for this evening,' said Jason. 'Get drunk, get high, enjoy all the pretty ladies.'

The doorbell announced the arrival of the first guest.

7

The pictures of Birdie's first date with Dean appeared on www.Ohmygahd.com the following day. Birdie was delighted. She immediately linked the best of the shots to her own page on Facebook, appending them with the note, 'Can you believe this invasion of my privacy? Why on earth won't the paps just leave me alone?'

Justin was equally pleased with the exposure.

'You make a good-looking couple,' he told Dean. 'Her outfit notwithstanding. What was she thinking? You should go out with her again.'

'What?'

'Do it,' said Justin. 'The figures for the latest episode of *PCH* were shaky. It's all about getting the exposure your good looks alone won't manage.'

Dean dutifully called Birdie up and asked her out. The phone call lasted one minute and fifty-seven seconds. As soon as Dean hung up, Birdie spent one hour and fifty-seven minutes dissecting the call with Chipper. Word by word, they took the conversation apart, analyzing content and tone and coming to the conclusion that Dean was head over heels. Birdie would have liked to talk to Chipper for longer but the insistent ringing of the doorbell interrupted her.

'I don't know what the hell is going on,' she said to Chipper. 'That doorbell just keeps ringing. Will you excuse me a moment?'

Chipper said she would.

'Clemency!' Birdie yelled down the stairs. 'Clemency, will you get the frickin' door? What do I pay you for?'

Birdie had forgotten that Clemency had the night off. Her first one in a month. And so, eventually, Birdie had to go downstairs herself. She looked out through the spyhole and saw her gardener standing on the front step. When Birdie opened the door, he took off his baseball cap and twisted it in his hands like a Victorian manservant.

'What do you want, er . . .' Birdie couldn't remember his name.

'Mitchell,' said the gardener. 'My name is Mitchell, Ms Sederburg.'

'Well, Mitchell, what do you want? Is there something wrong with the sprinkler?'

'I've come to collect my wages, Ms Sederburg. I talked to Clemency about it. I'd really like to have it in cash this month.'

'What?' Birdie spat at him. 'Cash?' She made it sound like 'crack'.

'It's my little girl's birthday this weekend. I want to make it special.'

'And what's that got to do with me?'

'I arranged it with Clemency. She said she would talk to you about getting me the notes.'

'Well, she didn't.'

'Just a few hundred dollars to tide me over. I'm kinda short right now.'

'I don't ever carry that much cash. It ruins the line of your clothes.'

'Perhaps you could drive to a machine. I know there's one in the drugstore at the cross-section of Sunset and Laurel Canyon. I'd really appreciate it.'

'What?' Birdie narrowed her eyes.

'I've worked for you and your grandfather for eleven years, Ms Sederburg, and this is the first time I've needed a favour.'

'And the first time will doubtless lead to a second. I can't make an exception for you no matter how long you've been on my staff. If I give you cash, Michael—'

'Mitchell,' corrected the gardener.

'Whatever. If I give you cash, I'll have to give cash to everybody. You will get your wages at the end of this month, when my accountant pays everybody. And you will consider that pay packet as your last one from me. Don't bother turning up tomorrow.'

'What?' Mitchell was astonished.

'You heard me. You can pack up your equipment right now. Your services are no longer required.'

Birdie shut the door in Mitchell's face. Then she went back inside to finish her phone call. It didn't help her mood that Chipper had already hung up and sent an SMS saying, 'Going out.'

In a foul temper, Birdie called Clemency. Clemency didn't pick up.

'I don't know what you told that gardener,' Birdie said in her message, 'but he practically threatened my life. I suggest you sort it out first thing on Monday. And second thing on Monday, you can find someone new to mow the lawn. Or I'll find someone new to be you as well. Pronto.'

Feeling a little better after her outburst, Birdie went back to admiring the pictures of her and Dean on Ohmygahd. She really loved the shots taken just outside the restaurant where she was holding on to his arm to keep steady in her Louboutins. The silver ensemble had been a great idea, she decided. Birdie thought her tan glowed particularly well against silver. After gazing at the photos for another half hour, she spent a further hour in her dressing-room, picking out an outfit to wear to meet Chipper in the bar at the Chateau Marmont. She settled on an emergency orange jumpsuit and accessorized with a pair of diamond ear-clips that had once belonged to Christina Onassis.

8

Clemency had not grown up in Los Angeles. She was born in Denver and lived a thoroughly ordinary life there as a small boy, with no hint that in the future she would be a woman, working as a personal assistant to a ridiculously wealthy heiress. If someone had told four-year-old Frank that one day he would be heading out for a party in Los Angeles wearing a pair of gold leather hot pants, he would have been very surprised indeed (though more than a little intrigued).

Clemency was in a great mood as she drove out on Highway 10 towards the beach. Since she'd arrived in LA she had dressed her boss for plenty of parties, but this was the first one she would be attending in her own right. Admittedly, it wasn't a lavish bash being held by *Vanity Fair* or *InStyle*, but the invitation still meant a lot to her, proving as it did that at last she had an LA life of her own.

The party hostess was a girl called Melanie Delfont. Melanie and Clemency had attended elementary school together. As a small boy, Clemency had greatly admired Melanie's style. She loved her bouncy blonde pigtails and the little pink dresses she wore in the summer. Meanwhile, Melanie liked the fact that, unlike the other boys in her class, Clemency did not express her affection via the medium of Chinese burns. They had lost touch with each other when they both went off to college, but lately, thanks to Facebook, they were back in contact again. Melanie was the first person from Clemency's old life to hear about the sex change.

'I totally understand,' Melanie wrote in her heartfelt response. 'You gotta be who you want to be.'

There had followed a lovely correspondence in which Melanie confided that she had changed too. She had, she told Clemency, learned about the true value of life since becoming eco-conscious. 'I've grown a whole lot,' she confided.

Clemency looked forward to unveiling her new incarnation for the girl who had meant so much to her as a child. Once they were properly reacquainted via this party, Clemency hoped that Melanie would be happy to hang out as girlfriends. They could go shopping together. Clubbing. Maybe they could even double-date.

As she parked on the street where Melanie now lived with a chap called Jason, who came (according to Google) from a very wealthy family, Clemency checked out her reflection in her rear-view mirror. She was looking good, she decided. And she knew that her legs were amazing. If Melanie still had that great tiny waist and enormous boobs, then she and Clemency would be unstoppable. Melanie's blonde to Clemency's brunette. They'd be like two thirds of Charlie's Angels. Clemency slicked on some more red lipstick and prepared herself for the reunion.

The first hint that the evening might not turn out as Clemency hoped came when she found the address at which the party was being held. Though Melanie lived in an upscale neighbourhood, her house looked as though it had just blown in on a hurricane and landed on an empty plot in a hail of used car parts. The paint was peeling off the boards. At the windows hung tattered old flags and sarongs in lieu of curtains. It was so unexpectedly awful that Clemency actually got out her iPhone and checked the address against the one Melanie had sent in her last email. But there was no mistake. Melanie lived in a hovel.

Standing on the rotted front step, Clemency rang the bell. She had driven such a long way to be there, she might as well have one drink. Hearing footsteps heading for the door, she plastered on her best smile. And was rewarded by an incredible smile in return. The man who opened the door and ushered her inside was quite delicious. His good looks robbed Clemency of the power of speech.

'Is . . . er . . . '

'Are you here for Melanie's party?' he asked. 'Excuse the mess.'

'Oh no,' said Clemency, almost fainting with delight as the man offered her his arm to help her step into the house without falling down a hole in the floorboards right behind the door. 'It's just lovely.'

'I'm Nate,' said the young god.

'I'm Clemency,' she said, feeling in that moment she finally knew why she had bothered with all the painful operations, the trauma and the ridicule. Here was her light at the end of the tunnel.

'Clemency!' From inside the dark house, behind the celestial Nate, there came a croaky voice. 'Oh my God, oh my God, oh my God!'

Clemency was thinking exactly the same as she surveyed the raddled-looking woman heading straight for her. Her hair had the consistency of a well-used floor mop. She was dressed in rags and missing her two front teeth. Clemency estimated her age as early fifties.

'Oh my God! Haven't you changed!'

Clemency unwillingly submitted to a hug from the patchouli-scented monster, realizing with horror that this was her beautiful childhood friend.

'You've changed too,' was the only possible answer. Please, tell me that Nate isn't her boyfriend, Clemency begged inside.

'This is my roommate, Nate,' said Melanie.

Only roommates. A result.

'Nate, this is the girl from school I've been telling you about. The one who used to be a man . . .'

'The one who used to be a man . . .' How on earth do you come back from an introduction like that? Within seconds, Nate had excused himself. Clemency was crying inside as Melanie dragged her around the room to introduce her to the other roommates.

Her party mood all but gone, Clemency turned down a hit on the bong but accepted a beer. As she sank into a sofa (and kept sinking. It appeared to have no springs), she considered she should probably just leave right now. If she drove fast enough she could get home in time to watch *Lost*. But something in her decided to hang on. Perhaps, if she got the chance to talk to Nate again, she could convince him she wasn't that odd. Perhaps she could tell him that Melanie had hallucinated the whole sex change thing. She certainly looked as though she had spent a lot of time getting high since she moved to California.

Clemency stared at Nate from across the room. She remembered the smile on his face as he opened the door to her. He'd seemed impressed. It wasn't totally unfeasible that he should find her attractive. Though he wasn't rushing to be with her . . . Suddenly Clemency felt totally conspicuous in her loneliness.

When her phone started to ring, Clemency leapt to answer the call as though God himself were trying to get through. But it wasn't God. It was Birdie. Clemency let her boss go through to voicemail and then listened to her rant, safe in the knowledge that she wouldn't have to respond right away.

'. . . find someone new to mow the lawn or I'll find someone new to be you . . .'

'I might as well just end it now,' said Clemency to herself.

An hour later, the party was in full swing. Nate looked around the room. Most people seemed to be having a pretty good time, but the girl/boy that had been at school with Melanie was sitting alone on the 'sofa of doom', sipping from a beer can. After a minute or two she shook the can and, finding it empty, put it down on the floor beside her.

'Can I get you another of those?' Nate asked.

'That'd be great,' said Clemency.

He returned with another can.

'I'm afraid it's not cold.'

'It's really just something to hold on to, isn't it?' Clemency smiled.

Clemency expected Nate to blend back into the crowd but he didn't. Instead, he sat down on the arm of the sofa.

'So, you went to school with Melanie,' he began. 'Has she changed much?'

'She certainly has,' said Clemency, wincing as Melanie threw her head back in laughter and revealed yet more empty gum where there should have been teeth. 'But not as much as me.'

Nate's eyes crinkled but he said nothing.

'How about you?' Clemency asked. 'How did you end up in this place? Not that it isn't a lovely place,' she added hurriedly.

'It's OK,' said Nate. 'I know it's a dump. But Jason kindly lets me stay here for nothing. And that's great because right now, I'm in search of a job.'

'What kind of work are you looking for?'

'I have a law degree and no experience. Oh, and a criminal record as of the other night.'

'Criminal record?' Clemency was surprised.

'I was involved in a peaceful protest that went a little wrong. It doesn't look great on the CV. I guess I'll just have to offer my services around the neighbourhood. I could mow lawns, though our front garden isn't much of an advert.'

'Do you know much about gardening?' Clemency asked in a sudden light-bulb moment.

'I had to mow the lawn every weekend when I was growing up.'

'Me too,' said Clemency. It still galled her that her sisters had never been expected to do the same. 'You know,' she said then, 'I think that you and I could do each other a big favour. You need a job and I need to find a new gardener for the house where I work. Like, pronto. I'm a celebrity PA, of all things. You want to apply for the job?' Clemency made little air commas around the word 'apply'. 'I can totally make it happen. In fact, I would be incredibly grateful.'

'How big is the garden?' asked Nate.

'Enormous. But it's mostly lawn.'

'I don't have a lot of experience. Do you think your boss will want to see references?' Nate asked.

'Trust me,' said Clemency. 'I don't think someone as dumb as Birdie Sederburg will be bothered about that at all.'

Nate could hardly believe his ears.

'Did you say Birdie *Sederburg*? You mean the golf heiress? The one who . . .'

Clemency rolled her eyes. 'Don't tell me. You have a still from that video clip of her with her ex as a screensaver?'

'Well, no,' said Nate. 'I have a photo montage of Yellowstone National Park as my screensaver, but I'll be sure to check out this video if you think I should.'

'Yes, she is the golf heiress. And she's a pain in the butt. But she needs a gardener and it sounds like you need the money . . . If you think you could bear it . . .'

It was the opportunity Mother Nature's Avengers had been waiting for. A chance to get access to the family that was number one on their target list of eco-offenders.

Nate said, 'I'd love to.'

Clemency smiled. 'When can you start?'

9

Clemency was right. Birdie Sederburg wasn't worried about checking the credentials of a new gardener. When Clemency announced that Nate and Jason had arrived for an interview, Birdie simply said, 'I don't have time for this. Show them where to go and tell them to get started.' She had far more pressing concerns than hiring staff. She had spent much of the weekend with DD, looking for an outfit for her second date with Dean Stevenson. They were still searching for the perfect dress on Tuesday afternoon.

The Age of Aquarius theme had been abandoned. Instead, this time, Birdie put her foot down, just a little way, and insisted that her second date outfit be themed around her new Hermès Birkin. She had picked up the bag just a couple of days before and was longing for the opportunity to show it off properly. Made of pale pink ostrich leather (such a horribly skin-like colour it made Clemency think of the psycho in *Silence of the Lambs*. The one who made a jumpsuit out of his victims), this Birkin was utterly unique. Not even Kate Moss had a Birkin in the same fleshy shade (whether she would have wanted one was another question entirely).

With pursed lips, DD examined the bag.

'Difficult . . .' she murmured. She pressed her fingers to her forehead as though warding off a headache. 'But I have it.'

Half an hour later, a courier arrived bearing a box from hot new fashion designer Makiko Clark, whose influences, according to her website (which showed everything but her clothes), included manga and English country-house parties. Upon DD's recommendation, she had sent for Birdie's inspection a cross between a pair of hunting trews and a body-stocking, made up in the same nude colour as Birdie's bag. DD went into ecstasies.

'This is it, Birdie. This is the bleeding edge of fashion you're looking at here.'

'Does something go over the top of that?' Birdie asked.

'Are you kidding me? Do you know nothing about design? This is a comment on the state of society in one pure garment. Makiko Clark is a genius. Put it on.'

It took a while. There were no obvious openings to the curious thing. Eventually, DD had to consult a photograph for help.

'That decorative pizzle,' she said, pointing to an odd-shaped toggle that was roughly the size and shape of a penis, 'That goes on the left hip. You can use it to carry your phone.'

'How do I look?' Birdie asked Clemency when she had managed to get the body-stocking in roughly the right place.

Clemency dropped another pen on the floor to buy herself time as she thought of an answer other than: you look like you're wearing a fat suit stitched out of other people's actual fat. From a distance, Birdie looked as though she wasn't wearing anything at all and the shape of the hunting trews gave the impression that she'd put on twenty-four pounds. But DD pronounced it 'wonderful' and what DD pronounced . . .

'You could maybe try throwing a long jacket over the top?' Clemency suggested.

As Birdie walked into the restaurant, Dean couldn't help but wonder whether the anti-drugs lecturer who had visited his high school had been right after all. If you took acid once, just once, you might experience flashbacks for the rest of your life. But, alas, this was not an LSD-induced flashback. Birdie really was wearing a body-stocking with padding in all the wrong places. Dean could not hide his dismay.

'You're wearing . . .' he struggled to find the words.

'It's Japanese,' she said helpfully.

'Ah,' said Dean, as though it all made sense after that.

Once again, neither of the young lovers ate anything much that night. For Dean, it was slightly less difficult than it had been when they were at The Ivy. There was something of the corpse about Birdie's outfit that made it very easy for Dean to push his French fries around his plate without being tempted to lift a single one to his lips. Meanwhile, Birdie was too busy twittering on about the Japanese avant-garde (repeating verbatim the blurb on Makiko Clark's website) to eat anything herself.

Dean spent most of the meal wondering how best to shield Birdie from the paps as they exited. It was a matter of minimizing the damage. He would have to put his left arm around her so that he could obscure the curious penis-shaped toggle that hung from her belt. Perhaps he should suggest that she might be cold and lend her his coat. It was quite a long leather jacket. Most of the hideousness would be hidden.

'You must be cold,' said Dean, as they headed for the exit.

'Not really,' said Birdie. 'I'm actually feeling rather toasty.' In fact she was sweating. Large parts of the outfit were made from the type of neoprene that surfers use to brace themselves against the Pacific chill.

'Are you sure?' Dean started to take off his jacket anyway. 'I could just drape this around your shoulders?'

'Oh, Dean,' said Birdie, mistaking his embarrassment for gallantry. 'You are super-kind. If you're really so concerned about my welfare . . .'

Result! thought Dean as he wrapped Birdie in his jacket. Fortunately, it was big enough to cover her as far as her knees. If he could just get her to her car without anyone getting a snap of what was beneath that coat. The last thing he wanted was to be pictured with someone who had what appeared to be a penis sprouting out of her hip.

As they exited the restaurant, the paps were waiting. Birdie shielded her eyes from the flashes.

'Come on,' said Dean. 'There's your car.' He was seconds away from having successfully hidden her from view. But just then, one of the photographers called out, 'Birdie! Show us what you're wearing! You're always such a stylish gal!'

And like the crow that was conned into dropping the cheese when the fox praised its singing voice, Birdie opened the coat.

'Oh, wow!'

'Shock and *awe*!' said somebody.

'Is that a penis?' someone else asked.

'It's a pocket for my cellphone,' Birdie explained. 'Incorporated into a fertility symbol. A decorative pizzle is what the designer calls it.'

'Shit,' thought Dean as Birdie twirled and struck poses, oblivious to the mockery. He thought he might throw up with embarrassment. At least this would be the last time he had to see her. There was no way he could be compelled to go on a third date after this.

Or so he thought. The following morning, as predicted, there were pictures of Birdie all over the Internet and, as Dean had also predicted, most of the captions were scathing. But a day later, the very same pictures appeared in a fashion column in the *New York Times*, which took an entirely different view.

'Known for her outrageous fashion sense, rarely has Birdie Sederburg looked quite so on trend as she did exiting the Viscount Hotel in Santa Monica on Thursday night. Her ensemble, by Japanese-American designer Makiko Clark, is almost *beyond* fashion. Who but Clark would have put anyone in a skin-tone bodysuit with such evocative lines? Who but Sederburg could have carried it off? The addition of a flesh-coloured Birkin was a nod to the more traditional style of other heiresses less brave. A refreshing look from one of Hollywood's most pampered princesses. It's so wrong it can only be right. An edgy fashionista like Birdie Sederburg is the ideal arm candy for Dean Stevenson to give him the kudos he so badly needs if he is ever going to make the transition from soap opera to silver screen.'

'Did you read this?' Justin asked Dean.

'She looked like an uncooked wiener,' Dean replied.

'According to the *Times*, she looked like a fashion maven. And she gave you edge. This is exactly the kind of press you need if we're going to put you up for the new Scorsese.'

'Ohmigod, ohmigod, ohmigod!'

When Birdie found out about the article in the *Times*, she sent Clemency to buy a hundred copies.

And so Dean and Birdie had a third date, at a new restaurant by the sea in Santa Monica. Birdie's outfit was relatively toned down this time, comprising a golf sweater and a tutu accessorized with baseball boots. And to his surprise Dean found that he quite enjoyed the evening.

He really hadn't appreciated until that moment quite how big a deal it was to be with Birdie Sederburg. When, halfway through dinner, he mentioned that he liked playing poker, Birdie made a quick call and the family jet was scrambled for a flight to Las Vegas. 'So you can show me how it's done,' she said. Once there, the best suite at the Sederburg Towers and Driving Range Vegas was put at their disposal, complete with a butler who handled everything from cocktails on their arrival to ensuring they had clean underwear the following morning (since they'd arrived with nothing but the clothes they had been wearing to dinner).

Dean was used to luxury. He had grown up in a wealthy family and attended a great private school in Pasadena, but this was something else. Birdie Sederburg's life was a real fairy tale. Having as much money as she did was almost as good as having magical powers. Whatever Birdie wanted became manifest almost by the click of her fingers. From a peanut butter sandwich to the use of a private jet. No door in the whole of the United States was closed to her.

The exact moment Dean's head was truly turned would have been obvious to any observer.

'I do all my own surfing stunts on *PCH*,' he told her on the jet flight back from Vegas.

'Have you ever been to Bora Bora?' she asked him.

'No,' said Dean.

'My grandfather has a resort there. I'll book the whole thing out to celebrate when you finish shooting this new series.'

The end of shooting wasn't that far away. Maybe Birdie Sederburg was worth another date.

Over the next few weeks, like a lobster in a pan of water that gradually warms from bearable to boiling, Dean Stevenson was trapped by Birdie's generosity. With each date that passed, her gifts to him grew more and more luxurious. He only had to glance in a store window as they walked by to be certain that a gift from that very store would be on his doorstep the following morning. He even swapped his favourite Breitling watch for a solid gold Rolex, which Birdie had sent to the *PCH* set.

'It's a classic,' he told himself. His father would understand that now he was twenty-four, he needed something a little more grown-up.

IO

Soon, Nate and Jason had been working the Sederburg gardens for almost a month. They arrived at the house every day at six o'clock in the morning. Jason was furious to have to get up so early but Nate explained to him on the very first day that it was essential to get the bulk of the work done before the sun came up.

'Are you telling me that we're actually going to do some work?' Jason couldn't believe his ears. He was not keen on the gardening project at all, but had found himself roped in, having drawn the short straw at a house meeting to find Nate a co-worker. The job was too big for Nate alone.

'We have to make her believe we really are gardeners,' Nate said.

'I thought we were just going to get access to the house and steal her laptop.'

'Jason,' said Nate. 'This is not something we can hurry. For today we're just going to be doing the job that Birdie Sederburg is paying us for. You can mow the lawn.'

'What? Hey, man. You never said we were going to be doing actual gardening,' Jason whined.

'For someone who claims to care so much about the natural world that you would kill to protect it, you have a worrying aversion to getting your hands dirty.'

Most mornings, Nate and Jason had been at work for almost four hours before there were any signs of life from Birdie's suite of rooms. Clemency was up at nine, fixing Birdie's breakfast how

45

she liked it. An hour later, Birdie came out onto the terrace outside her bedroom. Though it was ten, she still wasn't dressed. She wore a long silk robe. She stretched luxuriously before positioning herself on one of the loungers by the pool.

When he and Jason first started working at the house, Nate had been worried that Birdie might recognize him from the protest at the golf course, but, if she did, she wasn't saying anything about it. As Nate weeded the flower-beds or swept grass cuttings from the path around the pool, she looked at him with expressionless eyes. In fact, she pretty much looked right through him.

Often she didn't wait for Nate or Jason to get out of earshot before she picked up her phone and started making calls. It was as though Birdie didn't know they were there. No matter how close Nate got, she simply kept on talking on her phone without even lowering her voice. No matter the subject. On several occasions he heard Birdie talking money with her accountant. She talked about altogether more intimate things with her friends.

'Of course I had a Brazilian,' she said. 'Do you think I'm some kind of European?'

Nate quickly understood how Birdie's supercilious behaviour might have pissed off the previous gardener, but to be able to move about the place like a ghost was exactly what Nate wanted. And to discover that Birdie was so terribly indiscreet as a matter of course was wonderful! Sooner or later, he assured Jason, she or one of her hideous friends would let slip with some information that was actually useful.

Meanwhile, Clemency watched Nate from behind her big black sunglasses. Telling him about the gardening job was the best move she had ever made. If he could hang on for long enough without doing something that prompted Birdie to fire him, she felt sure they would become proper friends, and after that . . .who knew?

* * *

'Are you sure she used to be a guy?' Jason asked as they stopped for a break and Clemency brought them coffee, as had become her habit.

'That's what Melanie said,' Nate reminded him.

'I can't believe it,' said Jason. 'I think she's incredibly cute.'

Jason wasn't the only one who thought Clemency had something about her. She had another secret admirer who frequented the Sederburg house, but he compensated for his feelings of affection and confusion by acting like such an arsehole she would never guess.

'Clemency!' Birdie screeched from her bedroom window. 'Clemency! Dean needs you to wash his car while we have lunch.'

Birdie was on Cloud Nine. No, make that Cloud Ten! She and
Dean Stevenson had been an item for thirty-three and a half days.
Sure, their actual date count was still in the single figures (they'd
had nine) but Birdie could feel that they were getting serious. She
just knew that Dean wanted to spend more time with her. It was
simply that his shooting schedule for *PCH* was so hectic right
then. He was the show's male lead. He appeared in every episode.
He was expected to be on set every day, starting early in the
morning, which was why he didn't like to stay over at Birdie's
house. Or have her stay over at his.

Birdie wanted very much to visit the set of *PCH*. Since falling
for Dean at that party, Birdie had watched every single episode
of the soap at least five times and thus she felt she really knew
his fellow actors.

'You don't want to come on set,' Dean told her when she asked.
'It's really very boring.'

'It wouldn't be boring to me,' said Birdie.

'There would be nothing for you to do. You'd get under
everyone's feet.'

'Ah, well. I've been thinking about that and I've come up with
the craziest idea! I think you should call your producer and tell
her you want me to do a cameo.'

'What?'

'You know, make an appearance in a couple of episodes.'

'I know what a cameo is,' said Dean. 'But you're not an actress.'

'No, but I am a *celebrity*, Dean. And it's not as though I've
never been in front of the camera.'

Dean winced as he thought about the only one of Birdie's on-screen appearances he'd ever seen: a very blurry piece of footage that had been posted on the Internet by a particularly cruel ex-boyfriend. Birdie wasn't thinking about that, of course. She was thinking about her appearance in *Chip off the Old Block*, a reality show in which five heirs and heiresses went to work at the very bottom of the family firm. Birdie was supposed to spend a month working as a chambermaid at her grandfather's very first golf resort: the Sederburg Atlanta. She lasted a day, claiming that switching pillowcases had given her RSI.

'Talk to your producer,' she persisted. 'I know she'll jump at it. It would be great for the ratings.'

'We don't need any help with the ratings.'

'That's not what I heard . . . This will take it all the way to the top. Imagine the publicity. Real-life lovers on screen. I've already come up with a few ideas for what I could do.'

Birdie reached into her Birkin and brought out her iPhone to show Dean her notes.

'I can do accents, so I thought I could play your old college girlfriend just flown in from England who makes you doubt your connection to Shannon and break-up with her and go back to—'

'That's not going to work,' said Dean.

Birdie bristled. If there was one character on *PCH* that she hadn't warmed to, it was Shannon. Shannon was Dean's on-screen love interest, played by one of that year's most talked about actresses, Emily Branson.

The coveted role of Shannon on *PCH* was Emily Branson's first-big time job. Before that, she had been seen in a couple of teen movies. Usually playing one of the girls who hung out by the pool in the obligatory party scene. But it was *PCH* that had put her on the map. In the run-up to the show's first airing, the PR machine turned Emily into a national celebrity. She was featured in all the fashion mags, talking about her personal style (which was very Banana Republic, DD derided), and in all the men's mags wearing a variety of small but colourful bikinis. She was voted as having the 'hottest body in Hollywood'. And as the woman that most readers of *InStyle* wanted to emulate.

Birdie hated Emily B (referred to as such to avoid confusion with her co-star Emily D) long before she fell in love with Dean Stevenson. Now she hated her even more. Especially since Dean would not say a bad word about her. Not one. On the contrary, he raved about his perky co-star at every opportunity.

'She is a talented actress and a great person,' he said when Birdie asked about her on their first date.

'You're not doing an interview for *US Weekly* here,' Birdie reminded him. 'You can tell me what she's *really* like.'

'She is a talented actress and a great person,' Dean simply said again.

Birdie smiled but inside she was growling. She had been thinking of a way to loosen Emily's grip on her boyfriend ever since.

'I think it would be a great idea for me to play your old flame,' Birdie persisted.

'The storyline between my character and Shannon has been written for the next three seasons,' Dean said simply.

'And you're telling me they wouldn't do a few minor tweaks to accommodate a celebrity? It happens all the time, Dean. I know. Look at the celebrity cameos they had in *Sex and the City* and *Desperate Housewives*.'

Dean sensed an argument coming on.

'If you're not happy with me playing your old college girl-friend, then how about this? You have some kind of accident that results in a bump to your head. When you come to, I have replaced Emily B as Shannon. A few episodes later it can be revealed that the transformation was due to the fact that you hadn't woken up at all but were actually fact still in a coma. And the part can go back to Emily. If that's what people want at that point.'

'Birdie,' said Dean. 'That is absolutely ridiculous. Nobody goes for that 'it was all a dream' bullshit.'

'They did it in *Dallas* and I think you'll find that the popularity of *Dallas* will long outlast your hokey little show.'

'I'll ask,' he said. 'But I absolutely cannot promise anything.'

'OK.' Birdie was mollified. 'In the meantime, I'll take an acting class. A refresher. Oh, it's going to be so exciting! Can you imagine? Dating and working together!'

As soon as she got home that night, Birdie posted the news that she was 'considering a part in *PCH*' as her Facebook status message, then she called Chipper and they discussed the ideal outfit for meeting a producer until late into the night.

Meanwhile, the thought of putting Birdie's idea to his producer was a long way from the top of Dean's list of priorities. He went from his date with her to a bar where his co-stars on *PCH* were on the VIP list. He drank champagne until dawn.

'What is this?' Marie the producer asked Dean the next morning. 'You've told your girlfriend she can have a spot on the show? Did you even think to ask me first?'

'What?' Dean had no idea what Marie was talking about. It was a moment before he even remembered the conversation he'd had with Birdie the previous night. It was deeply buried under the soft snow of a hangover.

'Apparently she broke the news on Facebook, where it was picked up by one of her Facebook friends, a tabloid journalist, who called the PR here at *PCH* this morning to ask exactly when Birdie is going to be on and what part she's going to be playing. The news was already on Ohmygahd.'

'So, you just told them she was joking, right?'

'Wrong, because right before that PR called, I negotiated a deal with the Sederburg Hotel Group to use their new hotel in Long Beach as the location for that scene in which Shannon sees her high-school sweetheart for the first time in six years at the wedding of his mother to her father and you fly in to break things up. You have no idea what a good deal I got. Birdie is going to have to have a walk-on.'

Dean clutched his forehead.

12

'I want to shoot myself,' said Jason.

'Why?'

'I can't do these early mornings.'

'You get to sleep all afternoon,' Nate pointed out.

'I don't know how much more crap I can take. Does she ever talk about anything else but *PC* Fricking *H*?'

Nate had to agree that they didn't seem to be getting terribly far with 'Plan Sederburg'. So far they had gathered no valuable secrets. Even when she seemed to be talking to her grandfather – the great Julius Sederburg himself – Birdie's conversation remained mind-numbingly banal. As a result, Jason grumbled endlessly. He didn't see any point in continuing to get up so early to trek to the Sederburg house on a daily basis.

'Nate,' Jason whined, when they were back at the house, 'it's been five weeks. Last week you hauled my ass up there to do gardening when the girl wasn't even in town. What's up with that? Face it; this plan is taking us nowhere. We are no closer to knowing Julius Sederburg's confidential business than we were before we started.'

'She's back in town now,' said Nate. 'We're bound to hear something soon.'

'The only thing we're hearing is a bunch of stupid gossip about no-brain soap stars,' said Jason.

'Hey,' said Melanie, suddenly perking up. 'How come you don't pass any of it on?'

'Who wants to know what colour underpants Dean Stevenson wears?'

'I do,' said Melanie, Then quickly looked shamefaced.

'How do you even know who Dean Stevenson is?' asked Jason with disdain.

'Sometimes I have to watch his show while I'm in the launderette,' said Melanie by way of an excuse.

Jason tutted.

'Hey!' said Melanie. 'I'm not supporting that show in any way.'

There followed a debate about whether the members of the commune should watch soaps at all. Even if it cost them nothing to do it.

'Soap operas are the way the government softens people's minds,' Jason announced after a while. 'And we do not need that.'

'You're right,' said Nate. 'Because you're softening your mind already with that.' He nodded towards the bong.

'You know I use that for medicinal purposes,' said Jason.

'I've got an idea,' said Melanie. 'Maybe all this stuff that Birdie is saying isn't such useless information after all. There are websites that pay for gossip. We should start selling it. Real insider stuff. It would be priceless!'

'Why does anybody want to know about Birdie Sederburg?' asked Jason.

'Are you kidding? She's, like, always in the tabloids.'

'How do you know?'

'I read them at the launderette,' Melanie claimed again, hoping that no one would ever find the secret stash of celeb mags under her futon. 'She is serious fodder for those magazines. Nate and Jason – you need to start writing notes on everything you hear. I'll call the stories through to the magazine. That way, she won't make the connection between you guys and the way the stuff is being leaked. The money we make can go towards our mission. And believe me, there is big money in this. One of the magazines I read – when I'm doing the laundry – offers a thousand bucks a time for a celebrity tip-off.'

Jason was excited. 'Melanie, that is the best idea you have ever come out with.'

Melanie looked pleased, like a little cat that was getting a scratch behind the ears.

'Can you get hold of one of those magazines right now?'

'There's one under my bed,' Melanie admitted. 'It was already here when we moved in. I'll go and fetch it.'

'This is going to be great,' said Jason.

Nate shook his head. 'I don't know,' he said. 'It doesn't seem ethical to me. Birdie Sederburg's life is her private life. We are only eavesdropping on her at all to find out about her grandfather's business practices.'

'You mean if we found out that her grandfather was boning some pool-boy we wouldn't use it against him?'

'Of course we wouldn't. Julius Sederburg can live his private life as he chooses, except with respect to the environment. I don't care if he *is* boning a pool-boy. That's got nothing to do with how many golf courses he's intending to build. Likewise, I don't think we should be selling Birdie Sederburg's secrets to the press. We've got to keep our consciences clean.'

Melanie snorted.

Jason continued. 'If we work there for a hundred years, I predict that not one intelligent word will come out of that woman's mouth.'

'Perhaps we need to try a different tack from just hanging around eavesdropping,' Nate suggested. 'If we could engineer it so that we actually get into conversation with her from time to time, then at some point soon we might be able to ask her a few leading questions.'

'You think she would strike up a friendship with a gardener?' asked Jason. 'You're nuts.'

'It's worth a try.'

Nate did try. The following day, when Birdie came out of the house and set herself up by the pool, Nate put down his secateurs and headed across to talk to her.

At first, Birdie didn't even look up. Not even when Nate was right next to her. Eventually, when it was clear that she wasn't about to tear herself away from her gossip mag without prompting, Nate cleared his throat.

Birdie pulled down her sunglasses and looked up at him.

'Can I help you?' she asked.

'I thought I would talk to you about your plans for the garden,' said Nate. 'I mean, whether there are any particular plants you would like to have in the beds for the summer. We should really be thinking about that now.'

'I'm sorry?' said Birdie. 'Did you just say we?'

'Yes. Do you have any preferences?'

Birdie pressed her fingers to her forehead. 'Do I look like I have time to think about the garden?' she asked. 'That is your job.'

'But you must have a preference?'

'Just do whatever's fashionable in the world of gardening right now. I really don't care as long as they don't attract bugs.'

'Most flowers do,' said Nate. 'That's the idea of flowers.'

'Not in my garden.'

Birdie pushed her sunglasses back up her nose and turned back to her magazine, signalling that the conversation was over.

'How about pink . . .' Nate began.

Birdie looked up slowly. 'I pay you to think of that sort of thing for me. I also pay you not to get in my face when I am trying to read.'

Nate shrugged and gave up.

'Ain't no way we're infiltrating family Sederburg,' said Jason. 'I quit.'

And that was the last time he ever went to the house.

Nate, however, would not give up. If he couldn't get through to Birdie, there was still a possibility that she might tell Clemency something useful and Clemency might let it slip. The following morning he drove from the MNA house to the Sederburg mansion alone, leaving the others to a day of setting the world to rights over the bong.

13

'I am so excited!' Birdie bounced out of bed.

The day of her appearance on *PCH* had arrived. Dean had spent the past week in a state of shock, as had his co-stars. But the show's PR had to admit to her bosses that the news the heiress was going to be appearing had generated a lot of interest and even if most of it was of the disbelieving and sneering kind, at the very least it meant that the *PCH* website was getting hundreds of hits a minute, and that in turn meant that the advertisers were very happy indeed.

On Birdie's big day, Julius Sederburg's assistant, Mary, laid his schedule on his desk at seven thirty sharp. The old man looked at that day's events with a sigh. The morning was easy enough. He would spend most of it barking at the members of his board, but lunchtime brought something he dreaded.

'I'm having lunch with my granddaughter?' he said with a sinking heart.

'Yes,' said Mary. 'You are. It's been in the diary for almost a month.'

'Didn't I see her five weeks ago? Where have I got to go this time? Do I even have to go? Tell her if it's about money, she should email Jim Smith at his office and let him know what she thinks she needs. As usual. He knows what the parameters are.'

'It's not about money,' said Mary. 'You're supposed to be meeting her at the resort in Long Beach. Along with the cast of *PCH*. They're shooting at the resort all this week.'

'What's *PCH*?'

'*Pacific Coast Highway*. It's a top teen entertainment show, as I understand it. About surfers.'

Julius Sederburg looked blank.

'Good publicity for the resort,' she added. 'And the PR team are really pleased with the way it fits in with their new campaign to get more young people playing golf. The stars of this show are considered great models for their demographic.'

'In that case,' Julius sighed, 'I'd suppose I'd better go. Block my diary out for an hour.'

Birdie was almost as excited by the prospect of her grandfather coming to lunch as she was about her on-screen scene with Dean later that afternoon. Birdie was proud of her grandfather. For as long as she could remember, she had carried the family legend of his rise from rags to riches in her heart. The one book she had read with any enthusiasm was her grandfather's biography: called *A Whole in One*, the book charted his career from the early days as a child during the Great Depression, when his father sent him out to collect lost golf balls to earn a few cents, to the early twenty-first century, when the Sederburg empire spanned the globe and he was pictured with such luminaries as Donald Trump and Mohammed Al Fayed.

Birdie was Julius Sederburg's only grandchild. She was the daughter of his only child, a son, christened Paris, who had quickly become known as Par to fit in with the family golf theme. Julius's disappointment that his first grandchild was a girl had been somewhat softened when Par announced that he and his wife would be calling the little girl 'Birdie', in honour of her grandfather's obsession.

Julius told himself that a grandson would surely follow (for surely only a grand*son* could follow in the footsteps of so great a man). But it just didn't happen. And when Birdie was seven years old, her parents were killed in an avalanche while vacationing at the family chalet in Gstaad.

As the unfortunate orphan's only next of kin, of course Julius agreed that tiny Birdie should be brought straight to his home. But the needs of his business empire didn't leave much time for Julius Sederburg to spend on building a new family life for the little girl. Birdie rattled around the enormous mansions in California and Colorado and Florida, alone but for a succession of nannies (some of whom were much more interested in the welfare of their charge than others). And as soon as it was possible, Birdie was sent away to boarding school.

But her grandfather's extended absences from her life only made Birdie's heart grow fonder. It didn't matter to her that she didn't see him from month to month. She didn't think badly of the fact that she often had to stay at school for a few days after term finished because her grandfather was too busy to have her home at once. Birdie simply idolized the old man. She would not hear a word against him. Whenever she heard that some scummy eco-warrior had been rude to him, Birdie actually cried. Though the business community considered him a hard-ass and his own staff thought him a tyrant, he would always be her beloved grandad. She would always see, whenever she thought of him, the man who had dressed up as Santa Claus for her when she was five years old (even if he had only done it for an article in the Christmas issue of *Golf Monthly*).

Meanwhile, Julius had long given up hoping that Birdie would ever shape up to be a worthy successor. Instead he watched the progress of his cousin's children with great interest. Maybe control of the family business wouldn't have to leave the family altogether after all . . .

'Grandaddy!'

When she saw the familiar white-haired figure walk into the restaurant, Birdie leapt up to greet him. She pulled him into the room, hanging on his arm as she had done when she was six years old. She threw her arms around him for a hug. He returned it briefly, sending her away again with a pat of dismissal.

'Well,' he said to the cast of *PCH*, 'it sure is wonderful to have all you young people here. I hope that you'll be back to the Sederburg Golf Resort for your next holiday. Young people should play more golf.'

Birdie flitted around the table, introducing her grandfather to her new friends.

'And this is Dean Stevenson,' she said, finally. 'Dean is very special to me,' she said in a way that made Emily B roll her eyes. 'I hope that you'll consider him part of the family.'

It was a phrase that sent a shiver down the spines of both men. Julius cleared his throat.

'Do you play golf, young man?' he asked Dean.

Dean said he didn't. And the conversation stopped right there.

Julius stayed just long enough to eat a club sandwich, then he was gone.

14

'OK.' The assistant director clapped her hands. 'It's time for you lazy so-and-sos to do some work. Ladies and gentlemen, you have twenty minutes before I expect to see you on set.'

It took Birdie longer than twenty minutes. When she heard via Ohmygahd that Birdie was going to appear on *PCH*, DD took the rare step of calling her client. That hardly ever happened. A call from DD was the sort of thing you only got right after you got an Oscar nomination.

'I'm coming in with you,' DD insisted. 'Otherwise, how can you be sure that those people in wardrobe won't make you look like an idiot?'

'But this isn't *Sex and the City*,' said the show's official stylist when DD sucked her teeth at the outfit the stylist had chosen. They're meant to be young kids, ordinary kids, enjoying themselves on a So Cal beach. This is what kids on the beach all wear.'

'That's as may be,' said DD, holding the pretty sundress as though it were a mildewed dishrag. 'But my client is no ordinary kid on the beach. She's a trend-setter. What she wears this year, all your actors will be wearing by next spring. I want her in this.'

DD opened a garment bag and pulled out something that looked like the kind of protective tabard the checkout girls at Wal-Mart would wear.

The *PCH* wardrobe team looked understandably sceptical.

'Oh! I love it!' said Birdie, snatching it up. 'What do I wear underneath it?'

'Nothing,' said DD. 'Just these shoes.'

She handed her a pair of high-heeled Ugg boots.

'I can't work under these conditions,' the wardrobe mistress told the producer. The producer, aware that the *NYT* had declared Birdie to be a girl with 'edge', asked the wardrobe mistress to suck it up. Just this once.

'The scene goes like this,' said the director. 'Dean, you arrive at the party fresh from your fight with Todd. You're still angry. You can't see Shannon anywhere and that makes you angrier still. Where is she? You assume that she must be with another guy. You're seeing red. You down a couple of beers.'

Dean nodded. He had already squared his jaw.

'Birdie.' The director turned to her. He hesitated. It was the first time he had properly seen her costume. 'Right. Birdie. You are at the party with a group of girlfriends. You're having a great time. You're dancing. You spot Dean on the other side of the room. He looks up from his beer. Your eyes meet. You cross the room to be with him.'

'Er, wouldn't he cross the room to be with me?' Birdie interrupted.

'Not in my script,' said the director. 'You cross the room to be with him. You start to dance. Dean, you're reluctant at first . . .'

'Why would he be reluctant?' Birdie interrupted.

'Look, he just is, OK,' said Dean. 'He's come from punching a guy who hit on his girlfriend.'

'Well, if she's open to being hit on, then she's clearly not much of a girlfriend, so surely he wouldn't be all that bothered?' said Birdie with a look towards the dreaded Emily B.

'Emily B.' The director turned to the other actress. 'You come in. You see Dean dancing with Birdie. Without stopping to find out what's going on, you turn on your heel and run out into the car park. As Dean and Birdie turn around on the dance floor, he sees you leaving and follows at a run.'

Emily nodded. 'Do you want me to cry?'

'Do you think you can?'

'I can do anything,' said Emily. Birdie wrinkled her nose. 'Even that,' said Emily, catching sight of Birdie and wrinkling her nose right back at her.

That was a challenge if Birdie ever saw one. She was more determined than ever to show that stupid Emily B that whatever she could do, Birdie could do better. How hard could it possibly be to be an actress anyway? It wasn't even as though Emily changed her accent when she was in character as Shannon.

Well, Birdie wasn't going to be caught out like that. She was determined to prove to the director and the rest of the cast that she had *range*. She still liked the idea that her character could be a European student on exchange, so she decided that when she delivered her one line, she would deliver it with a cut-glass English accent.

'Rolling,' said the camera assistant.

Dean entered, slamming the door. He did a passable job of pretending to down a beer in one (the can was actually only a quarter full of water). Meanwhile, Birdie shimmied across the floor and said, 'Are you dancing?'

From behind the camera, Emily B sneered, 'In those shoes?'

'Cut!' shouted the director. 'What was with the voice?'

'That was my English accent,' said Birdie. 'Pretty impressive, huh? I was at school in the UK for a year.'

'You sounded like Kate Beckinsale,' said the director. 'Who sounds like she's never been anywhere near the UK. Just do the line in your normal voice.'

Dean looked annoyed.

'This is my first time,' Birdie reminded him. 'I'm a little nervous. I could use a hug.'

She wrapped her arms tightly around Dean, who looked over her shoulder to where Clemency was watching from the side of the set.

'You're moving my mike,' he said to Birdie. 'And you're supposed to be over there at the beginning of the take.'

Birdie slinked to the other side of the set. Watching the monitor, Emily B smirked. Then she smiled at Dean. Birdie saw it all. It made her all the more determined to wow everybody on the set. The camera began to roll. Dean entered the party, brow furrowed, looking every inch the young guy who had just punched his rival in love. The camera focused on Birdie. She flicked back her hair and licked her lips.

'Cut!' shouted the director.

'What?' Birdie asked. 'I haven't said my line yet.'

'What was with the hair flicking? You're not auditioning to be in The Pussycat Dolls. Just act like you're at a real party.'

'You haven't seen her at a real party,' said Emily B.

'OK,' said Dean. 'Can we just get on with this?'

Birdie took her place again. This time when the camera panned over to her, she stood still, just letting her eyes seek Dean out.

'Cut,' said the director. 'Now you look like you're in a neck brace. Act natural!'

The scene took twenty-four takes. By the twenty-third, no one on the set was pretending to find it funny any more. Least of all Dean.

'How did I do?' Birdie asked him.

'You did fine,' Dean lied.

'Do you think they'll extend my role?'

'I couldn't possibly say.'

'Can you sneak away now? Shall we go and have a cocktail to celebrate my first day as an actor?'

'I have to have an early night,' said Dean. 'Big day of filming tomorrow.'

'Oh, OK,' said Birdie. 'I suppose I should have an early night too. It's pretty tiring, isn't it? Being in front of the cameras all day . . . Tell you what – we could have an early night together . . .' Birdie gave Dean a nudge.

'I'll see you tomorrow morning,' he said. Then he headed off in the direction of the cameras, where the director was deep in conversation. With Emily B.

Birdie felt her heart sink.

15

Clemency drove Birdie home. When they got back to the house, Birdie was irritated to see that the gardening truck was still in the driveway. Really, how much could there possibly be to do in that tiny garden? The last guy may have got stroppy about being paid on time but at least he got the job done quickly. Birdie would have to get Clemency to talk to the new guy about it. Birdie hated to have people messing about in the flower-beds when she wanted to relax.

She walked into the kitchen and barked a couple of instructions at the maid, whose name she had never bothered to learn let alone remember, then she took her laptop out onto the deck by the pool. She wanted to update her Facebook status and check out Ohmygahd while perfecting her tan.

Nate the gardener was doing something to the borders closest to the pool. He was tying some of the plants to sticks. When Birdie emerged from the house, he called out, 'Hi'. She gave him a weird head flick/nod in return. She did not feel like making conversation. At least, not with a member of staff.

'Good day?' he asked.

'Are you going to be here for much longer?' Birdie asked him in reply. 'I don't understand what's taking so long. Am I paying you by the hour or something?'

'No,' said Nate. 'You're paying by the job. But I imagine we're taking longer than your usual guys. It's because we don't use pesticides and weedkiller and other quick fixes like that. I could have cleared that lawn of weeds in an afternoon with some nasty spray,' he explained. 'But the earth would be saddled with the legacy of my laziness for much longer.'

Birdie pulled a face that said, 'Weirdo'. She said, 'Fine. Just as long as the weeds are gone.'

Birdie didn't have time to dwell on the weeds. She was very worried about her relationship with Dean. Just the previous day, Ohmygahd had run an article titled 'Which Hollywood romance is going off the boil?' The text that followed explained that insiders on the set of *PCH* were suggesting that all was not well with the show's lovebirds. Birdie immediately called Chipper and shrieked with pain.

'Relax,' said Chipper. 'Perhaps they're referring to some other couple. After all, you're not actually a regular on the show.'

'And neither am I likely to be after today! I swear to you, Chipper. That bitch Emily did everything she could to ruin my scene. It was so hard to find my focus with her staring at me the whole time.'

'You're a great actress,' Chipper said in an attempt to buoy Birdie up.

It didn't work. Birdie put down the phone and gave a dramatic sniff. Moments later, she was properly crying. Great honking sobs that reverberated around the entire garden.

Nate wondered whether he was supposed to notice. He was the only person in the vicinity. Was she trying to catch his attention by crying so loudly? Should he ask her if she felt OK? Or would that just get him sacked?

Nate hesitated. Birdie continued to cry as though nothing on earth could ever console her. It was horrible. Nate hated to see anyone crying. Even if she was the granddaughter of the evil Julius Sederburg and a pretty shallow person herself. To see anyone in such distress tugged at Nate's kind heart. Eventually, he could stand it no longer. And that was when he saw it. Almost a sign from above that he should enquire about the state of Birdie's heart. It would be sure to cheer her up. He picked it up and walked to the pool.

'Look at this,' said Nate, opening his hand to reveal what was inside. 'Isn't that just the most beautiful thing you have ever seen?'

'Ohmigod! Get that thing away from me!' Birdie shrieked. She jumped up from her lounger and knocked the pitcher of margarita flying. 'Get that bug out of my face.'

Holding her laptop against her chest like a shield, Birdie ran back into the house, leaving Nate standing there with the caterpillar still on his hand. He didn't get a chance to tell Birdie how special this particular caterpillar was and how, one day soon, it would turn into a truly beautiful moth. A moth that could only be found in California. She wasn't interested. Of course.

'And clear up that spilled margarita!' was her parting shot.

Nate shook his head. Perhaps he had been over-optimistic, thinking that he could befriend Birdie Sederburg and persuade her to use her influence over her grandfather. It was clear she saw him as nothing more than a member of staff and he was unlikely to be able to interest her in his cause while she considered him to be so far beneath contempt.

Perhaps the others were right. There was no point trying to persuade people to come round to the right way of thinking. You had to scare them. But Birdie Sederburg wasn't going to be scared by the prospect that in a very short space of time, the humble caterpillar that Nate cradled in his palm might be extinct. The loss of a single moth meant nothing to her. She didn't see moths the way he did: as part of the complicated jigsaw of life. To her they were just bugs. A nuisance. Something to be shooed out of the house or perhaps even squirted with a noxious chemical spray. In fact, right then Birdie was coming out of the house with a can of Deet. Nate quickly set the caterpillar down where he had found it.

'Did you get rid of that thing?' she asked. 'It will be

impossible for me to relax by the pool if I know that critter is still out there.'

'I put it down over here,' said Nate. 'It won't get you.'

'What? You mean it's still alive?' She handed Nate the can of bug spray. 'Deal with it. Or I will hold you responsible if the moment I shut my eyes it crawls up my nose and eats my brain.'

'If it can find it,' Nate muttered.

Birdie shot him a look.

'I'll do it,' said Nate, shaking the can in the direction of the flower-bed but making the 'sssssssssss' noise himself. One hundred per cent eco-friendly.

Even though the bug was gone, Birdie was not in the mood for relaxing. She called Chipper who was over in a moment.

Chipper was less disappointed to see Nate than Birdie had been.

'I wish you'd told me,' she said. 'I totally would have brought a different bikini.'

'Chipper,' said Birdie. 'He's one of the staff. Anyway, this afternoon is not about getting you some action. I want to talk about Dean.'

'Of course.' Chipper was suitably chastened.

Birdie ran through the day's events on the set of *PCH* again. Chipper made appropriately sympathetic noises and inserted phrases like, 'She didn't!', 'The cow' and 'Bitch' wherever necessary.

'I hate the way she looks at him,' Birdie complained. 'And he looks back at her. I've seen it. He thinks I don't notice.'

'Maybe it's just because they have to pretend to be in love all day. She knows you're with him. She wouldn't dare tread on your toes.'

'He said he couldn't see me tonight because we have such a heavy day on set tomorrow. He keeps cancelling dates, Chipper. It doesn't matter what I suggest we do. You know how much he likes motor racing? Well, I suggested that we fly to see the Grand Prix in Singapore in September but he just said he couldn't commit to that right now because it's seven months away. You know what that means, Chipper. It means he doesn't see me with him in seven months' time!'

'That's quite a conclusion,' Chipper said, though the look on her face told Birdie all she needed to know. Chipper agreed with her prognosis.

'What am I going to do?'

Chipper offered the usual advice that girls give under the circumstances.

'You've got to make him want you again. Be elusive. Don't pick up the phone when he calls. Don't respond to his text messages. Pretend you're busy when he asks for a date. Before long he will be eating out of the palm of your hand.'

And Birdie responded as girls in unrequited love always do. She put up all the usual reasons why she should actually call Dean right that minute and beg him to come round because they needed to have a serious *talk* about the state of their relationship. Because surely the moment he realized just how deep her love for him was, he would quit the behaviour that made her unhappy right away. He just had to see the real Birdie and everything would be all right.

Chipper was unconvinced. Though she herself had put forward all the same arguments just a couple of months before when Birdie counselled her about an unrequited crush.

'We need to talk to Clemency,' suggested Chipper in the end. 'This kind of situation is really beyond me. Clemency will know whether the way Dean's reacting is normal behaviour for a guy and exactly what you should do about it. As a man.'

'Good idea,' said Birdie. She used her cellphone to call Clemency out from the kitchen to the side of the pool.

Clemency was not best pleased to be interrupted on a rare evening off, but Birdie promised margaritas and, in all honesty, since her dream of discovering LA with Melanie by her side had come to naught, Clemency had nothing better to do.

'OK,' she relented. 'What is it you want to know?'

'I'm going to tell you what's been going on with my boyfriend,' said Birdie. 'Then I want you to give me your honest opinion. As a man.'

16

'It's like this,' said Clemency, paraphrasing Chipper. 'He's starting to take you for granted. And when a guy starts to take you for granted, he starts to feel uncomfortable. So he pulls away and then you chase him, which only makes him pull further away until you yourself finally pull back and he chases after you. It's the age-old dance of the sexes. Trust me. He wants you to make him work for you.'

'Do you think so?' asked Birdie. 'But how can I do that?'

'You have to make him think that he's in danger of losing you. Let him know that there are other guys sniffing around.'

'But there aren't,' said Chipper.

Birdie shot her a look. 'There so are!'

'Whatever,' said Clemency before a fight could erupt. 'It doesn't actually really matter whether there are or not. You just have to make him think that there are. Be unavailable next time he calls to ask you on a date.'

'He has never asked me on a date,' said Birdie sadly. 'I make all the arrangements. He's too busy filming *PCH*.'

'Well, don't make any arrangements for a while. Trust me, he'll notice.'

'But if I don't make the arrangements, I won't get to see him.' Birdie was alarmed.

'If you keep on making the arrangements,' said Clemency ominously, 'then eventually, he won't want to see you at all. That's your choice.'

Birdie bit her lip. 'Are you sure?'

'Absolutely. Next time he calls, just be a little evasive. It's Wednesday now, right? Say you can't see him until next Wednesday.'

'A whole week!'

'You know what will happen if you don't. Remember, next time he calls, you're busy.'

Birdie didn't like to admit that since those first two calls, prompted by his agent Justin, Dean had never actually phoned her.

'Anyway, I can't not see him for a week. We're both on the *PCH* set tomorrow. What am I supposed to do? Not turn up for my scenes? Or pretend he isn't there?'

'Just be cool when you're around him.'

'I can't be *cool* when I'm around him,' said Birdie. 'I am in *love*.'

Clemency and Chipper both swayed backwards at the force of Birdie's exclamation.

'OK,' said Clemency. 'Then how about this? You've got to see him tomorrow, so use it as an opportunity to put this plan into action. Call the florist now and arrange to have some flowers delivered to the set tomorrow afternoon. When the flowers arrive, look delighted but slightly furtive. You'll soon have him wondering who the flowers are from and making more effort to make sure some other guy doesn't steal you away.'

Birdie's mouth dropped open at the simplicity of the plan. 'Do you think it will work?'

'Of course.'

'What kind of flowers do guys send?' Birdie asked.

'You mean you never had a guy send you flowers?' Clemency asked.

'No. I mean, of course I have. Just . . . not lately,' she admitted.

'Roses,' said Clemency, casting a longing look in Nate's direction. 'Roses are for love. They've got to be red, of course.'

So, feeling that she had no choice but to try Clemency's plan, Birdie called her florist and arranged for a bouquet to arrive on set at the *PCH* studio the following afternoon.

'Roses,' she said. 'Red.'

'A dozen?' asked the florist.

'Yes. No, wait. Two dozen,' said Birdie.

'Two dozen. Twenty four.'

'Make that ten.'

'Ten roses?'

'Ten dozen.' Birdie knew that this was one important shot at reigniting Dean's ardour. The gesture needed to be a big one.

'Ten dozen. You realize that's one hundred and twenty roses?' said the florist.

'I can count,' said Birdie.

'Are you sure you want that many?'

'Yes, I am.'

'Most people don't have the vases for it.'

'This girl does.'

'OK. One hundred and twenty roses it is. And what would you like on the gift card?'

'Just a love-heart and a question mark.'

'A love-heart and a question mark?' the florist repeated.

'Hang on. I've got a better idea. Put 'Thanks for the best night of my life'. *And* a love-heart and a question mark. Leaves it anonymous.'

'But surely,' said the florist, 'if you're thanking someone for the best night of your life, there's no point being anonymous? I mean, unless you gave them Rohypnol.'

It was a good point.

'OK. Put an initial. Put . . .' Birdie hesitated. 'BN.'

'BN.'

'No! Wait. Put DS.'

'DS?'

When Birdie heard the letters repeated back to her, she realized immediately that she had subconsciously chosen Dean's initials. That was no good. 'I mean, SK,' she corrected. 'Yes, SK is good.'

'Right,' the florist said slowly. 'One hundred and twenty red roses.'

'Long-stemmed.'

'Of course. One hundred and twenty long-stemmed red roses with a card attached that says 'Thank you for the best night of my life' from SK.'

Birdie agreed.

'And those roses are going to Miss Birdie Sederburg on the *PCH* set at Sundowner Studios. That will be four hundred dollars. And the name on the credit card is . . .'

'Birdie Sederburg,' said Birdie in a whisper.

'Birdie Sederburg,' repeated the florist. 'Fine. OK. I need the long number first . . .'

Birdie completed the formalities with a rising sense of shame that brought colour to her cheeks. She was sure she'd heard a snigger at the other end of the line when the florist parroted her name back to her. It was clear that the people at Fantasy Flowers knew exactly what was going on. But Birdie told herself it would be worth it. One hundred and twenty red roses would definitely get Dean thinking about how much she really meant to him. A little embarrassment now could save her relationship.

17

Next day on set, Dean seemed a little distracted. He told Birdie it was because he had a lot of lines to learn and she took him at his word and tried not to be too worried about it. Even though he went off to learn his lines in Emily B's Winnebago.

'I have to stay calm,' she reminded myself. 'What I don't need will come to me,' she added, paraphrasing one of the affirmations that Clemency had suggested she use if she started to feel out of control. 'I do not need Dean Stevenson. I do not need him. Oh, but I *want* him,' she sighed.

There was a lot of hanging around to be done that afternoon. There was some sort of continuity problem with the set. Some joker had stolen a bottle of champagne that had appeared in all the day before's shots and the director, who was a perfectionist and aspired to much greater things than a mere soap, would not proceed until everything was exactly as it had been twenty-four hours earlier.

Birdie chewed at a cuticle.

'You nervous?' asked one of the extras.

'Yes,' Birdie nodded but she wasn't nervous about the scene. There were just twenty minutes to go until the flowers were due to arrive. Would Birdie be able to feign realistic surprise when she saw them? Of course she would, she told herself. It was time for another affirmation; 'I am a great actress. I am a great actress.'

Twenty minutes later, the flowers had still to arrive but the director was finally pleased with his set and called for everyone to take their places. Birdie, wearing the same outfit as the day before, took her spot on one side of the set. Dean was having his nose powdered on the other side, in readiness to burst through the door in a Shannon-induced rage. The camera was about to roll when . . .

'I'm sorry to interrupt,' said one of the production assistants to the director. 'There's a man here with a delivery of flowers for Birdie Sederburg.'

'What the . . .?' The director scowled. 'Just tell him to leave the flowers and go. We are working.'

'I already suggested that, but I'm afraid he's absolutely insistent that he must see her. In person.'

'I won't have this on my set. Such interruptions are intolerable!'

The producer stepped forward to remind him, as gently as possible, whose grace and favour would be taking them to Sederburg Resort in Kauai later that month.

'OK.' The director put his hands in the air. 'Let the man in. Quickly.'

The florist staggered onto the set, weighed down by Birdie's flowers. He was not so much a man as a pair of legs sticking out from a mutant rose bush.

'Birdie Sederburg?' he announced.

There was a murmur of admiration from the extras as they took in the ultra-extravagant blooms. The regular actors feigned indifference but soon they too were drifting closer to Birdie and the action, eager to see if the flowers were from Dean to make up for having been so mean to her the past couple of days. Everyone had noticed that much.

Birdie skipped lightly from the stage.

'Ohmigod,' she shrieked. 'All for me?'

The ball of roses seemed to nod.

'But it's hundreds and hundreds of flowers. Roses. Red ones. My favourite.' She inhaled. 'And they smell so good!'

She turned to Dean and wagged her forefinger. 'You naughty boy. You didn't . . .'

'No,' said Dean flatly. 'I didn't.'

A whisper went through the crowd: a mixture of disbelief, excitement and surprise.

'Then I wonder who did,' said Birdie. 'Who on earth could have been so generous?'

'Just open the fricking card,' said the director.

Birdie plucked the little white envelope off the cellophane that wrapped one of the bouquets (there were three, in all. Forty roses in each). She started to read the message out loud.

'Thank you for the best . . .'

She stopped abruptly and pressed the card against her chest. 'Oh, my . . .' She shook her head and smiled a little secretively.

Dean's eyes narrowed. At last his curiosity was piqued.

'Thank you for the best night of my life . . .' Birdie continued.

'Who are they from?' Dean asked at last.

'Oh, no one. At least, no one you know,' said Birdie, looking suitably flustered.

'Let me see that.' Dean snatched the card from her hand. 'SK? Who's SK? Steven Krane?' He named one of his fellow stars on *PCH*. Steve backed away with his hands in the air.

'No way, man,' he said. 'I wouldn't touch her. No offence,' he added for Birdie's benefit.

'Seb Kochrane?' Dean continued.

'Cochrane is spelt with a 'c',' said Seb helpfully.

'Look, I hate to interrupt you, Ms Sederburg,' the delivery guy butted in. 'But I'm going to need to take an imprint of your credit card. When you called to place the order yesterday afternoon, my colleague must have took your number down wrong.'

'I . . . I . . .' Birdie was rumbled.

'Oh my God,' said Emily B, almost snorting with contempt. 'You're telling me she sent those flowers to herself?'

18

'I'm losing him!' Birdie wailed later that night. 'I can feel it. He's further away than ever before. That stupid idea with the flowers just made me look like an idiot. I ought to sack Clemency.'

'It wasn't a stupid idea,' said Chipper. 'I would have put money on it working. I think you should sue the florist for embarrassing you like that.'

'That's not going to alter the fact that Dean knows I sent myself flowers! A hundred and twenty red roses at that! ohmigod. He's probably on the phone to Emily B right now reliving the whole sorry scene. He's laughing at me. She's laughing at me.'

'But he didn't actually dump you?'

'Not in so many words. He didn't say anything. He just sort of walked off.'

'Then you still have a chance to pull this back. Rescue disaster from the jaws of victory,' Chipper insisted.

'Huh?'

'I think perhaps I meant to say that the other way round.'

'Whatever.'

'My opinion is, you've got to leave town,' said Chipper. 'It's the only way. You've got to make him miss you. Go somewhere hot and have a great time. Get your picture in all the magazines. Make him see that you can have a good time without him. That is one guaranteed way to drive a man crazy with desire.'

'Chipper, how do you know? You've never even had a boyfriend.'

'I so have . . .'

'Kissing that guy who passed out at your cousin's wedding in 2004 does not count.'

'Let's not get into that now,' said Chipper.

'We won't. I called you to talk about me. You say I need to leave town but where can I go?' asked Birdie mournfully.

'Birdie,' Chipper sighed. 'Your family own one of the biggest hotel chains in the whole fricking world! You can go anywhere you like. Let's go to the South of France. I'll come with you. I've got nothing in my diary for next week except a manicure and it will be good for me to get away from my mother. You would not believe how unreasonable she is being about that Birkin.'

'Did she find out about the vomit?' asked Birdie.

'Unfortunately she did. And she threatened to cut off my allowance. So I told her it was you. '

'Thanks a lot.'

'She says you're never to come to our house ever again.'

'What?'

'I'm sorry,' said Chipper.

'It's not such a big deal. Your pool is half the size of mine.'

'It is so not! Anyway, I am totally up for a trip with you. How soon can we go? Can we get a flight tomorrow?'

'Chipper, I'm not sure that leaving town right now is such a great idea.'

'Absence makes the heart grow fonder.'

'They say that, but I know of just as many instances where someone has gone absent and just been forgotten.'

'I don't see what choice you have. Have Clemency book us onto a flight.'

It was midnight. Quite reasonably, Clemency was in bed and did not expect to have to deal with her boss. But Birdie couldn't wait until the morning to ask her to book their passage to France. When Birdie Sederburg was on a mission, she was truly on a mission, and a mission to save her relationship with Dean Stevenson was far more important than her employee's time off.

'I need two seats, first class, on the first available flight to Paris.'

'Paris?' murmured Clemency. 'For you and Dean?'

'No,' Birdie harrumphed. 'For me and Chipper. Oh, and I suppose you'd better book yourself onto the same flight too.'

'You want me to go to France? How long for? I'm supposed to be at my cousin's wedding on Saturday.'

'You may not be back in time. Or you'll be unemployed.'

Birdie hung up.

'Shit.' Clemency closed the book she was reading and picked up her laptop instead.

The following morning, Clemency reported for work bright and early. Unusually, Birdie was already up. She was in a panic. Her bed was covered in items of clothing.

'I need you to pack,' she said. 'I need three changes of clothing a day for at least a week.'

'OK,' Clemency shrugged. She didn't know why Birdie ever bothered to pack, since whenever she travelled, she inevitably hit the shops and came home with four times as much as she'd taken in the first place.

'Now, remember,' said Chipper, when she arrived with her own bags (all five of them), 'You must not tell Dean where you're going. Or even that you're going anywhere at all. He's been acting like you don't matter. Well, you have to give him a taste of his own medicine. Make him think that he's been relegated to the status of mere friend. Let him find out *accidentally*.'

'How?'

'Facebook?'

'Of course.' Birdie changed her status message to 'wondering what I should pack for my trip to the South of France.'

'That's great,' Chipper approved. 'Now, do we know anyone who has a decent-sized yacht in the Med right now? I mean, the penthouse at your family's hotel will be nice and everything but it's pretty paparazzi proof.'

'Good point,' said Birdie. 'I never thought of that. Give

what's-his-face a call. Paris Hilton's old fiancé. I'm sure he's forgotten that time you vomited all over his shoes in Ago by now.'

It took a very long time for Birdie to be ready to leave the house that day. Thank God she was flying first class and the usual check-in times didn't apply. It was different for Clemency, who would have to join the hoi polloi at security. As it was, she made it to the gate for departure with seconds to go. The girl on the counter was counting up boarding passes.

'You have to let me on,' she begged.

'Gate's closed.'

'My boss is already on there. In first class. If I don't make this flight, she'll fire me.'

'Who's your boss?' the girl asked.

'Birdie Sederburg. And, yes, she had a nose job. In Poland, so she could hide out at the new Sederburg hotel there. I made the arrangements.'

Open-mouthed at such a great snippet of gossip, the girl on the counter waved Clemency on through. As the last passenger to board the plane, she was greeted with a round of disdainful applause as she slunk to her seat. She hated that so many people thought she was the kind of selfish person who might hold up a flight because she was busy shopping in duty-free.

Up in first class, Birdie and Chipper brainstormed their strategy for turning the French sojourn into a publicity coup that would make Dean Stevenson realize exactly who he was dealing with.

Their mile-high planning session was aided by a bottle of Krug. Two bottles. Eventually, Birdie and Chipper fell asleep. Birdie's snores competed with the volume of the jet's engine as she dreamed of her triumphant return to LA and a suitably chastened boyfriend.

At the back of the plane, Clemency was just dreaming (awake and dreaming) of the moment when she would be able to crawl into bed and catch up on the sleep she was missing with this transatlantic flight. Having been the very last to check in to the flight, hers was the very worst seat. Right at the back by the toilets, in the middle of a row of five, sandwiched between two people who were oozing out of their own seats and under the armrest to encroach on her space. It was going to be a long flight.

19

Birdie was disappointed that there were no paparazzi to greet the plane when it landed at Charles De Gaulle. Sure, there were paps, but the French paps weren't there for an American heiress. They were there for their own president and his newish wife.

Birdie and Chipper slipped by unsnapped while Clemency pushed the luggage trolley behind them. (Another advantage of having a gender-reoriented personal assistant was that she had enormous arm muscles, Birdie confided to Chipper.)

They would spend a night in Paris before heading down to Cannes. Birdie and Chipper had adjoining suites in the Paris Sederburg. Clemency had a much smaller room downstairs in the part of the hotel that was still undergoing refurbishment and thus rang with the sound of electric drills from six in the morning till seven at night. So much for catching up on that sleep.

Unable to lie in, Clemency was up at six and set to checking all the press for any news about her boss. Unsurprisingly, there was nothing in the *International Herald Tribune* or *Le Figaro*.

'Are you sure?' Birdie asked. 'Look again. I don't trust your French.'

Meanwhile, Birdie checked her iPhone at least twice a minute for anything, anything at all, from Dean. But there was nothing. Not a call, not a text, not an email. It wasn't as though he hadn't been online. Birdie knew that he had because he had changed the status message on his Facebook page to 'Dean Stevenson is loving Chinese food.'

'What does that mean? Just who is he eating Chinese food *with*?'

Birdie was tormented.

'He's just playing the game,' Clemency assured her. 'It's a man thing. He senses that you're holding back and he's trying to wait you out. You've just got to make sure you're not the first to buckle.'

'Right,' said Birdie, reluctantly turning off her phone as they boarded the short flight from Paris to Nice airport. She turned her phone back on again before the plane's engines stopped running. Still nothing . . .

It should have been a nice break. The Sederburg Hotel in Cannes was one of Birdie's favourites. It reminded her of happy childhood holidays before the avalanche killed her parents. If only the avalanche had happened in the afternoon, they would both have been too drunk to be on the slopes. Still, Birdie had very happy memories of that part of the Côte d'Azur, where she had once built sandcastles while her parents raced each other to finish their dry martinis.

Birdie and Chipper arranged themselves by the pool and discreetly scanned the other guests from behind their sunglasses. Meanwhile, Clemency got down to her task for that afternoon which was to wade through the thousands of Google hits for Dean Stevenson and see whether there was anything new to report. Nothing. Nothing. Nothing. Then suddenly there was something . . .

'What is it? What is it?' Birdie was all at once as excited as a child on Christmas Day and as nervous as a student awaiting exam results. She covered her eyes. 'Good or bad? Tell me, quickly. Chipper, hold my hand in case it's bad.'

'It's, er, neutral,' said Clemency. 'I think.'

'Neutral?' Birdie uncovered her eyes. 'What do you mean it's neutral?'

'It's just a picture of Dean from the *People* website. It's a focus on watches. What are the bright young stars of Hollywood using to tell the time these days?' Clemency read out loud. 'For a while, it seemed that no one wore a watch any more. Why bother when you have one clock in your Mercedes and another on your iPhone? Dean Stevenson spearheaded the return to old-fashioned time-keeping with the Breitling diver's watch he received as a gift for his twenty-first birthday. But what's this? He's upgraded. Last week in Santa Monica, Dean was seen out and about in a solid gold Rolex Daytona.'

'Oh my God.' Birdie clutched Chipper's wrist so hard that she left a pale ring where the blood couldn't get through. 'Oh my God. Show me the picture.'

'Birdie,' said Chipper, grasping the significance. 'It's the watch that you gave him.'

Birdie nodded. It took a while before she regained the power of speech.

'As a pre-engagement present!' Chipper shrieked. 'Which means . . .'

'He loves me. He still wants to be with me. He's wearing my watch. It's a signal to everyone that we are a serious item.'

'A pre-engagement present?' said Clemency. 'I don't think I've ever heard of that.'

'It's quite common,' Chipper assured her.

'Not where I come from,' said Clemency.

'Keep Googling him,' Birdie instructed. 'I want to see every single new picture.'

'OK,' said Clemency. While Birdie and Chipper continued to discuss the significance of the 'pre-engagement watch', she trawled through another thousand Google hits. At four in the afternoon, early morning LA time, the front page of Ohmygahd.com was refreshed. And there was Dean.

He was pictured sitting at a table outside a restaurant with his co-star Seb Cochrane and a third unnamed man (who was actually Justin). The three looked deep in conversation. The story was ostensibly about Seb Cochrane's new tattoo, which could be seen beneath his rolled-up sleeve. It was supposed to be the Chinese character for 'fearless'. Ohmygahd's researchers had discovered that it actually said 'wheatgrass'.

Birdie didn't care about Seb Cochrane's tattoo. She was studying the photograph for other clues. Dean was still wearing the Rolex. Birdie and Chipper high-fived when they noticed that. Now Birdie was looking closely at the background of the shot. They had quickly worked out the restaurant: The Newsroom Café on Robertson Boulevard. Chipper recognized one of the waiters in the background. Beneath the table was a whole stack of shopping bags. One of the boys had been going nuts with his credit card. A connoisseur of Los Angeles' best boutiques, Birdie soon had every bag worked out. Except for one. You could just see the corner of a small bag in duck-egg blue.

Clemency was called to help work out the conundrum. She brightened the screen of her laptop and suddenly the blue was unmistakable.

'Tiffany,' Chipper breathed.

'Ohmigod, ohmigod, ohmigod!'

Clemency had to flap a magazine over Birdie's face to give her some air. 'It might not be Tiffany,' she pointed out. 'Or maybe it wasn't his bag.'

Birdie didn't care. 'Tiffany . . . the engagement watch . . . Tiffany . . .' she murmured. 'Don't mention this to anyone,' she warned Chipper. 'Not one word. If what I've said to you this afternoon finds its way onto the Internet, I will have you hunted down and killed.'

Birdie might as well have changed her Facebook status to 'getting engaged to Dean Stevenson'.

20

'Dean and Birdie about to tie the knot?' said the headline on Ohmygahd the following morning. A pap photograph of Dean exiting the Tiffany store in the Century City mall substantiated Birdie's suspicion about the Tiffany bag. The store had refused to confirm details of Dean's purchase for confidentiality reasons, which, coupled with more exclusive info about the engagement watch from a mysterious 'overseas caller' could only mean one thing – or so the writers at Ohmygahd decided.

Reading the website in the South of France, Birdie was outwardly indignant at her best friend's betrayal (who else knew the real story behind the Rolex?) and inwardly delighted.

'Chipper!' Birdie put a call through to Chipper's suite. 'How could you have done that to me? You blabbed about the engagement watch! While you're staying here as my guest!'

'I swear I don't know how it happened,' said Chipper. 'I didn't mention anything to anyone. Maybe one of the hotel staff overheard us talking and called someone in Los Angeles.'

'Sometimes I feel like Princess Diana,' said Birdie dramatically. 'I can't sneeze without the whole world asking whether I have a cold. I'm living in a goldfish bowl.'

'Perhaps the best way to kill this story is to say nothing more about it,' suggested Clemency.

'You're right,' said Birdie. 'I will act as though this has not happened.'

Still, after breakfast, she had the fine jewellery store on the ground floor of the Sederburg Hotel Cannes send up a tray full of diamond engagement rings so she could check the size of her ring finger and work out the perfect number of carats for her dainty hands, just in case. The number was fifty-seven.

'It is extremely important that no one knows I asked to see this jewellery,' Birdie told the store over the phone, within earshot of four maids who were tidying the room. Four maids who knew that they would be fired for selling a story about any member of the Sederburg family but who were nonetheless all weighing up in their heads the financial pay-off. Lose a job that paid a thousand euros a month for a hundred-thousand-euro lump sum. Now that was a risk worth taking.

The maids had a conference in their staff-room later that day and decided that the story probably wasn't worth that much. Instead, they went back to deciding which one of them would take the rap if they sold a story about another, much bigger, star who had been sharing a room at the hotel with a mystery man who was most definitely not his wife. They decided by rolling a die.

Meanwhile, having made up with Chipper about the website leak, Birdie asked her best friend to accompany her on a little shopping trip. There were a couple of bridal boutiques in Cannes. Birdie had Clemency call ahead and make sure that no one, but *no one* would be admitted to the stores while she was inside trying on dresses.

'It is extremely important that nobody knows you have Birdie Sederburg in your store this afternoon,' Clemency explained in her very best French. It was more for Birdie's benefit than anyone else's, since the staff at each of the stores Clemency called assured her that they wouldn't have alerted the paparazzi because they didn't have the faintest clue who Birdie Sederburg was.

Of course, the next call Clemency made was to a picture agency in LA. Birdie would be very disappointed if there were no photographers waiting at all.

Having asked the stores to close on her behalf from ten in the morning onwards, Birdie and Chipper were finally ready to see what was on offer at three in the afternoon. To preserve her anonymity, Birdie donned the kind of enormous sunglasses that say 'Don't look at me, I'm a *celebrity*' in twenty-three different languages. Chipper did the same. Clemency trailed behind them in a pair of twenty-Euro specs she had bought at the airport, having left hers back in California. She carried a clipboard, for making notes, and a digital camera to take photographs that Birdie could send back to her grandfather for approval.

Birdie was already imagining how her big day would be. She brainstormed the details with Chipper. With a bit of luck, if they moved quickly, she and Dean could be getting married by Labor Day weekend. Birdie imagined a wedding at her grandfather's most prestigious golf resort: the Sederburg Santa Barbara. They'd have the ceremony on the terrace overlooking the sea. The entire cast of *PCH* would be there. She had asked Chipper to be a bridesmaid, of course. Perhaps she should ask Emily too. Just to see her face. A wicked smile spread across her lips at the thought.

'I can't believe I am actually trying on a wedding dress!' Birdie was wide-eyed with excitement as they entered the second shop. 'If my grandfather could see me now, he would be so proud.'

And relieved that he was about to be shot of you, Clemency thought to herself.

Birdie had the store assistants bring out their dozen most expensive dresses. Never mind what style the dresses were (they ranged from milkmaid to mermaid). Birdie just wanted those that cost the most.

While she was halfway into a dress that looked one hundred per cent Disney heroine, Birdie's cellphone rang. It was DD.

'I heard all about the engagement,' she said. 'I hope that you will not even *think* about buying your wedding dress without me. Makiko Clark says that she would be happy to create something absolutely unique for you, perhaps incorporating style elements from the all-in-one you were wearing when Dean first realized he was in love.'

'Of course I'll wait to take your advice,' said Birdie as Chipper zipped her up.

'How do I look?' Birdie twirled in front of the mirror.

'You look incredible,' said Chipper.

Birdie looked at the price tag on the dress. The price was four thousand euros. 'I think I can get something similar to this made up in New York for around four hundred,' she said with some satisfaction.

'But mademoiselle,' said the sales assistant, 'these crystals are applied by hand. The workmanship required to produce a garment like this would make it impossible to create it for anything less.'

'Oh, I know,' said Birdie. 'I was thinking four hundred *thousand*. I mean, I'll have to have real Swarovski crystal. Not this *glass*. Clemency, will you take a photo for Vera to work from?'

Realizing that she wasn't going to get a sale, the assistant was a great deal less helpful after that.

Outside the shop, a lone photographer waited on his motor-bike. When Birdie came out, he gamely fired off a few shots of her inadequately hiding behind her Birkin. Birdie took an ineffectual swing at the photographer with her bag to make sure that he got at least one proper shot of her face. Then, as Birdie stalked off to a waiting limo, Clemency negotiated with the photographer to ensure he didn't send in a pic of Birdie looking like a Rottweiler.

'She'll like that one,' Clemency said, as she slipped the pap a hundred-Euro note and made sure that he had the right URL for Ohmygahd.com.

21

Birdie was suddenly very much enjoying her holiday in France. 'It was an awesome idea to get away,' she told Chipper. 'It completely made Dean see the light.' But back in Los Angeles, Dean Stevenson was in an altogether blacker mood.

When he saw the headline on Ohmygahd, Dean almost choked on his breakfast. By the time Justin called to congratulate him, Dean was ready to go into hiding.

'You might have called me first,' said Justin. 'I mean, the news broke on a website. I could have made sure it came out in a magazine that would have paid for it.'

'Jesus, Justin. I'm twenty-four years old. I'm not getting married,' said Dean. 'Not to anyone, but especially not to her. You know I only went to Tiffany to get a keyring for your assistant's birthday.'

The item on Ohmygahd about the 'engagement watch' really pissed Dean off. When he got to the set that day, everyone was talking about it. Seb Cochrane insisted that the whole gang should go out that night and celebrate.

'There's nothing to celebrate.'

'Hey, come on, man,' said Seb. 'You're getting married.'

'I am *not* getting married,' said Dean. 'This is just another example of something being taken totally out of context. You know I only bought a keyring in Tiffany because I asked you what you thought of it at lunch. And I don't suppose Birdie said anything about getting engaged at all. She's not that stupid.'

Seb kept a polite silence.

'Someone just put two and two together when they saw me

coming out of Tiffany and made seven. Whoever heard of an 'engagement watch', for Christ's sake?' Dean was conspicuously wearing his twenty-first-birthday Breitling once again.

'Whatever,' said Seb. He walked off humming, 'Here comes the bride.'

Meanwhile, Emily B was acting weird. Ordinarily, she and Dean would meet for breakfast with the rest of the crew but that morning, she was already in her Winnebago when Dean arrived and told him, when he asked her to join him at the breakfast truck, that she would just sip some orange juice while she went over her lines. Dean sensed that she was jealous, which gave him something of a thrill. Until that moment, he hadn't been sure that she cared. That was a silver lining to the stupid rumour, Dean supposed.

But by the time shooting had finished for the day, things were looking far worse for the commitment-shy soap star. When he came out of his trailer, he discovered a bunch of people huddled around one of the juniors from the production team. As Dean got close, someone alerted the junior to the fact that Dean was coming and she quickly snapped her laptop shut. Everyone tried to look nonchalant. But it was too late – and they were a terrible bunch of actors. As the rest of the crowd dispersed, leaving the production assistant all alone. Dean insisted that she show him what everyone had been laughing about. Slowly, guiltily, the girl opened her laptop again and the page she had last been reading flickered onto the screen.

'What the . . . ?'

Dean sat down on the folding chair next to the production assistant and pulled her laptop over onto his own knees. Half the screen was taken up with a picture of Birdie, exiting a store and wielding one of her stupidly expensive handbags like a medieval knight's mace. Underneath, the text explained the exact nature of Birdie's shopping expedition for anyone who hadn't already guessed from the mannequins in meringues that graced the shop window.

'Earlier this afternoon Birdie Sederburg was snapped exiting a high-end bridal store in Cannes in the South of France in the company of her friend and fellow heiress, Chipper Dooley. Though Birdie was anxious not to be photographed anywhere near the bridal boutique, Ohmygahd can reveal, exclusively, that the shop assistant confirmed Birdie tried on three wedding dresses and took photographs of her favourite. The dress Birdie liked best was by French designer Chantal l'Amour. It's an elegant full-skirted number in cream silk dupion with gold lace overlay on the bodice and sleeves. We're sure it will look fabulous with Birdie's blonde hair. All we need to know now is whether Dean will be wearing a morning suit or tux.'

'I'm sorry,' said the production assistant.

'It's not your fault,' said Dean automatically. He handed back the laptop. And almost simultaneously, his cellphone rang.

'Dean,' said Justin. 'I need you to speak to Birdie right this instant. Do you think she has any idea how much money I could be getting for these photographs? I could have easily got six figures for photos of your future wife trying on dresses in some store in the USA. Jesus, Dean, it breaks my heart. Some paparazzi shot in France? That store gets free advertising and we get nothing. Zip.'

'Justin,' Dean interrupted his manager's rant. 'I am not getting married to Birdie. We are *not* engaged. I am going to break up with her when she comes back from Cannes.'

'Are you nuts?' asked Justin.

'I don't want to get married to her! She's a lunatic. I should never have gone on that first date. I blame you.'

'Calm down,' said Justin. 'No one said anything about you actually having to get married. But there is money to be made from this, Dean. Just a few photo shoots, then everything will go quiet again. You can set the wedding date for eighteen months away.'

The words 'wedding' and 'date' in such close proximity made Dean's bowels feel loose.

'You set the wedding date for eighteen months away,' Justin repeated, 'and in six months or so you announce your break-up. Quietly. Nobody will care. Everyone will be on to the next hot thing by then. But in the meantime, we will have made a nice chunk of change. Just roll with it. For me.'

'What's the alternative?'

'You could look terribly ungallant and say the whole engagement thing was just a rumour. Then I suppose I'll just have to go back to trying to convince people you definitely do like chicks . . .'

Dean told Justin that he understood and that he would follow Justin's instructions for dealing with the whole thing to the letter. But the incident had really rattled him. That very evening he took his co-star Emily B to dinner. Over sizzling fajitas and several cold beers, Dean poured his heart out. He explained that he just wasn't ready for commitment. He didn't even know who he really was, deep inside. He needed to find himself and there was no way he could do that within the confines of marriage. What on earth was he to do?

Emily B laid her hand over Dean's and looked deep into his eyes.

'Follow your heart,' she said, which was exactly what her character Shannon would have said at that point. '*You need to be true to the true you you need to be* . . .' (That line actually did come directly from the *PCH* script.)

'I don't know how I would get by without a friend like you,' Dean told her, quite sincerely.

Then Dean took Emily B outside and kissed her and kissed her in the parking lot until someone, thank God, finally, used a cellphone to take a picture of the soap stars snogging.

'Hey! Are you going to try to sell that photo to the media?' Dean asked the passer-by.

The passer-by said he probably would, and so what if he did? It was his right to do so.

'If you want to keep things quiet then get a room,' the jerk continued. 'Public displays of affection are in the public domain as far as I'm concerned.'

'Good for you,' said Dean. 'I totally agree. Call this man.' He scribbled down a number. 'He'll get your picture onto Ohmygahd.'

22

Clemency discovered the photograph taken on a cellphone had been posted on Ohmygahd while Birdie and Chipper were taking advantage of their last day in France and tanning their under-arms down by the pool.

When Birdie saw the photograph of her boyfriend kissing another woman, her first instinct was to throw up. She didn't (she had already thrown up her lunch in an altogether more controlled way in the bathroom of her hotel suite). Instead she told herself that the picture must be a still from an episode of *PCH*.

'It says it was taken in a parking lot in Santa Monica,' said Clemency.

Birdie's next tack was to decide that the guy in the photo was not really her boyfriend.

'This is a composite photo,' she assured Chipper. 'Look at the background around his head. It's very slightly blurred. I can see exactly what they've done here. They've taken a picture of Emily B kissing her own boyfriend and Photoshopped Dean's head on top.'

'Why don't you just call and ask him about it?' Clemency suggested.

'I will not,' said Birdie. 'Why on earth would I dignify such nonsense with a reaction and make Dean think that I don't trust him? Trust is the cornerstone of any relationship, right?'

'Right. Do you trust him?'

'Of course.'

*   *   *

But the holiday had come to an abrupt end. Birdie gave up on browning her underarms at once. She dressed in her most sober shirt-dress and asked Clemency to bring their flights home forward. Then she had Clemency pack up her luggage. And Chipper's too.

'Do you really think we need to go back early?' Chipper asked. The guy at the pool bar had been flirting with her and she was anxious to know what might develop if she hung around. Chipper hadn't been properly kissed since her Bat Mitzvah and that was by a cousin.

'I have to go back,' said Birdie. 'Dean and I need to present a united front right now. There will be gossip if we're not seen together.'

Birdie had tried to call Dean but was having no luck getting past his voicemail. She hadn't said in any of her five messages exactly what it was she wanted to talk about, but he must know by now.

The flight from Paris back to Los Angeles seemed to take forever. Eleven hours stretched into years.

When the flight landed at LAX, Birdie prepared for the paparazzi that were always hanging around the nearest exit to the first-class lounges. Chipper helped her stick on her fake ponytail, as though Birdie were Joan of Arc getting into her armour.

'Whatever they say,' she advised her friend, 'just keep walking. Don't stop to chat.'

'Birdie!' they shouted. 'What are you going to say to Dean when you see him? Does this mean your engagement is over?'

'Was the engagement ever really on?' asked another.

Birdie gave a large anguished gulp.

'You don't have to talk to them,' Clemency reminded her. But Birdie would not keep quiet.

'All I want to say is that I love Dean very much and I will do everything in my power to make our relationship work.'

'He said in an interview on *E! Live* that he never really

considered you had an actual relationship. He thought it was just casual dating. What do you think about that?'

Birdie wailed in agony.

Eventually, Birdie had to call Dean and hear the news from the horse's mouth.

'Are you really seeing her?'

'I am,' said Dean, feeling almost sorry for his most recent ex-girlfriend. 'I guess we discovered we had chemistry on set and it just developed from there. We went for a couple of cocktails, and that lowered our inhibitions, and . . .'

'Stop,' said Birdie. 'I don't need to hear any more.'

Birdie went straight into a decline.

She flew into her bedroom and locked the door behind her. She refused to admit either Chipper or Clemency. She refused offers of company and of food and drink. She didn't want a sandwich and milk. She didn't want champagne and Ben & Jerry's. She just wanted to be alone.

'Birdie never wants to be alone,' said Chipper worriedly.

Well, she did now.

'I think the only thing we can do is leave her in her cave,' said Clemency.

'Isn't that what you *guys* are supposed to do?' said Chipper. 'Girls don't go into their caves.'

Clemency tried not to be upset by Chipper's intimation that she didn't understand feminine emotions.

23

Birdie stayed in her room for five days solid. Clemency didn't worry too much for the first forty-eight hours but by the end of the third day, she was starting to be concerned. Birdie refused to touch any of the food the maid or Clemency herself prepared for her. Clemency would deliver the meal trays and retrieve them, completely untouched, an hour or so later.

'Birdie,' she called through the door when she discovered yet another uneaten meal in the hallway. 'You have to eat.'

'I don't *have* to do anything!' Birdie responded. 'I am a Sederburg. In any case, it's not worth doing anything. The one man I ever loved is in love with someone else.'

'He's not in love with Emily B,' said Clemency, trying to be helpful. 'I'm sure its just sex.'

A wail came from Birdie's bedroom. 'I don't want to think about them having *sex*!' The worst of it was that Birdie had never got beyond second base with Dean. There was always some reason why he wouldn't or couldn't stay the night. Birdie had hoped that refraining from making love was Dean's way of showing that he respected her more than previous boyfriends had. She had convinced herself that it was a sign that their union would have longevity. It was a non-verbal way of telling her that there was no need to hurry their love. They had forever. How could she have got it so *wrong*?

So many emotions fought for space in Birdie's mind right then. Loss, sadness, embarrassment. They took it in turns to prevail. Birdie could find no solace anywhere. In anything. She couldn't watch any of the usual entertainment channels for fear of catching sight of her lost love in a trailer for the new series of his show. She couldn't even watch the Discovery Channel because the mere sight of the channel's logo reminded her of her second date with Dean when she asked him what he liked to watch on TV and he said he liked the Discovery Channel's documentaries on sharks and Nazis. She couldn't read gossip magazines for obvious reasons. She couldn't read a book because . . . well, she didn't have any books in the house.

With the curtains drawn tightly shut, Birdie lost track of time as another day became night became day.

'Birdie, come on.' On the sixth morning of Birdie's self-imposed solitary confinement, Clemency knocked gently on the bedroom door and pushed it open. 'I have a visitor for you. It's time to get up.'

'I can't get up,' Birdie whined from beneath the duvet.

'You've been saying that for the past five days. Come on.'

Clemency opened the long drapes to let some light into the sour, still room.

'No.' Birdie pulled the duvet over her head.

'Come on.' Clemency pulled the duvet back.

'I'll fire you!' Birdie warned her.

'And your grandfather will have you *committed* if you don't show your face outside this bedroom soon. He's very worried about you.'

'Is he?' Birdie asked. She sat up a little against her pillows. 'I don't want to worry Grandaddy. Is he my visitor?'

'No,' said Clemency. 'It's Lindsay Lohan.'

'You can't let her in here while I look like this!' Birdie squealed. 'I haven't washed my hair in five days!'

'It's not *the* Lindsay Lohan,' Clemency elaborated. 'It's Lindsay Lohan, Chipper's dog. She thought if you didn't want to see her, you might at least want to see her Chihuahua.'

'OK.' Clemency opened the bedroom door again and Lindsay scampered in. Birdie managed a smile and Lindsay licked Birdie's face as though to praise her for her efforts. 'Is Grandaddy really worried?'

'Of course he is,' said Clemency. 'He's been calling every day to see how you are.'

'He could have called my cellphone.'

'I guess he thought it would be better to go through me in case you were sleeping,' Clemency lied.

Birdie didn't need to know that her grandfather hadn't called at all, or that when Clemency had started to panic and phoned him at his office, his only reaction to Birdie's predicament had been to roll his eyes and say, 'Can't someone take her shopping or something?'

'I don't want to worry Grandaddy,' said Birdie.

'Then why don't you jump in the shower and come downstairs for breakfast as soon as you like.'

An hour after Clemency told Birdie that she was worrying her grandfather, Birdie found her way downstairs for the first time since getting back from France. Locked in her room for all that time, allowing only Gatorade and Chipper's dog past the door, Birdie now looked a shadow of the girl who had tried on wedding dresses on the French Riviera. Those few pounds that she could never quite seem to shed on a proper diet had just slipped away. Her tan had faded. The skin under her eyes was grey, betraying the fact that she had hardly slept, despite having access to a lovely stash of prescription sleeping tablets (courtesy of Chipper's mother, who never understood how she got through her prescriptions so fast).

Seeing Birdie in daylight, out of the gloom of her bedroom, Clemency was shocked by the alteration in her young boss's appearance and demeanour. Birdie looked much younger than Clemency had ever seen her. Clemency was surprised to feel something akin to a genuine desire to protect the poor girl.

Since joining Birdie's staff, Clemency had had little to do with Julius Sederburg himself. Over the past four days he had spoken to Clemency more often than ever before, but not because he was concerned with his granddaughter's welfare. His tone when he discussed Birdie's state of mind had been disturbingly disinterested, Clemency thought. At best he seemed impatient and frustrated. She had previously assumed that Birdie had it all. Now she knew that she was blessed in a way that Birdie most definitely wasn't.

Clemency had grown up in a family full of love. Many Middle American families might have had difficulty discovering that their beloved son wanted to become a beloved daughter, but Clemency's folks had stood by her through it all. She spoke to her mother every single day. In fact, it was her mother who had first expressed how sorry she felt for Birdie.

'So sad and with no mother to turn to. That's why she made such a mess of things with Dean. She's got no one to ask for advice.'

'She's always asking for *my* advice,' said Clemency. 'As a *man*.'

'Turn the other cheek, dear,' said Clemency's gentle mother.

And so Clemency decided that she would try a different tack with her boss. She would try to treat Birdie not as someone who needed to be continually hoodwinked in recompense for the measly wages she paid, but as another ordinary girl, trying to make her way in a cruel world, who deserved a little compassion.

'Who knows?' thought Clemency. 'Perhaps if I play this right, Birdie will take me to some of her parties.'

'You need to eat,' she said to Birdie then, pushing a milkshake across the table. She had loaded it with bodybuilder's protein. In fact, she always loaded Birdie's shakes with bodybuilder's protein, but for once it wasn't because she wanted to scupper her weight-loss plan out of spite.

'And don't think that's all you're having for breakfast,' said Clemency firmly. 'I've decided I'm going to look after you.'

Birdie looked up from the table. She smiled. A wavering little smile that took fifteen years off her already newly youthful face.

Clemency felt an odd pain in her heart as she imagined the little girl who had come home from Gstaad all alone.

'Thank you,' said Birdie in an unusually tiny voice. 'I know it's not part of your job description, but I really appreciate your support.'

24

Since her break-up with Dean, Birdie had decided that the media was no longer her friend. Checking the Ohmygahd website ten times an hour was definitely not the pleasure it had been while Birdie's romance with Dean was going well (or at least, while it was *ongoing*). Now, each time she opened the site she was greeted with an image of the man she loved with someone else. Barely an hour went by without someone adding a new pic of Dean Stevenson and Emily B swooning over each other. There were pictures of them kissing outside restaurants, in malls, at baseball games, even while exiting a drycleaning shop. To make matters worse, it was the week of Ohmygahd's best dressed/worst dressed awards.

Of course, Emily B was riding high in the 'best dressed list'. A page on her personal style featured Hollywood's hottest new actress in a variety of elegant and graceful dresses by every designer from Armani to Zac Posen. Everyone who was anyone in the fashion world clamoured to dress the beautiful *PCH* star, whose long lean body could make a sack look like Dior. Meanwhile Birdie, whose slightly shorter than average legs invariably made Dior look like a sack, had also crept up the ratings.

'Worst dressed in Hollywood?' ran the text beneath a picture of Birdie with that chiller bag hung over her arm. 'How about worst dressed in the *world*?'

It was all so cruel. Seeing her name right there at the top of the worst-dressed ratings was enough to send Birdie back into her room, but Clemency would not hear of it.

'Is that how your grandfather would react to a little bit of bitching?' she said. 'Who cares what Ohmygahd think about your fashion sense? The website is run by a man from Iowa, for goodness' sake. He's catering to the provincial tastes of his high-school pals. People like us know *real* fashion.'

Clemency was glad to see that Birdie showed no hint of surprise when Clemency said 'people like us'. 'It's hard to be a true individual,' Clemency continued. 'But it's worth it. You've got to get back out there, Birdie. You're only a loser if you stay down.'

'She's right,' Chipper agreed. 'It's time you got back out there! Let's go to some parties. Do you know of anyone who's having a party anytime soon?'

Birdie could think of only one.

It was the launch of the new series of *PCH* at Shutters on the Beach in Santa Monica. Birdie had received an invitation. It had been sent to her on Dean's behalf, before they split up and had remained in pride of place on the mantelpiece ever since.

'Uh-uh. You can't go to that,' said Clemency, when Birdie told her what she was planning to do.

'Why not?' Birdie asked. 'If I'm going to drag myself out of this funk, I've got to do it in style. I can't think of a better way to give the finger to Dean Stevenson than to show up at the *PCH* party looking like a million dollars plus change.'

'But . . .' Chipper wasn't terribly sure it was such a fantastic idea either.

'There's no reason why I shouldn't go. I'm going to be in the next series after all.'

Chipper didn't have the heart to tell her that she'd heard none of Birdie's scenes made the cut.

'Come on, girls,' Birdie tried to drum up enthusiasm. 'first you say you want me to get out there again and now you're trying to clip my wings. If I can go to the *PCH* party and have a great time, I will know that I am cured.'

* * *

Chipper and Clemency only became more worried for their friend when they heard that DD had offered to find Birdie's 'coming out again' outfit.

'We are going to show that boy what he's missing,' DD assured her.

It seemed she meant that quite literally. One of the get-ups she suggested was nothing more than a surgical robe, completely open down the back. 'The appliqué on the front yoke was hand-sewn by Tibetan monks,' DD explained.

'Not that one,' Chipper and Clemency begged.

'Then how about this?'

DD showed Birdie a prom dress made entirely of cling film.

'Not that one either,' Clemency prayed.

Birdie settled on a shaggy sleeveless jacket over what looked like a shortie wetsuit. It wasn't exactly conservative but at least she wouldn't be arrested for exposure.

'Are you sure this is a good idea?' Chipper asked one more time as they climbed into Birdie's Mercedes for the drive down to the beach. 'We could just go to the Chateau Marmont. Get some cocktails?'

'No,' said Birdie. 'We're going to the party. At the very least, I want to show Dean that there are no hard feelings,' she continued unconvincingly. 'We're going to be friends and a friend would support the opening of his show, right? No matter what had gone before.'

Chipper nodded.

'Plus,' said Birdie, 'how can he see what he's missing if I don't show him? How do I look?'

'You look fantastic,' said Chipper.

'Do I look so good he will fall down on his knees and beg me to come back to him?'

'Sure,' Chipper nodded again.

Birdie certainly set the camera bulbs flashing as she stepped from her car onto the driveway of the hotel. She stopped and posed, fluffing up her hair, turning one hip towards the camera to present a slimmer yet somehow more curvaceous silhouette. The jerkin was actually quite slimming, though from a couple of angles it did give the impression that Birdie was being attacked by a cat. Still, she pouted and grinned and the paps fired off thousands of pics.

'How are you doing, Birdie?' someone shouted. 'Still pissed about your break-up?'

'Do I look like a girl who isn't enjoying being single?' Birdie asked. 'I am loving my life right now. Dean Stevenson just did me a favour.'

So far, so good. She really was giving the impression that she didn't give a toss about Dean.

Then Birdie began to walk towards the door, which was flanked by two enormous guys in black and a small, pin-thin blonde with a clipboard. Birdie didn't even look at her and so she nearly fell off her Louboutins when the blonde threw out an arm to prevent Birdie's passage.

'I'm sorry,' said the blonde. 'You can't come in.'

'What are you talking about?' asked Birdie.

'You can't come in.'

'Do you know who I am?'

'Of course,' said the door Nazi. 'Everyone knows who you are. You're Birdie Sederburg.'

'Exactly. And I have an invitation.'

'*Had* an invitation,' said the blonde. 'I'm afraid it really wouldn't be a good idea for you to come to this party tonight. Dean has specifically requested that we ask you – respectfully – not to attend, in order to avoid any embarrassment.'

'What?'

'I'm sorry, Ms Sederburg.' The blonde attempted a smile. 'I'm sure you understand.'

'No I do not. I have an invitation.'

'Come on, Birdie,' said Chipper, taking hold of the back of her jerkin. 'I knew this was a bad idea.'

'I am not going now,' said Birdie, as she shook Chipper off. 'I have a right to be here. I am appearing in the next series, for goodness' sake.'

The blonde on the door sniggered.

'Actually,' Chipper whispered to Birdie, 'you're not.'

'What?'

'Ms Sederburg,' said the door Nazi. 'You're going to need to move out of the way. You are preventing other people from entering.'

The two bouncers stepped to physically hide Birdie from view as Emily B emerged from her limo to take her photo call. She looked amazing. She was wearing a floor-length gown by Marchesa. All shimmer and chiffon, it might have looked over the top on anyone else but Emily B, who had no stylist, had accessorized with flat Roman sandals that brought the outfit down to earth in a way that made it perfectly wonderful for a party by the beach.

Birdie saw red.

'Hey! You!' she shouted. 'I understand you got me banned from tonight's party? What's your problem, Emily? Are you worried that if the door Nazi lets me in, I'll steal your boyfriend back from you?'

Emily pretended not to hear. She carried on posing for the photographers, turning this way and that, making sure they got all her best angles.

'Are you listening to me?' Birdie tried again.

Emily continued to ignore her.

'I said . . .' Birdie stepped forward and poked Emily in the middle of the chest.

'Get your hands off me,' said Emily. She gave Birdie a little shove.

Birdie shoved back. Much harder.

'Are you pushing me?' Emily asked. 'Because you really do not want to be doing that.' Emily adopted a ju-jitsu position.

'I'll do what I want,' said Birdie, poking Emily again. 'See? I am Birdie Sederburg and I do exactly what I want! I'm going to call my grandfather and have him place an embargo on *PCH*,' Birdie announced to the gathered photographers. 'They will not be allowed to use any of the scenes filmed in Sederburg resorts.'

'Tell your grandfather to do whatever you like. They've all been pulled anyway, you idiot,' said Emily. 'None of them came out right. Mostly because you can't act for shit.'

The paps were having a field day, firing off thousands of shots as the two girls squared up to each other.

'You're lying,' said Birdie, giving Emily another push. 'You're a boyfriend-stealing slut.'

'You're a lunatic.'

'Your tits aren't real.'

'Neither are yours.'

Birdie swung a punch and before long Emily had her by the hairpiece. It took three men to part them. Somehow Emily managed to look even more beautiful than before with her hair all over the place and her cheeks pink with the exertion of fending off her boyfriend's mad ex. Birdie looked only that: mad. And half bald without her fake ponytail. A couple of cops turned up and bundled her into a squad car with the intention of giving her a moment to calm down, before they sent her on her way. But Birdie didn't calm down and she called the female cop a 'fat bitch' for suggesting that Birdie accept Emily was Dean's girlfriend now.

Birdie ended up at the police station.

Birdie's grandfather refused to find bail, so Chipper put the full amount (fifty thousand dollars) on her credit card. Clemency drove them both home.

The photo that appeared in all the gossip magazines later that week was one of Emily B looking serene and elegant while Birdie prodded at her like a troll. In interviews, Emily explained that she would not be pressing assault charges because it was clear that Birdie had 'mental issues'.

'Mental issues! I am going to sue that bitch from here to Christmas!' Birdie exclaimed.

'Birdie,' said Chipper. 'Don't you think this is getting a little over the top?'

'I don't know what else to do,' said Birdie. 'He was the love of my life. He *is* the love of my life.'

'You have to move on,' Chipper begged her.

'No,' said Birdie. 'More than ever, this episode has made me realize that Dean and I should be together. Emily B is an evil, lying cow. It's for Dean's own good that I split them up. I have to get him back.'

25

The following day, Birdie once again quizzed Clemency about what might be going on inside Dean's head. Once again, she used the dreaded words, 'In your opinion, as a *man*.' Smoothing her pencil skirt across her knees, Clemency counted until she felt her anger subside, then offered Birdie her latest thoughts – made up, as usual, on the fly.

'Hmmm. I think the reason that Dean likes Emily B is that she's so fragile-looking. So vulnerable. Real feminine. You know, you don't have that air about you.'

'What?'

'I don't mean to suggest that you're not womanly or anything, but when it comes to making a man feel like a man, then you've got to quash some of that fierce independence. A man wants to feel needed. You were the one who made all the arrangements in your relationship. It was you who booked all the trips and had everything put on your Sederburg account. Really, what chance did that give Dean to show you that he cared? You took away every opportunity he had to be a man. You emasculated him. With Emily B, he gets to feel alpha again. She's less famous than him. She has less money than him. Men like to be able to show their feelings by taking action. Dean could never do that with you.'

Birdie cocked her head to one side and tried to make sense of what Clemency was telling her.

'So you're saying that Dean dumped me for Emily because I did too much for him?'

'Yes. And because you left him no space to do something for you in return.'

'Hmmm.'

'Trust me, Birdie. All men want to be a hero from time to time.'

Birdie nodded, as though Clemency had finally revealed the secret of life. 'Hero,' she murmured.

Clemency smiled. 'You got it, girl.'

There was a moment of quiet while Birdie considered the implications.

'You know,' she said. 'You are really wise. I guess it comes from having so many incarnations in one lifetime.'

'I like the idea of that,' said Clemency.

'You would never know that you were a man except that you come out with so much wisdom.'

'Thanks,' said Clemency flatly.

'My pleasure,' said Birdie.

'Birdie,' Clemency decided to strike while the iron was *soft*. 'You know how I've been saving up for my breast augmentation?'

Birdie nodded vaguely. She was already on her iPhone again, texting Chipper with the gist of Clemency's revelation about the real nature of men.

'Well, I've been saving as hard as I can for the past year or so but I'm still about a thousand dollars off. It's so frustrating to have got so far and yet . . . I would really love to get the op done in the next couple of months so that I'm pretty much healed for the summer. You don't know how much it would mean to me to be able to wear a bikini this year, to enjoy the season without fearing that my chicken fillets are going to fall out every time I jump in a pool.'

'Uh-huh,' said Birdie.

'But more than that,' Clemency continued, 'I feel as though a boob job would be the final part of the puzzle. It would make me the woman that I want to be. I've been living a half-life since I had my reassignment. I'm a woman from the waist down – no doubt about that – but from the waist up I'm still the weedy guy who got teased by the jocks all through high school.

'Right.'

'I know it's not your problem, Birdie, but I hope that you would agree with me when I say that since we've been working together, and especially since we got back from France, you and I have become friends. You know, sharing confidences. Giving each other advice about life and love. So I'm asking you, as a friend, if you might be able to loan me that last thousand dollars. It's a tenth of the cost of a Birkin I'm asking for, but it would change my life forever. What do you think?'

Birdie stopped fiddling with her phone for a moment and looked her PA in the eye. 'Did you just ask me for money?'

Clemency gave a nod so tiny you might have missed it.

'You just asked me for money?' Birdie repeated.

'A thousand dollars,' Clemency confirmed. Her voice tailed away at the end.

'A thousand dollars? Do you know how many times a day people ask my grandfather and me for money? Do you have any idea how it feels? Sometimes I feel like people see me as a walking wallet!' Birdie snapped her laptop shut and stood up to better expound her feelings. 'I get so much bullshit from people who claim to be my friend. They're all nice and sweet and then, suddenly, boom, there's the request for a hand-out. You see the name on my cheque book? It's Birdie Sederburg. Not The Birdie Sederburg Foundation for people who can't manage their own finances and need bailing out.'

'To be fair,' said Clemency. 'I wasn't asking to be bailed out. I've been saving really hard but I'm a thousand dollars short for an op that would make a real difference if I could have it now. I'd pay the money back as soon as I could.'

'You should have saved harder.'

'What? On the money you pay me?'

'I pay you the going rate.'

'You think so? Taking into consideration the hours and the aggravation, I figure you actually pay me slightly less than a cleaner gets at McDonald's.'

'Oh!' Birdie looked hurt. 'Aggravation?'

'Yes, aggravation. Calls in the middle of the night. Cancelling my time off at the last moment. Dragging me all the way to Europe just to carry your bags. Treating me like a slave! And all of it I put up with. Have I ever once complained?'

'You're complaining now.' Birdie pointed out. 'I trusted you, Clemency. I can't believe you could be so rude to me. Well, you know what you can do if you're not happy here. If you don't think I'm a good enough employer! You can take yourself elsewhere. I'll write you a reference. You can leave anytime you like,' she continued. 'I won't expect you to work out your notice. But perhaps you might want to wait until your next job is lined up. It's a hard labour market out there. Especially if you're a little *unusual*.'

Birdie gave Clemency a look up and down, as if to underline her 'unusual' qualities, then she went into the house to call Chipper and exclaim about the horror of being hit up for cash by your employees.

Clemency remained in the garden for a moment. That had not gone well at all. She had thought, lately, that she had seen a sweeter side to Birdie Sederburg, but it was clear now that the experience of being dumped by Dean Stevenson had not really altered her at all. She was still as self-obsessed as she had ever been. Clemency must have been temporarily insane to think that, since getting back from France, their relationship had turned the corner from employer/employee to genuine friendship.

'Unusual,' Clemency muttered to herself as she followed Birdie inside. She stopped to examine her reflection in one of the huge mirrors in the hallway. She put her hands on her waist and turned this way and that. She did have pretty legs. Her feet, thank goodness, were at least smaller than Chipper Dooley's. She had great ankles. Her knees were smooth. She had no cellulite. No saddle-bags. But . . . Clemency turned sideways on.

Despite the hormones she had been taking for the past three years, her chest was still as flat as the growth in the United States economy and would remain as such for another year at the rate she was able to save.

And then there was her face. Clemency leaned in close to the mirror now and concentrated on her nose. If her nose were a little smaller, would she look less like a guy? Perhaps she should just spend a couple of hundred on some collagen for her lips to balance things out until she could afford a rhinoplasty. Would she ever be able to afford a rhinoplasty?

Birdie was walking around on the landing, chatting animatedly to Chipper. Clemency couldn't help but tune in.

'So I said to it, fine. You walk out right now if you want to. I'm sure there are people all over LA getting excited by the thought of employing some weirdo half-man/half-woman freak with a typing speed of forty.'

It? Half-man/half-woman freak? Typing speed of forty!!! Clemency set her jaw. She felt the urge to run upstairs and punch Birdie hard on the chin but decided that would just prove Birdie's point. There was nothing ladylike about throwing a punch. Tears sprang to Clemency's eyes as she locked herself in the bathroom, which is where she decided that while there is no elegance in thumping another girl, there is something terribly ladylike about cruel and protracted revenge.

Of course, Birdie was totally oblivious to her personal assistant's personal pain. Later that same day, she was gratified to see that Clemency had sorted out the pile of admin that Birdie had left for her (mostly parking tickets). She assumed that meant Clemency had decided she was staying and all that nastiness about money was over. Chipper had agreed that it was a real liberty, asking for a hand-out like that. What did it matter that Birdie would drop a thousand dollars on knickers in the lingerie department at Barneys without so much as blinking? It was her money and she had the right to spend it on herself.

Birdie was much more interested in the conversation she'd had with Clemency before the nastiness about money. She pondered Clemency's theory on a man's need to be a hero as she drove to see her hairstylist to have her roots touched up. It made perfect sense, but how on earth would Birdie change the status quo?

The answer came to her as she was under the drier.

Whatever you want to happen, there's someone in Los Angeles who can make it happen for you. Or, at least, make it *appear* to have happened. Those Hollywood people can build a Taj Mahal. They can send a man to Mars. Making it seem as though someone had been kidnapped would be no sweat at all.

Birdie read the article in *Marie Claire* with an increasing sense of excitement. Freda, 36 (not her real name), had been complaining to her boyfriend Andy, 37 (not his real name either), that their love was getting a little stale. He tried everything to bring the spark back. Flowers, presents, weekends away. He even lost twenty pounds and gained a six-pack. Nothing worked. Freda was on the point of leaving for good when Andy came across the Dangerous Dreams website. Andy called up and paid five thousand dollars to have his girlfriend kidnapped from the car park beneath her place of work.

Freda was held in the basement of a house in the Hollywood Hills for three days before Andy burst in and 'rescued' her. Their love was rekindled in an instant and they got married in Vegas just three weeks later.

'Of course,' Andy admitted, 'Freda still doesn't know I actually paid to have her captured.'

Inside Birdie's well-coiffed head, the little cogs began to whirr. A moment of fantasy jeopardy had saved Freda and Andy's relationship by giving Andy the opportunity to behave like a hero and, possibly, for Freda to relinquish some of her control issues and allow herself to be the weaker half of the couple for once. Something she would never have countenanced otherwise.

Birdie pulled her fountain pen out of her handbag and stuck

the end of it in her mouth. She soon spat it out again. She was sucking the wrong end. But the article on fake kidnaps had given her an idea . . .

As Clemency had pointed out, the problem with her relationship with Dean was that he felt emasculated by her great wealth. She had taken the traditional male role in their time together by making all the arrangements on their exotic dates and by showering him with gifts. Birdie decided that she had contributed to her own downfall in this way by not allowing Dean to impress her. No wonder he felt weak and, ultimately, had to go off and prove his manliness by boffing someone else.

It was a brilliant theory. Birdie could think of no better explanation for the troubles she was having with that man. And now she had the solution. It was the perfect way to stoke up Dean's testosterone and reignite his manly passions.

Desperate times called for desperate measures. Birdie would have herself kidnapped . . .

26

'Ohmigod,' said Chipper when Birdie told her and Clemency about the new plan. 'ohmigod, ohmigod, ohmigod! Are you kidding me? That is crazy! In a good way.'

'What do you think, Clemency?' Birdie asked. 'As a man?'

Clutching her favourite heart-shaped pendant tightly to help hide her irritation, Clemency pursed her lips. 'Getting yourself kidnapped? It's so insane, I think it could just work,' she said.

Birdie was delighted. 'I've found the perfect way to let Dean be the hero he needs to be, haven't I? How clever am I?' she asked.

Chipper gave her a congratulatory hug. When Birdie tried to make it into a group hug, Clemency stepped back with a weak smile.

'I'm going for it,' said Birdie. 'It's going to be amazing. The article in *Marie Claire* said that the people at this company all have backgrounds in the stunt and special-effects departments of the film world. Either that or they worked in security. One of them was even chief of security for the Aga Khan! Clemency, will you look them up online?' She handed Clemency the note she had made in the hairdressers. Birdie's handwriting was atrocious, but eventually Clemency decided that the name of the company was 'Dreams of Danger'.

Clemency soon found the site. It looked unimpressive. 'Dreams of Danger' said the title in jagged white print on a simple jet-black page. 'Enter if you dare,' provoked the line beneath.

'Do we dare?' asked Clemency as Birdie and Chipper leaned over her shoulder.

Birdie was already clicking. 'This better not be porn,' she said.

It wasn't porn. The click led to the Dreams of Danger biography. It claimed to be a Los Angeles-based company, founded in 2007, specializing in making whatever you dreamed of come true, no matter how wild or wacky. 'Trust us with your darkest fantasies,' said the web page. 'We have heard it all before.'

'Shall I go for it?' Birdie asked.

While Birdie and Chipper discussed Birdie's crazy new scheme over margaritas, Clemency started the donkey-work to make it happen. She made an appointment for Birdie to meet the CEO of Dreams of Danger the very next day. In keeping with the fantasy nature of their operations, the owner of the company explained that he didn't meet potential clients in an office. They had to meet him in a neutral location to minimize the risk of surveillance.

'Just as though you were hiring a real hit-man,' Clemency relayed to her boss.

Birdie felt a small shiver of unease as she heard the word 'hit-man', but she managed a laugh all the same.

'I get it,' she said.

And so Clemency arranged a rendezvous between Birdie and 'Mr G' of Dreams of Danger in front of the Griffith Observatory.

'How will I recognize him?' Birdie asked.

'He said he'd be wearing a Dodgers cap,' said Clemency.

'You're not going alone,' said Chipper.

'I was hoping you would say that,' Birdie confirmed.

In the event, the baseball cap wasn't such a good way to mark Mr G out from the crowd. They were in Los Angeles. It was a sunny day. There weren't many people who *weren't* wearing baseball caps and Dodgers hats in particular were in abundance, on Angelenos and tourists alike.

Birdie had been altogether more imaginative with her attire. The clandestine nature of her business that afternoon naturally brought to mind old black and white movies starring private detectives called Sam. Birdie dressed accordingly. She wore a pale cream-coloured mackintosh from Burberry, a headscarf by Hermès (borrowed from Chipper's mom) and a pair of wrap-around sunglasses so dark she could hardly see where she was going, even in the bright California sun. She definitely couldn't see Mr G. Luckily, he saw her first.

He sidled up to her.

'Ms N?' he asked in a low voice with an accent she couldn't quite place.

'How did you guess?' Birdie took off her glasses in surprise. '*You're* Mr G?'

Mr G. did not look like the kind of man who could master-mind an effective kidnapping. He didn't look like the kind of man who could eat an egg without getting most of it down his front, as he obviously had that morning. Birdie recoiled from the sight of the yellow yolk drips on the front of his sludgy grey T-shirt.

Birdie's first instinct was to signal to Chipper and Clemency (who were hiding behind a tree dressed in burqas) that it was time to go. The whole thing was a waste of time. But then it struck Birdie that perhaps this was part of the set-up. Mr G looked so utterly ordinary that no one would have a hope of guessing what they might be talking about. What if his ordinariness was absolutely deliberate? She decided to go with that thought.

'Shall we walk?' he said then. 'We don't want anyone to get a fix on us.'

'Yes, of course,' said Birdie, putting her glasses back on.

The fact that he was concerned about such a thing as someone getting a 'fix' further convinced Birdie of his professionalism.

'OK. We're going to be heading east towards the picnic tables. We're going to sit down at the one on the far right. Just keep in step with me. Look natural. Don't look behind you. It might attract attention. Do *not* look behind you.'

Birdie looked behind her. She saw only Chipper in her burqa, giving her the thumbs up that let her know she and Clemency would be close behind to make sure nothing went awry.

They arrived at the picnic table. Mr G motioned for Birdie to sit down, then did what he referred to as 'a sweep of the immediate vicinity'. He even checked under the table for bugs.

'I think we're clean,' he said at last, just as Birdie discovered she most definitely wasn't. She had dog shit on her shoe from their walk across the grass.

'Euwww.' She tried to scrape it off. 'Can we sit somewhere else?' she suggested as the smell of dog mess wafted up at her.

'But I've cleared this area,' said Mr G. 'Moving will attract attention.'

'OK,' Birdie acquiesced. 'If you insist. But this smell is going to be annoying.'

'I can't smell anything,' said Mr G. 'I was born without a sense of smell.'

'Oh, right,' said Birdie. Perhaps that explained why he didn't smell too good either. 'Shall we just get on with it? Tell me what you can do.'

'So, you have a dream of danger,' said Mr G dramatically. 'Well, you've come to the right man to make all your dreams come true. I am the dream-maker.' He sketched clouds and raindrops in the air with his hands as though he were some kind of shaman.

'Yes, well,' said Birdie. 'I hope so.'

'Tell me your dream, little lady.' More clouds and rain with the fingers. Birdie hoped he wasn't going to keep doing that while she talked.

'It's like this,' she began. 'I have a very big problem.' Birdie explained exactly what she wanted. In hypothetical terms. She did not let on for now that the person to be kidnapped was her.

Mr G listened like a guru, cross-legged on the grass with his fingers steepled beneath his chin. From time to time he let out a 'hmmm' of affirmation, though there was a great deal of 'he said, she said' that made it hard for him to follow. Half an hour later, when she was certain that Mr G understood the import-ance of rescuing Dean Stevenson from his terrible romantic mistake, Birdie finished.

'Do you want the victim roughed up a bit?' Mr G asked.

'No!' Birdie said at once. '*Definitely* not.'

'But you want to scare her.'

'No,' said Birdie. 'I want to scare the people *left behind*. It's me, you see. The girl I want you to kidnap is me.'

'Oh wow,' said Mr G. 'I think I get it.'

'Do you think you can do that?'

'I can do anything,' he said.

Mr G insisted that they leave the park separately, for the purpose of bamboozling anyone who might be tailing them.

'I think we're safe,' he said. 'No one gets to listen in on my conversations without my knowing.'

Mr G pulled his baseball cap down low and hulked off in the direction of his Volkswagen Rabbit.

Birdie met the girls next to the Mercedes.

'Did you hear all that?'

'Every word,' said Clemency. 'And I got plenty of photos just like you asked me to.'

'Good work. I think I'm going to go with him. He seems like a professional guy.'

Clemency's veil hid her reaction.

Chipper pulled off her burqa and wrinkled her nose. 'Birdie, are you sure you got all that dog shit off?'

27

'Good day on the Interweb, dear?' asked Mr G's mother when she returned home from work to find her son sitting, as usual, in a room lit only by the flicker of a computer screen.

'It's the Inter*net*, Mom,' said Mr G, as he found himself doing with irritating regularity. 'It's the World Wide Web or the Internet. It is not the Inter*web*.'

'Whatever you say, dear. Have you eaten?' Mother G asked this as she opened a window and plucked the wrappers of three Snickers bars from the floor.

'I could manage a sandwich,' said Mr G, shutting the window again.

His mother beamed. 'I'll make it just the way you like it. Pastrami and jack cheese. You want some mayonnaise on it too?'

'OK,' said Mr G. 'But don't try to sneak any vegetables into it like last time.'

'Whatever you want, my love,' said his mother.

Mr G – real name Gareth Grimes – was very excited. He had known that Dreams of Danger would make his fortune one day. His friends had all told him that no one in their right mind would actually pay to be kidnapped, but Gareth had ignored the naysayers and at last he had been proved right. Having been in operation for the best part of three years, he finally had his first real customer. Even more unbelievably, when he'd told her that he wanted ten grand for his services (five times more than he expected to charge), she hadn't batted an eyelid. In fact, she had written him a cheque for half the amount there and then. Gareth pulled the cheque out of his wallet and looked at it again now. It definitely wasn't a joke. It was for real. All the right information was there. The amount of money. Her name. Her signature. This was a cheque he could actually *cash*, unlike the one pinned to his noticeboard. He had written that cheque to himself, for a million dollars, on the advice of a self-help book.

'Write yourself a cheque for the amount you deserve to be paid,' the book had insisted. 'Believe you're worth it and pretty soon someone else will believe it too!'

Gareth had looked at that fake cheque every morning for the past three years. At last, his wish had come true.

After leaving Birdie Sederburg at the Griffith Observatory, Gareth got straight to work with his plans for the kidnapping. Birdie had Clemency send an email outlining her movements for the next week to help Mr G choose his moment. It was Los Angeles fashion week and as a high-profile big spender, Birdie had been invited to many of the shows. Her day planner was full of Chanel and Marc Jacobs. Gareth Googled each of the designers and their venues, trying to decide the one show that might afford him the best chance of kidnapping Birdie with the right combination of high visibility and low risk. Kidnapping Birdie at a fashion show would certainly ensure that plenty of people saw it happen, but fashion events had notoriously strict security. Or so he heard.

Gareth would not be working alone, of course. Though he had a gym membership, he had yet to darken that particular establishment's door. He was, to paraphrase Michael Caine in *Get Carter*, a big guy but he was out of shape. There was no way that he would be able to pick Birdie up and get her out of the area quickly enough to avoid the police on his own. And so Gareth decided that his skills would be best utilized in the driving of the getaway car. The actual snatching would have to be left to someone more fleet of foot.

Unfortunately, Gareth moved almost exclusively in IT circles and he didn't know anyone fleet of foot. To that end, he had asked the two guys who came to do his mother's garden on Tuesdays and Fridays if they might care to do some more interesting work. On the down low? Cash in hand?

'What kind of thing you talking about?' they asked him. 'Smuggling? A hit?'

'A kidnap,' said Gareth tentatively, wondering if they would be shocked. They had been joking, surely, when they mentioned a hit?

'You want us to kidnap someone? Sure,' said the older of the two. 'We've done that before.'

'You have?'

'All the time. You want them roughed up?'

'No,' said Mr G. 'Definitely not.'

'We'll do whatever you say, boss,' said the younger guy, with a grin that suggested otherwise.

Gareth didn't feel entirely comfortable about the arrangement but he really had no choice. He couldn't do the kidnap on his own. And if he didn't do the kidnap, he wouldn't have ten thousand dollars to spend at the next IT Masters conference in Las Vegas.

'You have to do exactly what I tell you,' he told the gardening guys in a tone he hoped conveyed authority.

'Sure,' the younger one promised again. 'Whatever you want.'

With the heavies on board, Gareth called Clemency and told her to tell Birdie to be ready to begin her 'ordeal' the following Tuesday, after the Morrie Ray show, which was being held in the Disney Theater in downtown LA. Gareth had chosen this show because he thought it would be easy to park a getaway vehicle nearby. He gave Clemency strict and explicit instructions to ensure that the kidnapping ran smoothly.

'She has to exit through the door closest on the left of the auditorium,' he said. 'Two Latino guys will be doing the actual pick-up. They will be dressed in black and wearing Disney character masks. I will be waiting in an unmarked white Chevy van.

We will be taking Ms Sederburg to the following address, where she will hide out until such time as she wants to 'escape' . . .'

Mr G gave Birdie the address of his friend Marty's condo in Long Beach. He had thought about keeping Birdie at his own house – he liked the thought of that – but he had no idea how he would explain it to his mother. Fortunately, his old high-school pal and fellow geek Marty was also only too pleased by the prospect of having the heiress in his bedroom. He'd had a photograph of Birdie on his bedroom wall for years. Ever since she came to public consciousness when a clip of her taking her bra off found its way onto YouTube.

'Make the place nice for her,' Mr G told Marty. 'Get supplies in.'

Marty went to Costco right away and returned with a bumper-sized bag of tortilla chips, six tubs of ready-made salsa and a small round sheepskin rug to cover the indeterminate stain on his bedroom floor. He even cleaned the bathtub, which turned out to be avocado in colour and not, as he had always thought, brown.

The only thing left for Mr G to do was hire the van. Alone in his bedroom, while his mother prepared his dinner, Gareth went online and started looking for a rental bargain. He took a Chevy Uplander for a fortnight. He made the booking with his mother's credit card, which he had slipped from her purse while she dozed in front of *Prison Break* the previous evening. He'd already used it to buy a complete box set of series two of *Babylon 5*.

Fifteen minutes later, Mrs G popped her head around the bedroom door again. She was carrying her son's sandwich on a plate – pastrami and jack cheese with mayo, exactly as he liked it – garnished with potato chips and a side-serving of salsa (which was the only way she could get him to eat his veg, unless he was in the mood for guacamole). Gareth, who hadn't told his mother about his business venture, hurriedly hid the cheque from Birdie Sederburg in his lap. He didn't want to have to explain.

'Gareth,' his mother wagged her finger. 'I do hope you haven't let Mr Winky out to play again.' She craned her head to see what was on the screen of Gareth's computer but if she hoped to catch her son watching a skin-flick, she hoped in vain. Even if Gareth had been looking for MILFs on the Internet, he could switch between pages in the blink of an eye. In fact, he flicked to screen-saver automatically every time he heard the tell-tale squeak as his mother stepped on the loose board outside his bedroom door. It had become a reflex. Living with his mother had taught Gareth the need for subterfuge.

'Of course not, mother!' Gareth responded in mock horror. 'I don't believe you would think such a thing of me.'

'Good. Because you know what will happen if you let him out once too often?'

Mrs G picked up a small piece of pastrami from her son's nutritious dinner and waved it menacingly. She needed to say no more. She set the beef down again and turned to leave.

'Now don't stay in front of that screen for too long! Don't want to end up with square eyes!'

'Square eyes and a shrivelled dick,' Gareth muttered to himself. Living with his mother was driving Gareth nuts. But the day was fast approaching when he would be able to afford a place of his own. Gareth got Birdie's cheque out one more time. Oh yes. He was going to make all her dreams come true.

28

The following lunchtime, Birdie, Clemency and Chipper went through the fine details of the plan.

'I can't believe you're really going through with this,' Chipper lamented, as they went through every step of the procedure. 'I have to admit I'm a little bit worried.'

'What can possibly go wrong?' Birdie laughed. 'You girls know who is going to kidnap me and exactly how it's going to be done. You know where I'm going to be held. Apparently Long Beach is quite civilized,' she added as an aside. 'And you know that as soon as Dean springs into action and makes an effort to find me, I'm going to escape and be found wandering looking dazed and confused near the pier on Huntington Beach.'

Clemency had come up with that last part of the plan. In order to make sure that Sederburg's heavies didn't haul Mr G and his team in as soon as Dean started to look concerned, they were going to make it appear as though they'd got cold feet and dumped Birdie by a roadside. That way, she got the drama of the kidnapping, the reassurance that Dean cared, and the Dreams of Danger crew got to remain completely anonymous, thus protecting Birdie from any embarrassing revelation that she had paid for the kidnap herself.

'So the kidnappers will be carrying guns,' said Clemency. 'But Mr G has assured me they will not be loaded. Or they will be replicas or something like that.'

Chipper bit her lip. 'That sounds dangerous. I mean, if the police see you being dragged off by men with guns, won't they just open fire?'

'But how else would anyone kidnap me? I'm not going to get into the car if I'm not in fear of my life, am I? How realistic is that?'

'Good point,' said Clemency.

'But guns, Birdie? How about knives?' said Chipper. 'Couldn't they just threaten to stab you instead?'

'Knives!' Clemency exclaimed. 'Now that really is a way to get killed.'

'I'm just not sure about this,' said Chipper. 'I foresee all sorts of bad stuff happening and I don't know if Dean Stevenson is worth it.'

'What?' Birdie's mouth dropped open.

'You heard what I said. I don't know if Dean is worth you taking all these risks.'

'Chipper,' said Birdie. 'Don't you want me to be happy?'

'You know I do.'

'Well, getting Dean back is the best way for me to be happy, and this is the best way to get Dean back. Isn't that right, Clemency?'

'Right,' said Clemency. 'In my opinion, *as a man*,' she added slyly, 'this is indeed the best way to ensure that Birdie regains Dean's interest. It would have worked for me before my operation.'

'Well, if it's what you want.' Chipper nodded warily but continued to bite her lip. 'But really, who are these people you're dealing with?'

'Mr G is a very nice guy,' Birdie insisted. 'I could totally tell from the moment I saw him. He was so nice and polite. Called me 'ma'am'. I liked that about him.'

'Oh well. If he had nice manners . . .' Chipper decided that she had to let it go. Hadn't Oprah said just that week that the role of a good friend was not to judge but to support?

'It'll be fine,' said Clemency. 'I promise you that this is going to be the most amazing experience of Birdie's life. I'm sure that Mr G and his people will pull it off with the utmost professionalism.'

In reality, Clemency was far from convinced that Mr G knew what he was doing. The fact that he had not noticed he was being followed by both her and Chipper (wearing the by now incredibly commonplace 'burqa' disguise) strongly suggested to Clemency that the geek was an idiot. If he couldn't outfox her and Chipper Dooley, he had no chance against the thuggish team that worked for Julius Sederburg. Clemency predicted that Mr G's own team would be foiled before they could get their van out of the Disney Theater car park.

In her seven-hundred-square-foot bedroom, Birdie lay back on her bed and contemplated the day's events. She flicked on the television, which was tuned, as always, to E!. And within minutes, as had been the case for the last few days, she was confronted by a trailer for the new series of *PCH*. But this time, Birdie didn't throw herself face down into her pillows and sob when she saw the man of her dreams (and his new dream girl). Instead, she watched closely as Dean's character took a wave and then walked up the beach with his surfboard, salt-water glistening on his perfect pecs. She touched her fingers to her lips and blew a kiss towards his beautiful full mouth.

'I am going to get you back,' she told him. 'Dean Stevenson, you *will* be mine.'

29

But Chipper and Clemency were not the only ones who knew everything about Birdie's big plan. Nate heard all about it too. As usual,
it didn't seem to have crossed Birdie's mind to be more discreet as
she talked to her friends by the pool. She acted as she always did.
As if the people who worked for her weren't really there at all. Or
else they were mute automatons who would never dream of taking
the things they learned while eavesdropping straight to the gossip
columns.

Well, Nate wouldn't have gone to the gossip columns. And
ordinarily, he would start to tune out when Birdie and Chipper
got onto the subject of Dean, but this whole kidnapping thing
was just too weird. And interesting. He couldn't help but start
sweeping his way up the garden path and closer to them, to better
hear what was going on.

Later, back at the commune, Nate relayed to Jason the gist of
the bizarre conversation he had overheard.

'I mean, that girl is totally insane. Her boyfriend has gone off
with another girl so she's going to have herself kidnapped in
order to win him back. She got the name of these would-be
kidnappers off the Internet, for fuck's sake. I don't think she has
any idea how badly that could go wrong.'

Jason listened to the story with a curious smile on his face.

'You know what,' he said to Nate, 'you are so right. That girl
has absolutely no idea how wrong her plan could go.'

'Are you thinking what I'm thinking?' asked Nate after another
moment's silence.

'I imagine I am,' said Jason. 'House meeting?'

*　　*　　*

Soon Mother Nature's Avengers had come up with a plan of their own. It was a plan that would get people to take them seriously. And, as a bonus, it was a plan that did not involve sitting in mud for three days wearing adult diapers.

The scruffy beach house buzzed with excitement as everyone considered his or her part in the upcoming adventure. Without knowing it, Birdie Sederburg had given Mother Nature's Avengers the inspiration and the opportunity for their most daring and dazzling protest yet. Mr G and his mother's gardeners were not the only people who were looking forward to bundling Birdie into a van after the Morrie Ray show.

'If we dress the same as those other jokers, there's every chance we'll get to her first,' said Jason.

'Where are we going to keep her once we've got her?' asked Melanie. 'We could put her in the cellar!' Melanie's eyes glittered at the thought.

'We can't keep her around here,' said Nate. 'It's too obvious. When Birdie gets kidnapped, the first people to be interviewed will be her staff and that will bring the police straight to Jason and me. The cops will be all over this place in a second.'

'Good point,' said Jason.

Instead, they made arrangements with another chapter of Mother Nature's Avengers who had their own small commune in the high sierras near to Bakersfield. The Bakersfield chapter of MNA had been growing top-quality grass out there for the past fifteen years undisturbed. If Nate and his gang could get that far without being intercepted by the cops, they could easily hide an heiress in those hills for a couple of weeks. Long enough to persuade Julius Sederburg to consider his plans not only for the Marshlands site but also for several other sites earmarked for golf courses all over the world.

'Do we get to torture her?' Melanie asked.

'No!' Nate said quickly. 'Definitely not. Even though this particular situation will involve our first hostage, we, Mother Nature's Avengers, are going to bide by our code of honour.

No one will be hurt. Peaceful protest for a peaceful world. Remember?'

'Aw,' Melanie groaned. 'Can't we at least cut off her ear and send it with a ransom note?'

'No,' said Nate. 'Absolutely not.'

Sometimes there was a distinct lack of peace and love among these old hippies.

'Now, let's go over these arrangements one more time. Tony, you're in charge of getting the Disney masks from Toys Я Us. We need a Mickey and a Donald. We also need some toy guns. Realistic as you can get. Jason, you're going to source those fake number-plates to disguise the van. Melanie, you're painting signs for the distraction protest that you will be staging outside the Disney Theater while we three get Birdie into the van and out of there. I'm going to study the plans of the theatre and work out the fastest route from Downtown to the 405. Now, is everybody clear on what's happening tomorrow? We've got to be ready to leave the house at nine in the morning. There's going to be no time to get high before we go.' He addressed that last remark to Tony. 'In fact,' he said sternly, 'we better stay off alcohol and anything else tonight too. We need our reactions to be lightning sharp.'

'Don't worry,' said Jason. 'We won't let you down. This is going to be our moment of glory.'

Jason raised his fist in the official salute of MNA. The others looked bewildered. They had no idea that MNA had an official salute at all.

30

The day of the kidnap dawned bright and sunny: a perfect California day. The wind blowing in from the desert was warm as a caress. It lifted the scent from the flowers Nate had planted in Birdie's garden and carried it into the house.

Birdie didn't notice how lovely a day it was. She had been awake for hours. She sat at the kitchen counter, playing with a plateful of scrambled egg.

'I can't eat,' she said finally. 'I'm too nervous.'

'It's not too late to back out,' said Chipper, who had stayed over to keep her company. 'We can call Mr G right now and tell him you want to call the whole thing off.'

'No,' said Clemency quickly. 'She can't do that. Show some guts, Chipper. You're telling her to call off the best and most daring plan I have ever heard about.'

'It's going to be a disaster!' said Chipper.

'It'll end with a wedding,' Clemency promised. 'I can feel it in my bones.'

Birdie looked from her friend to her PA and back again as they each argued their case.

'I'm doing it,' she announced finally. 'I've come this far. Everything is in place and I am psychologically prepared to go through with it. Dean is worth the risk.' She gazed at a picture of her former boyfriend in the latest edition of *US Magazine*. 'I would give my life for this man,' she added dramatically.

'Then I need to call Mr G and tell him what you'll be wearing,' said Clemency. 'So the guys have the best chance of finding you quickly.'

How to describe what Birdie was wearing that day? What does a girl about town wear to her own kidnapping? Fortunately, DD was on hand, though she didn't know the full story of why Birdie was so especially nervous that day. DD assumed that it was because she had an invite to the Morrie Ray show. It was the most sought-after ticket in LA Fashion Week. Everyone who was anyone would be there, and there was a strong chance that Birdie might get photographed in the vicinity of the Olsen twins.

People often asked DD if she styled the Olsen twins. Though she couldn't lay claim to their particularly quirky style, their grandad cardigan/glam shoes combo in particular was a look that DD especially admired.

DD decided that she would find a similarly edgy look for Birdie. She eschewed her favourite avant-garde designers and settled on a vintage housecoat, of the kind that fifties house-wives wore while letting the cat out at night. It was one hundred per cent nylon. The label on the inside carried a big warning about the danger of sitting too close to open fires. And it was the kind of pink that is never seen in nature.

'It's a bit big,' said Birdie, when she put the housecoat on.

'That's why you'll also be wearing this.' DD went into her enormous handbag and came out with a piece of red rope, like the ropes that hung outside hip clubs. DD wrapped it twice around Birdie's middle and pulled tight.

'I'm liking it,' she said, standing back and taking in her han-diwork. 'This really works for me.'

Birdie stood in front of the mirror, catching her breath.

'Could it be a little looser?' she panted.

'It's a little bit geisha meets cyber-punk,' DD explained to her client. 'And once you've put these shoes on,' DD motioned Birdie towards a pair of stacked wooden clogs, 'the look is complete.

That is perfect. Let me take a Polaroid,' she said. 'I think I can see Tilda Swinton in this at the Oscars.'

'What do you think?' Birdie asked Chipper.

'Totally out there,' said Chipper. 'You'll definitely get noticed in that.'

'Hold on!' said DD. 'I forgot about the purse.'

She handed Birdie a hollowed-out coconut that had been halved then put back together with a solid brass clasp. It had no handle.

'It's a kind of clutch,' DD explained.

'Ah,' said Birdie. 'I see . . . But my iPhone doesn't fit.'

'Put it in the pocket of the housecoat.'

'I feel kind of underdressed now,' said Chipper, peering critically at her own reflection. She was wearing a black shift dress with an asymmetric hem and a pair of red heels.

'I have just the thing for you,' said DD. She went out to her car and returned with a Carmen Miranda-style bonnet of fruit.

'Genius,' said Birdie.

Clemency thought of another word entirely. But she wasn't going to say it out loud. It was unladylike. 'You look good enough to eat,' she said instead.

'You're in a good mood this morning,' said DD, noticing the change in Clemency's demeanour at once. 'What happened?'

'Oh, nothing,' said Clemency. 'I just have a feeling that today is going to be fun. I mean, I'm excited for Birdie. Turning up at the Morrie Ray show in such a fabulous outfit is the perfect way to turn Dean Stevenson green at the thought of what he's lost. Are you girls ready to go? The driver is waiting.'

Chipper nodded, shedding a couple of cherries and a kiwi fruit in the process. The kiwi fruit fell to the marble floor with a splat.

'Oh wow,' said Chipper. 'I had no idea the fruit was real!'

'Of course it's real. The whole hat will have rotted away by the end of the week. It's a comment on the ephemeral nature of life,' DD explained. 'And the futility of consumerism.'

'That's amazing,' said Chipper.

'It's eight hundred dollars,' said DD, making a note to invoice Chipper for that amount the minute she got back to her office.

'Come on, ladies.' Clemency tapped her watch. 'The car is outside. If we don't get on the road in the next three minutes, you might miss the beginning of the show. And we want everything to go according to plan today, don't we?'

31

The Morrie Ray show really was one of the hottest tickets in LA Fashion Week. The English designer, who had turned around the fortunes of a staid French fashion house with his avant-garde designs and now had his own label, had never shown in the States before. Until now, LA and New York socialites had been required to make a trip to Paris to get their hands on his deconstructed T-shirts and icing-bag-shaped trousers. But finally Morrie Ray had agreed to make a capsule collection available through Neiman Marcus.

Because it was Morrie's debut in the States, front-row seats were more valuable than ever. Without a front-row seat at this show, you were officially nobody in Los Angeles. So Birdie was not best pleased to find that she and Chipper were in the second row. Right behind Emily B.

Still, the thought of what was going to take place that day filled Birdie with adrenaline that made her fearless. She quickly switched the place cards and sat down in the front row, between two of Hollywood's brightest new stars, leaving Chipper to sit next to Emily B. Chipper was altogether more nervous.

'What is this?' asked Emily when she walked in and found herself in the second row.

Fortunately, Emily had left it so late entering the auditorium (too busy posing for the paps outside) that the first of the models was already stalking down the catwalk, wearing an army surplus parka and what looked like half a chicken on her head. On her feet she wore surgical boots with calipers. The crowd applauded rapturously.

The chain-store buyers (who were mostly seated in row five) wondered how on earth they were going to sell that look to the good people of Cleveland.

'Sederburg,' Emily hissed in Birdie's ear. 'I do believe that you are sitting in my seat. If you persist with this aggressive behaviour, I will be taking out a restraining order.'

Birdie stared straight ahead.

A second model stepped out. The high prancing step so beloved of catwalk models was all but impossible in her moon-boots, which had wheels in the heels. The crowd applauded not just her outfit but also her valiant efforts to stay upright.

The truth was, not many of the celebrities in the front row were all that interested in the clothes. They were far more interested in checking out who was on the front row on the other side of the catwalk. They looked up at the models from time to time when they thought that a camera might be on them. It was a good look for the aspiring starlet, gazing up into the lights: always a flattering angle, guaranteeing no unsightly double chin. Or, even better, you might be caught chummily whispering in the ear of the slightly more famous starlet to your left or right.

Birdie wasn't whispering chummily (not that Emily's friends, who flanked her, would have chatted anyway). She was more than a little preoccupied. She was trying to work out which of the exits from the auditorium was the one that Mr G had spoken of. She checked the details on her iPhone again. Did he mean her left as she walked out of the auditorium or left from the point of view of a kidnapper looking at the building from outside? It was impossible to remember. Birdie had a vision of herself leaving by the wrong exit and having to walk all the way around the building before her kidnappers picked her up.

The show seemed to last forever. Forty models graced the catwalk that afternoon, each of them processing more slowly than the one before, thanks to Morrie Ray's current obsession with unsuitable footwear. The final model, in what was supposed to be a wedding dress but looked more like a crocheted toilet-roll cover, was actually wearing ice-skates beneath her voluminous skirt. She grimaced with every ankle-turning step.

When the designer himself came out to accept the crowd's congratulations, Birdie clapped along.

Emily B leaned forward over the back of the chair Birdie had stolen. 'Nice stunt, Sederburg. But rest assured you won't be in the first ten rows of any fashion show anytime soon.'

Birdie ignored her. 'Come on, Chipper. It's really starting to stink in here.' As she exited the row, Chipper stepped hard on Emily's foot.

'What?' she said, when Emily gave her a shove in retaliation. 'It was an accident.' It was true. Chipper's enormous feet often seemed to have a mind of their own.

'I'll see you both in court!' Emily hissed.

Birdie flipped the finger at her rival and kept walking. It was just a matter of time before Emily B was history. The moment had arrived. Birdie simply hoped that everyone was in position.

32

Mr G's men had been in position for half an hour. He had dropped them off at the back of the theatre, where they were to wait for the end of the show. The idea was that they would make a straight shot across the front of the place, coming at Birdie from behind, grabbing her before she had a chance to turn round and whisking her straight to the van which would be waiting with its back doors open. Guido and Hector assured Mr G that everything was under control. All he had to do was keep the engine running.

'You know,' said Guido to Hector as soon as Mr G was out of earshot. 'I think our Mr G is missing a trick. This stupid girl wants to be kidnapped. What if we really kidnapped her? We could make a ton of money. Do you know who her grandfather is? How much do you think he would really pay to get his little girl back?'

'What are you suggesting? You think we should cut Mr G out of the equation?'

'I think that sounds like a good idea. He asked two guys he doesn't know to help him kidnap an heiress? He's an amateur. But he can help us to get the girl out of there first. It's a high-risk situation we've got here. If we do get stopped, we've got him to take the rap. The girl explains she paid to be kidnapped and we walk away,no questions asked. But if we get away with it . . . If we can get as far as Long Beach, I don't see why you and I shouldn't go a little further.'

Hector smiled in agreement. 'This is going to be fun.'

From inside the theatre, they heard the sound of rapturous applause.

'Do you think that's it?' Guido asked. 'Show over?'

'Let's hope so.'

The men put on their Disney masks. Guido was Mickey Mouse. Hector, to his annoyance, was Minnie.

'I look like a dork.'

'You always look like a dork.'

They were too busy arguing over who looked the dorkiest to notice that Jason and Nate were getting in position too. Tony was driving the van belonging to Mother Nature's Avengers. He pulled up at the kerb at the back of the theatre. Jason and Nate, already wearing their masks, jumped out.

Both of them were carrying rags dosed in ether when they crept up on their rivals. It was the work of seconds to overpower the two unsuspecting men and bundle them into a dumpster.

Nate felt a little bad about knocking the guys out, but Jason rather enjoyed it. It was more fun than wearing an adult diaper, that was for sure.

'Now what?' said Jason, when the two original kidnappers were safely out of action.

'We just wait here until she comes out. Melanie will radio us as soon as she sees her and then she'll make sure she gets in the way so Birdie can't go anywhere until we've got to her.'

'I think we did pretty good at that,' said Jason, nodding towards the dumpster. 'What a couple of amateurs they were.'

Nate shot him a warning glance. 'We are not going to be making a habit of this, you understand. And you are not to rough-handle Birdie like you did with those two scumbags. We're not going to harm a hair on her head, remember.'

Jason nodded. 'Whatever, man.'

Outside the theatre, Melanie had been staging her one-woman protest on behalf of the environment for the past forty-five minutes. She wasn't drawing much attention. While the fashion show was going on inside, the forecourt of the theatre was largely deserted, apart from liveried drivers waiting to whisk the models and heiresses on to the after-party, which was to be held in an old abattoir downtown. The drivers weren't bothered by Melanie's shouting. A nutter holding a lonely protest march was all part of the average LA day. Most people just tuned such things out. One guy, driving a stretch Hummer, tried to drown Melanie's chants with his car stereo.

But Melanie was unperturbed and at long last, she spotted their target. She whispered the news into the microphone she had attached to her collar then went on dancing with her signs. She signalled to Tony, who had brought the van to the front of the theatre, that he needed to be ready. Birdie and Chipper were moving quite slowly because of their outfits. Birdie could not get used to the Japanese clogs and Chipper had just three grapes left on her elaborate and expensive fruit bowl of a hat.

'I swear the guy sitting behind me ate half my hat during that show,' Chipper complained.

'We'll get you a new one. Can you see any kidnappers yet?' Birdie whispered.

Spotting her paid abductors was not going to be as easy as Birdie had hoped. The courtyard outside the hall was soon seething with people as the guests exited the auditorium and made their way to their cars past camera crews recording show reports and paps stalking starlets. Scanning the road in front of the theatre, Birdie could see not one but two white vans that fitted the description Mr G had given her. And now there was some bloody madwoman waving a sign in front of her face.

'No to Sederburg Golf in the Gulf!' the girl was shouting. 'No to Sederburg Golf in the Gulf. No to the rape of America's natural heritage. No to Sederburg! No, no, no!'

It was the last thing Birdie needed.

'Get out of the way.' Birdie gave the girl a shove but she kept on shouting and then she actually lifted up her filthy top and flashed her tits!

* * *

It was the sign Mother Nature's Avengers had been waiting for. Nate and Jason covered their faces with the Disney masks and made a run for their target.

33

The rush from behind took Birdie's breath away. She threw an ineffectual punch in the direction of the guy in the Mickey Mouse mask. She was somewhat shocked when that punch was blocked in a forceful and very professional manner.

'Get off me!' Birdie struggled dramatically. Then, suddenly, there were four guys upon her. Two Mickeys, a Donald Duck and a Minnie, whirling around and around her like a nightmarish ride at Disneyland.

'Hey!' she exclaimed, rubbing her arm. The force with which one of the kidnappers, a Donald Duck, was holding her wrist and twisting her arm up behind her back stunned her. Chipper, who had launched a couple of kicks at a passing Mickey and received a very hard slap in return, ran screaming from the scene. It wasn't supposed to be like this.

'You're hurting me,' Birdie complained to her captors.

'Just get walking,' said Donald Duck. 'Towards the white van.'

'Let go of my arm. You know I'm coming with you. Loosen off.'

'You think I'm going to do that? Just do as you're told and you won't get hurt. Get moving. Come on, bitch. Pick up the pace.'

'I didn't pay to be insulted!' Birdie told him.

The kidnapper in the Donald mask just squeezed her arm hard.

Birdie walked. Though she had been preparing for this moment for the past week, there was something surprisingly frightening about the whole experience. The previous night, in front of her dressing-table mirror, she had worked on an expression of fear and shock to convince the crowds who would watch this moment that she really was being kidnapped, but in that moment, she didn't need to fake it at all. The faces of the people in the crowd as they backed away from the kidnappers' guns fed Birdie's fear back to her. Their mouths dropped open in horror. Their eyes popped out of their heads. She wanted to scream.

'I want to scream,' she said out loud.

'Scream and I will shoot you,' Mickey Mouse whispered in her ear. 'Just walk.'

'I'm going to walk,' Birdie conceded. It seemed like the right decision. 'Please let go of my arm.'

'Faster than that.'

'I'm going as fast as I can in these shoes!'

'Take them off.'

'I will not! They cost a thousand dollars!'

Her captors dragged her along.

They reached the white van on the left. The back doors were already open. Donald Duck shoved Birdie inside. She banged her shin hard on the tailgate of the van as he did so.

'For fuck's sake,' she yelled at him. 'I thought I said no rough stuff.'

'Shut up,' said the guy, pushing her down onto a pile of blankets. Two more guys jumped in behind her. The doors were closed and the van skidded away.

'Help!' Chipper shouted belatedly. 'My friend has been kidnapped! Someone call the police!'

'What was that?' asked a fashionista. 'Was it part of the Morrie Ray show?'

'It was a kidnap!' Chipper shook her arm. 'Call the cops! Someone call the police.'

Clemency, who had been sitting outside the theatre in the limo that had taken Chipper and Birdie to the show, checked a text on her mobile, then she put in a call to the LAPD.

'Thanks a lot,' said Birdie as the van headed down the 405 at warp speed. 'That was one hell of an experience. But I really could have done without the rough stuff. Would you look at my shin? I'm bleeding like a pig. For fuck's sake, guys. This will take weeks to heal. Do you have any arnica?'

'Shut up,' said the guy with the Donald Duck head.

'No, you shut up,' said Birdie. 'Mr G,' she addressed the driver, who was wearing a Pluto mask. 'Where the hell did you get these jokers from? I do believe I specifically asked you to make sure there was no rough stuff. And while I understand that you wanted to make the whole thing look authentic, I have to tell you that I am not in the least bit happy and when I find out what trade union regulates pretend kidnappers, you can rest assured that I will be making a complaint.'

'What the fuck is she on about?' asked one Mickey Mouse.

'Mr G!' The driver of the van did not look round. Birdie knocked on the partition. 'Excuse me. I am fed up of this. You people are freaking me out. Mr G, will you please tell them that there's no need for the role playing any more?'

The driver of the van turned slowly, lifting the mask as he did so. Birdie didn't recognize him.

'Huh?' she said. 'Where's Mr G?'

'We don't know who the fuck you're talking about,' said Donald Duck.

Birdie made a grab for the door handle. Within seconds she was in handcuffs with a piece of duct tape over her astonished mouth.

Breathing heavily behind his Mickey Mouse mask, Nate looked into the eyes of the terrified girl sitting opposite him. The van screeched through a red light, heading in the opposite direction to the route Nate had planned so carefully. Something had gone horribly, horribly wrong.

34

'OK, people!' Thirty-five minutes after Birdie's kidnappers had screeched away, a police detective was holding an impromptu press conference on the steps of the auditorium. 'Everybody, we're going to need your help. My team is just getting here and they want to take statements from anyone who thinks they might be able to accurately describe what went on out there. I hope you'll all cooperate. It's very important that we get to work on this right away.'

'Don't worry, ma'am,' a female police officer was comforting Chipper, who now had nothing but a net on her hair. 'Most kidnap victims are returned to their families unharmed very quickly indeed. The California Highway Patrol has been informed. They're on the lookout. And if they can't catch that van then nobody will. Your best friend will be absolutely fine.'

Chipper was surprised to find that she was shaking. Though she knew very well that Birdie should be fine (she'd hired the hoodlums, after all), the whole experience had been so much more violent than she'd expected. Clemency, who had seen the whole thing and was a little surprised herself, wrapped her arm around Chipper's shoulder.

'Chipper, you have to get a grip on yourself,' she said. 'You know that Birdie is going to be fine.'

Chipper nodded. 'I suppose,' she whispered to Clemency, 'the fact that I'm so shaken up will add authenticity to the whole thing. Make it look like I didn't know what was going on.'

'Good point,' said Clemency. 'In that case, keep shaking.'

'But, you know, I'm still a little worried. It was all so sudden and they were really rough. Look what they did to me!' Chipper rubbed at her own arm, which had been battered black and blue in the kerfuffle. 'Clemency, we let Birdie choose her kidnappers off the Internet. We didn't meet any of them except Mr G. What if the ten thousand dollars she offered them isn't enough and they try to extract more by cutting off her ear or something?'

Clemency grimaced.

'I'll never forgive myself if she ends up coming home in a series of matchboxes.'

'Chipper, don't even think like that. Nothing bad is going to happen. Stay calm.'

'I have to tell the police what really happened. I've got this awful feeling in my gut.' She underlined the sentiment with a small burp. 'I'm going to tell them.'

Clemency looked panicked now. 'For God's sake, not yet. Birdie will be furious,' she added.

A detective interrupted. 'We need to take your statements.'

'Have you spoken to Birdie's grandfather?' Clemency asked.

'A member of our team is on the way to him right now.'

Julius Sederburg was not best pleased to be interrupted in the middle of a planning meeting. When Mary, his assistant, put her head round the doorway to the boardroom and mouthed, 'It's about Birdie,' his immediate reaction was to roll his eyes. Then he shook his head. 'I'm busy.'

'It's urgent,' Mary mouthed again. 'Real urgent. The police are here.'

Julius stood up. 'Gentlemen, would you excuse me for just a moment?'

Two detectives were waiting in the lobby. Detective Bryden, who was the more senior of the two, told Julius to take a seat.

'What do I need to take a seat for? I don't have time to sit down.'

'Sir, I have some shocking news,' said Bryden. 'Your grand-daughter has been kidnapped.'

'She what?'

'From outside a fashion show at the Disney Theater. The kidnappers were wearing masks.'

'How on earth did it happen? Why did no one intervene?'

'It seems that people didn't know a kidnap was in progress. They assumed, given the avant-garde nature of the designer whose show they'd been watching, that Birdie's kidnap was just another part of the entertainment.'

'For heaven's sake,' said Julius. 'This is most inconvenient.'

'You must be very worried,' said Bryden.

'I am. I have the Malaysian ambassador arriving in my office in half an hour. I am negotiating the largest golf course in South East Asia. The last thing I need to be doing is dealing with a kidnap.'

'I understand, sir,' Bryden assured him. 'But I'm afraid we really are going to have to take up some more of your time.'

Julius Sederburg looked at his watch. 'You have fifteen minutes. And if I find out that my granddaughter is pulling some kind of stunt, I will disinherit her at once.'

'Mr Sederburg, with respect, I don't think this was any kind of stunt. Eyewitness reports say that she was bundled into the back of the van quite violently. Her assailants appeared to be carrying guns.'

'Huh,' Julius looked faintly impressed.

'OK. Let's start. We're going to need the names of everyone you can think of who might hold some kind of grudge against you or your granddaughter.'

'Why would anyone hold a grudge against me?'

'My question exactly,' said Bryden, more out of politeness than because he believed it. 'But we need to rule a few things out. For example, can you think of anyone who might have missed out on a great deal because you got there first? Or how about staff? Have you sacked any staff in the past few weeks? Has your grand-daughter?'

'How am I supposed to know whether my granddaughter has sacked any staff?'

'I thought perhaps she might have mentioned something to you. We'll need to see the names of everybody on her payroll.'

Julius was getting more and more agitated. 'Mary, I need you to deal with this.'

'Thank you, Mr Sederburg,' Bryden nodded. 'Rest assured that we're going to be working hard to sort this situation out. We'll keep you directly updated.'

'You can leave messages with my assistant,' Julius Sederburg replied.

Dean Stevenson was on the set of *PCH* when Justin called to tell him that Birdie had been kidnapped.

'He's in the middle of a shot,' said the production assistant.

'I have to talk to him right now,' Justin insisted.

When Dean picked up the phone, Justin told him to find a very private corner to take the call. Justin had already known about Birdie's disappearance for an hour. During that time, he had come up with the perfect strategy.

'So?' said Dean when Justin told him that Birdie had been snatched by masked men outside the Morrie Ray show. 'Why should I care?'

'Wrong answer,' said Justin.

'But she's my ex-girlfriend,' said Dean reasonably. 'This doesn't impact on me.'

'Wrong again. Dean, we have to handle this very carefully. At the moment, we don't know why Birdie was kidnapped or by whom. It may all be over in a matter of hours. It may take months. Either way there is a strong chance she comes out of this looking like a heroine. It will improve her profile. People will feel sorry for her. When she does come out, every newspaper and TV show in the land will want to interview her about her experiences. And when they move on to talking about her life in general, your name will come up. You want it to come up in a good way, right?'

'But last week, after she punched Emily outside the *PCH* party, you said I had to distance myself from her.'

'That was when the general public thought she was a brainless heiress who brought all her worries upon herself. That is going to change. Particularly if the kidnappers cut off her ear or something like that.'

Dean shuddered. 'What do you want me to do?'

'I'm sending a camera crew to the *PCH* studios. They should be outside any minute. I need you to come out looking distressed. You'll stop and give a small speech about your concern for your ex-girlfriend's safety. You'll say that you are going to do everything you can to ensure her safe return.'

'Emily is not going to like this,' said Dean.

'Emily? Who's she? You're going to break-up with her . . .'

Less than two hours after Birdie's disappearance, Dean gave a press conference on the matter.

'I am absolutely out of my mind with worry about Birdie,' he assured the assembled journalists.

'Hadn't you broken up?' asked someone.

'Didn't you say you thought she was mad as a cut snake and you were happy to be rid of her?' asked another.

'Birdie and I had our differences, it's true,' Dean admitted. 'But that doesn't mean to say that I didn't always hold her in the highest regard. I've been thinking about Birdie a lot in these past few weeks since we've been apart and this incident has just brought it home how much I've been missing her and how much she really means to me.'

'What about Emily B?' came a shout from the back.

'Emily and I have parted ways,' Dean muttered.

As he said it, Dean could almost feel the stinging sensation of Emily's open hand as it landed 'slap' upon his cheek.

Within five hours, the kidnapping of Birdie Sederburg had become world news. A posse of journalists set up store outside the Sederburg Golf Resorts headquarters in Beverly Hills, ready for any announcement the family cared to make. Meanwhile, the California Highway Patrol sent out an 'all points' alert for the white van, which was already over the state line and into Nevada.

The police questioned Chipper and Clemency several times immediately following the kidnap. The two girls stuck to the same line. They didn't have a clue who might hold a grudge against their dear friend, with the exception of Emily B, who had stolen her boyfriend.

'But she's unlikely to have set up a kidnapping as a result,' said one of the detectives. 'If Emily B went missing then Birdie would be a prime suspect. But the other way round? It doesn't make sense. Emily already has what she wants.'

'Perhaps she wanted to make sure,' Clemency suggested.

At the end of each interview, Chipper was a little more agitated.

'I don't understand it,' she said to Clemency when they found themselves alone. 'I would have expected to hear something from her by now. Just an SMS or something to reassure us that she's OK. But there's been nothing. Have you called Mr G?'

'I did,' said Clemency. 'But he isn't picking up.'

'You don't seem at all worried. How come this isn't bothering you?'

'Because I am certain that everything has gone according to plan.'

'It's no good,' said Chipper. 'I can't keep this up a moment longer. I just have such a bad feeling. I know something awful has happened to Birdie. I'm going to tell the cops that she set the kidnap up herself.'

'She wouldn't want you to do that.'

'I think you're wrong. Birdie and I have been best friends since we were little kids. We've always been like sisters to each other. We've had a bond so special, I can sometimes read her mind. And right now I'm reading her mind and I can tell that she's frightened. I'm telling you, Clemency. Something is not right.'

35

As it happened, Chipper did not have long to wait for confirmation of her fears. The police investigation started simply. CCTV footage revealed that three white vans answering the description of the kidnappers' vehicle had been lurking around the theatre that day. It was the most basic police work to take down the registration numbers and use those numbers to track down the registered drivers.

Mrs G was all smiles when three detectives walked into the office where she worked as a chiropodist's secretary. She prided herself on being a good Christian woman but there was nothing she enjoyed more than a little scandal. When the officers flashed their badges, she welcomed them warmly, assuming they must have come to arrest her boss for evading taxes. She was absolutely speechless when the officers explained that they had come to take her to the nearest station for questioning. She was under arrest.

'But I've never done anything wrong in my entire life!' she insisted. 'This is a travesty!'

'Your credit card was used to hire a van that was used in a kidnapping attempt,' the female detective told her. 'Please come quietly, Mrs Grimes. It'll make life so much easier for all of us.'

'Young lady,' said Mrs G. 'There is no need to address me as though I am a criminal. Just who do you think you're talking to? You can't have been out of high school for more than a month. I want to speak to your senior officer.'

'I am the senior officer on this team,' said the young woman.

'But how can you be? You're a girl . . .'

It wasn't long before Mrs G found herself being led through

the chiropodist's waiting room in handcuffs, as regular customers, who had done battle with Mrs G's arcane appointments system for years, quietly gawped and gloated.

'This is so humiliating!' she cried. 'Couldn't you have covered my head?'

While Mrs G was being arrested in Torrance, a team of officers screening the area around the Disney Theater for more clues discovered Hector and Guido in the dumpster, still asleep and still wearing their Disney masks. When they were taken in for questioning on their version of events, it was found that they were both working in the United States illegally. They were more than happy to finger Mr G in return for lenience. So they told the detectives all about the plot and Mr G was duly brought in. After that, they found themselves being sent right back to the border. Seeing Mr G in the waiting area at the police station, Hector promised Mr G that they would be back.

'We're coming for you.' He made a slashing motion across his neck. 'You won't even know that it happened. We know where you live,' he reminded him.

Mr G paled. His mother, who had been released from handcuffs and further questioning thanks to Guido and Hector squealing, was sitting beside him. She complained to a detective.

'That man just made a threat against the life of my son! Aren't you going to do something about it?'

'Lady,' said the officer, eager to avoid any more paperwork, 'as far as I'm concerned, I didn't hear nothing.'

'Why! Sir, that is a bald-faced lie.' Mrs. G got to her feet, holding her handbag in front of her like a shield.

'Mom,' Mr G pleaded. 'Please don't make this any worse.'

But she would. When Detective Bryden came to fetch her son for his interview, Mrs G began her rant at once.

'I don't understand why my son is here at all. It seems clear to me that he and Birdie Sederburg had a perfectly legitimate contract. It's hardly his fault that it didn't go according to plan.

If my son had managed to kidnap Birdie then I'm sure he would have looked after her very well indeed.'

'Mrs Grimes,' said Detective Bryden. 'We need your son's version of events. Without coaching.'

It wasn't much of a story. Gareth explained how he had never truly expected Dreams of Danger to come to anything. It was just a hobby. A way of practising his web-design skills. Web design was his real job, he assured them.

'We'll be talking some more about that when we have finished investigating the content of your computer,' the detective confirmed.

'My son has nothing to hide!' Mrs G interjected.

Gareth cringed as he thought about just how much he did have to hide. The detective smirked as he read Mr G's facial expression.

'Anyway, Ms Sederburg and her personal assistant called me and we set up a meeting.'

'Where did the meeting take place?'

'I arranged to meet her near the Griffith Observatory,' said Mr G. 'She turned up wearing a disguise. She had a scarf over her head and sunglasses. I didn't recognize her, even though I'd seen that video of her that went around the Internet a few years ago.'

Both Mr G and the detective looked faintly wistful as they remembered the video clip.

'Anyway. The meeting went like I expected it to. We talked about what she wanted and I told her what I could do. She gave me a cheque for five thousand dollars.'

'Five thousand dollars!' Gareth's mother gasped. 'You took five thousand dollars off that poor girl?'

'She's a multi-millionairess, Mom.'

'I'm ashamed of you,' said Mrs G.

'With all respect,' the detective interrupted, 'I'd appreciate it if you would keep your moral judgments for later on. We are conducting a time-sensitive investigation. So, getting back to that day. You're telling me that this was the only time you and Birdie Sederburg actually met face to face?'

'Yes,' Mr G confirmed.

'And you're sure that she was alone that day? There was no one there who might have overheard your conversation?'

Mr G looked pensive. 'I don't think so,' he said. 'I'm pretty careful about that. But now I think back . . .'

'He has a photographic memory,' said his mother.

'Now I think back, there was someone. A woman. Dressed in one of those Middle East things. What are they called?'

'A burqa?' said the detective.

'That's it. Wearing one of those. A burqa.'

'Thank you,' said the detective. He turned to his assistant. 'I need you to get on to Julius Sederburg's office and find out about his projects in the Middle East. We need to see if he has upset any mujahidin.'

'Can we go?' asked Mrs G.

'You can,' said the detective. 'But don't leave the state. We'll be in touch.'

'I am so ashamed of you,' said Mrs G as they crossed the car park to the bus stop. 'I raised you all on my own after your father left and I raised you to respect authority and stay out of trouble. And now this! I was arrested because of you. I was taken from my office in handcuffs in front of several well-respected members of the community. You've brought our good name into disrepute!'

She batted him around the head. Mr G decided it was not the best time to remind her that he was hardly the first member of the family who'd made a mistake. His father had skipped town to avoid trouble after amassing huge gambling debts.

'Now that poor girl is out there somewhere, being held by heavens only knows who . . .'

'She wanted to be kidnapped, Mom. It was to impress her ex-boyfriend.'

'You should have counselled her, Gareth. You should have sent her towards the consolation of the Church. In fact, I think that's where we should go right now so that you can contemplate what you've gotten that poor child into.'

Despite her small size compared to the hulking bulk of her only son, Mrs G had no trouble whatsoever steering him towards the bus. She took the top of his arm in her claw-like grip and pinched so hard that it made him want to cry.

How had it all gone so wrong? All Gareth had ever wanted was to impress his friends. To be in the papers. Now he would be all over the papers, but as the incompetent who got Birdie Sederburg kidnapped by al-Qaeda. When he got home that night, he attempted to hack into the Disney Theater's CCTV system in order to get a proper look at what had happened on the day of the kidnap. He spent three hours trying to find a way to access that information online. He got nowhere, of course. In reality he didn't have the first clue how to do anything more complicated than pick up his email. So he went back to browsing the usual MILF sites while his internal critic took up its position at the back of his mind again and made the 'Loser' sign.

When she heard the latest development in the investigation, Chipper was beside herself. 'Birdie has been taken by terrorists!' she wailed.

'Chipper,' Clemency reminded her. '*You* were the girl in the burqa that day.'

36

Just as the police were realizing that Mr G and his merry men had not kidnapped Birdie, the same realization was coming to Birdie herself. After they'd handcuffed her and stuck tape over her mouth, Birdie's real kidnappers had gone one step further in their efforts to shut her up. While Birdie signalled panic with wide-open eyes, one of the men in the Mickey Mouse masks brought out a syringe and jabbed it into Birdie's arm. Mickey was not a trained nurse. When Birdie awoke after what seemed like a week-long sleep, the first thing she noticed was that her arm was throbbing. The second thing she noticed was that she couldn't see. At all.

'Aaaah! I've gone blind! What's happened? I can't see anything. Aaaaaah, aaaaaah, aaaaaahhhh!' she shrieked in panic.

'It's OK,' came a voice from the darkness. 'You're not blind, you've got a blindfold on.'

'What?'

Birdie went to pull the blindfold off but couldn't. Her hands were tied.

'Ohmigod, ohmigod, ohmigod.'

'Stay calm,' said the disembodied voice.

'I can't be calm! What's going on? Who are you? Where are you? What am I doing here?'

Birdie sat up, promptly thumping her head on a ceiling that was considerably lower than she'd expected.

'Oh yeah,' said the voice in the darkness. 'You're on the top bunk of a bunkbed so you might want to stay lying down. And don't roll.'

Birdie lay straight back down.

'Who are you?' she asked the voice. She curled into a ball, fearful of the answer. Though the voice in the darkness sounded oddly familiar, which made her think that perhaps she wasn't tied up in a strange place after all. Perhaps this was a dream. Any minute now she would wake up and Clemency would bring her breakfast on a tray.

'It's Nate,' said the voice. 'Nate Hathaway.'

'Do I know you?'

'I'm your gardener.'

'Oh, then this is definitely a dream. How else would I have ended up trussed up like this with the gardener?'

'You don't want to know,' said Nate. 'But I'm afraid it isn't a dream.'

'In which case,' said Birdie, with a hint of panic in her voice, 'you should know that I am not comfortable in complete darkness and I think you should take this mask off and let me out of here before I freak out.'

'I can't do that,' said Nate.

'You have to do that,' said Birdie. 'I'm your employer.'

'Not any more. The status quo has rather changed since you were last awake.'

Birdie's head thumped. Partly through dehydration, partly because of the strain of putting together the fragments of memory that were drifting back to her now. How long had she been asleep? Why did her arm hurt? And her leg, too? She remembered hitting it as she was bundled into the back of the van. Sure enough, when she felt her right shin it was tender. She remembered that there were three men in Disney masks, not two as Mr G had told her there would be. And then she remembered that the driver had turned out *not* to be Mr G.

'You kidnapped me,' said Birdie with sudden clarity. 'Oh God!' she wailed. 'I was kidnapped by my gardener.'

'Yes and no,' said Nate.

* * *

'Yes and no' was what Jason said to the cops when they questioned him about the kidnap too. 'Yes, we did intend to kidnap Birdie Sederburg. But no, we didn't manage it.'

After the kidnap fiasco, he and Melanie had run to the right van and Tony had driven them out of the vicinity like the devil's own driver taking them straight to hell. It was a couple of minutes before they realized that not only had they failed to get Birdie Sederburg, they didn't have Nate either.

'What the fuck?' said Jason.

Back in Santa Monica, they'd gone over the afternoon's events in disbelief.

'Nate must have set us up!' was the only conclusion Tony could come to. 'He had no intention of taking Sederburg up to the Bakersfield MNA. He got us to cause a distraction while he took off with her and a whole different bunch of guys.'

'I always knew he wasn't one of us,' said Melanie. 'Look at the way he dressed.'

'Yeah,' said Tony. 'And he doesn't like the Grateful Dead.'

'Neither do we,' Melanie and Jason chimed.

Still, when it came down to it, the remaining members of the Santa Monica chapter of the MNA had to concede that the only thing they'd really lost through the whole fiasco was a late night and a lie-in. The Bakersfield chapter was told to stand down (not that they had actually done all that much to prepare for their possible visitor) and life in Santa Monica regained its usual rhythm. A slow one.

Though not for long.

That very evening the police arrived. They came in three cars that screeched, with lights flashing and sirens blaring, into the cul de sac where the MNA lived. The entire street came out to watch. The yuppie guy who had just bought the house next door and considered the MNA to be bringing the value of his property down actually started a round of applause as Tony, Melanie and Jason were brought from the house in cuffs.

'How did you find us?' was the first thing Jason wanted to know.

The officer who had cuffed him snorted. 'Isn't it obvious? We checked the registration of your van.'

Melanie and Tony were furious.

'It was the only thing you had to do!' said Melanie. 'Change the plates. You didn't change the plates.'

'Hey,' said Jason. 'I didn't think we were going to get up in time to do the damn kidnap anyway . . .'

Soon it wasn't just Melanie and Tony who were furious with their friend. The police took Nate's laptop and, though he had done his best to delete the electronic trail he'd made, the police IT team quickly found the ghost of a file containing directions from the Disney Theater to the hideout in the hills. It was particularly bad news for the Bakersfield chapter, who had cops land a chopper on one of their most mature and profitable marijuana fields later that very same night. Their fifteen-year stretch of being undetected was over.

'Look,' said Jason, as his interview entered its fifth hour, 'there is nothing more we can tell you. I've spent more time talking to you than was spent organizing this whole stupid plot in the first place. You know that we planned to kidnap Birdie Sederburg. You know our plan went wrong. That is the long and the short of it. You have no grounds to keep me here.'

'Just tell us where Nate Hathaway has taken her.'

'I don't know,' said Jason. 'He never said. I still can't believe he took off like that. He was supposed to be my best friend.'

Unfortunately for Jason, the detective in charge of his interview did not take Jason's bewilderment as a sign of his genuine ignorance of Nate's whereabouts.

It took a lawyer, a good one, hired by Jason's family, a whole twenty-four hours to convince the detectives to let the Avengers go, albeit on bail with several charges relating to the possession of marijuana to their names. Jason's family found the enormous bail bonds.

But there still remained the mystery of the fourth avenger. Where was Nate Hathaway? Was he with the gang who had kidnapped Birdie? Perhaps he had double-crossed his old friends? The detectives ignored Jason's somewhat wild suggestion that maybe, just maybe, Nate had been kidnapped too and instead they put out a warrant for his arrest. The boy had form. Just a few weeks before the kidnap he had practically assaulted Old Man Sederburg at the opening of a golf course. It had been his idea that he and Jason take work as gardeners at Birdie's home. He was obviously the brain behind this ramshackle bunch, who were as clueless a gang of criminals as the police had ever seen. Nate must have used them to set up a distraction.

A photograph of Nate Hathaway, taken while he was at law school, was soon circulating on the police system. They would track him down and when they found him, they had no doubt that the mystery would be solved.

Back at the MNA house in Santa Monica, the general opinion was that the detectives were right.

'Nate double-crossed us,' said Tony. 'He got us to do the donkey-work. Now he's hiding out in Cabo waiting for Old Man Sederburg to fill up his bank account.'

'You know what I think?' said Melanie. 'I think that Nate is in league with Birdie Sederburg! How about this? He got close to her while he was up there doing that gardening and they've run away together! She's helping him to fleece her grandfather, then they'll take the money and set up home.'

Jason shook his head. 'I can't believe Nate would try to double-cross us. How long have we known him, guys? Has he ever given us any reason to think that he wasn't one hundred per cent behind our aims? He worked harder than any of us to spread the message about the environment. He's somewhere out there and he's in trouble.'

'What can we do about it?' Melanie shrugged.

'Yeah,' said Tony. 'Nothing. That's what. And we can't even light the bong to help us think.'

As far as Tony was concerned, that was the worst of it. They couldn't smoke. The house was still under police surveillance, of course. They knew that. The phones would be tapped too, just in case Nate tried to get in contact with them.

'This is the biggest fuck-up ever,' Jason sighed.

37

After they had sedated Birdie, there was no need for the kidnappers to keep their masks on any more because there was no danger that Birdie would see and remember their faces. She was dead to the world and would be for quite some time to come.

'I gave her enough to sedate a fricking horse,' said the guy who had injected her, proudly.

As Birdie slumped like a sack in the corner of the van, Mickey Mouse was the first to unmask himself.

'Jeez,' he said. 'I am glad to get that damn thing off. It was like a hockey player's jockstrap in there.'

Donald Duck went next, revealing a face that was hardly any less ugly or stupid than the mask had been. Which left only Nate in his own Mickey mask, sweating for many more reasons than the heat generated by wearing plastic over his face.

It was at that moment that the other kidnappers first cottoned on to the fact that something was not quite right. The man who had been Mickey pointed at himself as though to count, then he pointed at the driver, at the unmasked Donald Duck and then finally at Nate.

'Four,' he said. 'That's funny. I don't believe we were four when we set out this morning, do you, Fatman?'

'Robin, I don't believe we were,' said the unfortunately-named Fatman.

'Well, something very funny is happening here. Perhaps we moved into another dimension and I got multiplied. Take your mask off, Mr Mickey. Help me solve a mystery here.'

What else could Nate do? There was nowhere to run. Slowly,

he lifted the moulded plastic away from his face and all was revealed.

'Who the fuck are you?' asked Robin.

Nate started to explain. But his story of how he came to be in the wrong van didn't interest his new friends at all. There followed instead a short debate about what should be done with him. The van was by now travelling at quite a speed along an empty highway. Fatman's idea was that they should just open the doors and push Nate out the back. But that might not necessarily kill him, Robin pointed out, and now he'd seen their faces. They couldn't risk letting a witness free. The interloper would have to be shot.

'You want me to do it now?' asked Fatman, getting out his gun.

'You can't shoot him in the van,' said Robin. 'What if the bullet ricochets and hits one of us instead?'

'Good point,' said Fatman. 'We could stab him.'

'Blood,' said Robin simply.

'Hey, no blood,' said the driver. 'I got to take this van back to work on Monday morning.'

'Look, guys,' Nate interjected. 'I understand you're pretty pissed off to have me in your van and all that, but really, there's no need to kill me. After all, we're not enemies. We had roughly the same objectives back there at the Disney Theater. We all wanted Birdie Sederburg. I wanted her as a way to get to her grandfather and persuade him to get more environmentally friendly. You wanted . . .'

'Money,' said Fatman simply.

'Well, yes, of course. And I'm not going to stand in the way of that.'

'Your family got any money, Nate Hathaway?' Robin asked. 'Maybe we could put you up for ransom too?'

'My family don't have much,' said Nate. 'So how about this? You stop at the next truck stop and let me out of the van. I start walking in the opposite direction and never look back. I swear on my mother's life that you will hear nothing further of me or from me. If anyone asks where I've been for the past few hours, I will claim amnesia.'

'Amnesia, huh?' said Robin. 'Nice try. But no dice. We're going to have to kill you. It's simply a matter of when. I'm sure you understand,' he added. 'We're professionals. We don't leave loose ends. No matter how prettily they plead.'

Nate felt his bowels loosen. Thank God Melanie's insistence on bran in the morning meant that he had already evacuated his bowels that day.

'Fatman,' said Robin, 'have we got any more of that sleeping stuff?'

Fatman prepared another syringe and soon Nate and Birdie were sleeping side by side.

When Nate woke up, it was just as Fatman was laying him, almost gently, on the floor of the room in which Birdie now found herself.

'You're telling me that you've been kidnapped too?' said Birdie.

'I don't think they meant to get me,' said Nate. 'I'm like a dolphin that got caught in the tuna net.'

'And these are definitely not the kidnappers I hired?'

'I'm afraid not,' said Nate. 'My friend Jason and I took care of them before the fashion show was even over.'

'Then who are these people?'

'I have no idea,' Nate replied. 'But I don't think they're the good guys.'

38

Birdie didn't have to wait long to get to know their captors better.

'They're moving about,' came a voice from beyond the locked door. And soon the door was wrenched open by Fatman, formerly Donald Duck, who was as big as a house and blocked out most of the light he let into Nate and Birdie's dungeon as he whipped off their blindfolds. Robin appeared behind him. He had beady eyes above the surgical mask he wore to cover the bottom half of his face (Fatman was wearing a bandana across his mouth). Robin was obviously the brains of this team.

'Thank God you've opened that door,' said Birdie. 'Now, look. I understand that you are nothing to do with Mr G, who I hired to do this job, so clearly we need to have a conversation. I'm a wealthy woman. I'm sure we can come to some kind of arrangement to secure my immediate release . . .'

'Exactly,' said Robin. 'That is the whole point of taking a hostage. But we're not going to be doing any negotiating with *you*.'

Robin grabbed Birdie by the arm and yanked her out into the hallway. She had to shade her eyes, which stung from having been shut for so long.

'Shall I get him out too?' Fatman asked, jerking his head towards Nate.

'I don't see why not,' said Robin. 'He might want to see how a professional kidnap team works.'

Fatman dragged Nate out of the room. Birdie saw now that Nate was cuffed.

* * *

'We're going to make a nice little video for your grandfather,' Robin explained. 'I want you to sit on this chair and tell him how nice Fatman and I are being to you. For now. But I want you to tell him that we seem like the kind of guys who aren't very patient, so he might want to send a million dollars to our bank account pronto if he'd like to see you home in one piece.'

Robin and Fatman had already prepared a makeshift studio in which to record their broadcast. A dirty sheet, which might once have been white, hung from a washing line stretched between the door and the window.

'Don't want anyone getting any ideas about where we might be keeping you, do we?' said Robin as he manhandled Birdie onto a kitchen chair in front of the temporary screen. The chair, like the sheet, had seen better days. Stuffing was escaping from the lino-covered seat. Birdie instinctively recoiled from the thought of putting her bottom on something so ratty. But there was no point complaining.

Robin focused the camera on her.

'Want to see what you look like?' he asked, flicking the screen round so that Birdie could see her own frightened face. Old habits dying hard, Birdie couldn't help but scrutinize her appearance, even in this worst of situations. Her eyes looked very weird. It was a moment before she realized she was missing one set of false eyelashes. Her hair was all over the place.

She glanced at and caught Nate's eye. He gave a small smile that was intended to encourage her.

'Happy?' Robin asked.

'At least let me comb my hair,' said Birdie.

'Your hands are cuffed. We'll have to do it for you.' Robin pulled a greasy comb out of his back pocket. Birdie ducked away from it but Robin was intent on doing her hair.

'You're pulling,' she complained.

'Aw, sorry,' said Robin and pulled some more. 'That good enough for you?'

It was not the time to tell him that she ordinarily wore her hair parted on the other side.

'Then we'll begin. Read this.' He held a piece of card up in front of her. 'Now, be sensible, Birdie. Just what's on the card. Nothing more than he needs to know.'

Birdie squinted at the words.

'I can't read it,' she said. 'What have you written there? Is that supposed to say 'disarmed' or 'unharmed'? Because there's no such word as 'disharmed'.'

'Don't try my patience,' said Robin, 'I'm a very short-tempered guy.'

Still, he took the board and changed the word 'disharmed' to 'unharmed'.

'Read it,' he commanded again. 'Nice and clear.'

Birdie looked at the board but remained silent. She wasn't sure what she was supposed to do. Should she be compliant or defiant? If this were a movie, she thought to herself, I would definitely be defiant. But before she could set her jaw like one of Charlie's Angels facing death, Robin had decided enough was enough. He didn't feel like waiting. He brought a flick-knife out of his pocket and though he merely used it to clean his nails, Birdie got the hint.

'Read it,' he said again.

'Grandaddy,' Birdie began. 'I've been taken hostage by a very professional gang. They have been keeping me in very good conditions and you can see that I am unharmed.'

'Wave your fingers,' said Robin. 'To show you've still got them. For now.'

'I am unharmed,' Birdie started again. 'But you should know that these people mean business. If you deposit one million dollars in the offshore bank account detailed at the end of this message, then I will be returned to you in one piece. If you don't, then . . .'

Birdie hesitated as she read the last line.

'I will be returned to you piece by piece, starting with my . . .'

Her eyes widened. Nate held his breath.

'Starting with my *hair*!' The word came out like a wail. 'My hair! Oh no. Not my hair. Not my hair!'

The depth of Birdie's distress astonished the three men in the room. Robin snatched the card from Fatman.

'*Ear*. It's supposed to say ear.'

'It doesn't look like ear,' said Birdie.

'It's ear! Why would anyone care if we cut your fucking hair off?'

Birdie was equally surprised at the idea that anyone *wouldn't* care.

'Hair grows back,' said Robin.

'It takes for frickin ever,' Birdie explained. 'I had a disaster feather cut in 2004 and I'm only just getting over it . . .'

Nate tried hard to stifle a smile.

'For fuck's sake,' said Robin. 'Shut up. Do that last bit again. And say 'ear' this time. *Ear*. Whoever heard of a kidnapper sending hair?'

'I will be returned to you piece by piece, starting with my *ear*,' said Birdie.

'Thank you,' said Robin.

'Original,' said Birdie, just under her breath.

This time Nate did smile. It was comforting to see a flash of the Birdie who sacked gardeners on a whim.

'Then perhaps we'll start with your fingers,' said Robin. 'Wouldn't want to disappoint you with a lack of originality.'

'Look,' said Birdie. 'This is pointless. You don't even need to ask my grandfather for money. If all you want is a million dollars, then I can sort that out myself. Let me out of here and I will write you a cheque the minute I get back to Los Angeles.'

'Nice try,' said Robin.

'Or I'll have my assistant wire it to you. That way it'll be instant and you can have the cash before you let me go. But you have to drive me to the nearest town first.'

'What about your boyfriend?'

'I'm not her boyfriend . . .'

'He's not my boyfriend . . .'

Nate and Birdie chimed in unison.

'Look, sister,' said Robin. 'We are not driving you anywhere. We know you don't have access to that kind of cash without talking to your grandfather first. So, to cut out the middle man, you are staying right here until your grandfather pays up himself.'

'How do you know I don't have access to a million dollars?' Birdie protested. 'You know how rich I am, otherwise you wouldn't have kidnapped me.'

'It's all in trust. You get an allowance.'

'Where did you hear that?'

Robin smirked.

Nate interrupted. 'You know, she is pretty rich. I used to work for her. And getting her assistant to send the money would be a whole lot simpler than getting Julius Sederburg involved. You have no idea how ruthless that man is.'

'Not quite as ruthless as me, I would imagine. Get these people out of my sight, will you, Fatman?'

Fatman stepped up to Birdie, took the eye-mask that was hanging round her neck and pulled it up over her eyes again.

'No! No!' Birdie shrieked with panic. 'I can't do eye-masks. I don't even do an eye-mask when I'm at the spa.'

'Then this is a first for you,' said Robin.

'No, please! No!'

'Come on, man,' said Nate. 'Don't put the eye-mask on her. It's not like she hasn't already seen you. Give the girl a break. We're not going anywhere.'

Robin stroked his chin. 'Hmmmm. OK. I wouldn't want you to think I'm a man with no heart whatsoever. We'll forget about the eye-mask,' he said.

Fatman ripped it off. Birdie's expression was wild with panic.

'And we'll even take off the handcuffs.'

'Hey,' said Nate. 'That's really . . . er, kind.'

'But you'll have to stay in there.'

Nate and Birdie followed Robin's head-jerk in the direction of a narrow door.

'But . . .' Birdie began.

Before she could finish her sentence, she and Nate were locked in the otherwise empty cold store. No windows. No light. No way out.

39

Good guys Robin and Fatman most definitely were not. Now that they had their video clip of Birdie, they made their first demands of her grandfather. They were, as they had told Nate, consummate professionals when it came to kidnapping. They used an untraceable email address from which to send their missive. They sent it to Sederburg's personal assistant, Mary, who went white when she opened the clip attached. The detectives working on the case had been waiting for this moment. They pounced on this tiny shred of evidence and followed the electronic trail as far as they could, but it led to nothing. They were clearly dealing with clever guys. The plain sheet background to the video clip gave no clues at all.

'They're threatening to do to your granddaughter what those brutes did to poor young Getty!' Mary was distraught.

Julius watched the clip several times without a trace of emotion on his patrician face.

'What do you want us to do, sir?' asked Julius Sederburg's right-hand man, Jim Smith. 'We could just send the money. Apparently that happens quite a lot. I've been looking into your various security insurance policies and one may just pay out.'

'Do nothing,' said Sederburg. 'If they can put up with my granddaughter for more than a week, I'll send them a million dollars as a reward.'

'But . . .'

'How are things going on the Marshlands site?' asked Sederburg to change the subject.

'The Marshlands site?' The new development was the last thing on Jim Smith's mind, but not, it seemed, on his boss's.

'Yes. Tell me how my new golf course is coming along.'

Jim looked to Mary, who shrugged. Maybe this was Julius's way of dealing with the stress, his two staff decided independently. Just carrying on, pretending that all was business as usual. Acting as though the kidnappers were just another pesky supplier who wanted to be paid more than their services were worth. Inside, he must be as anxious as they were. More so.

'Well, sir,' said Jim. 'The site is pretty much drained by now and the earth-movers are in place. That old farmer who was refusing to sell his land – the piece that abutted the space earmarked for the tennis courts – was arrested in relation to an accusation of assault after he took a swing at one of our real-estate guys. His bail was set at seventy-five thousand dollars.'

Julius's mouth twitched upwards at the corners.

'He couldn't find the bail, of course, and he'll almost certainly have to sell to find his legal fees.'

'Good,' said Sederburg.

'Your granddaughter is being held by some very professional guys,' said Jim, bringing the conversation back to Birdie. 'They obviously mean business.'

'And so do I. If they think that targeting my family members is going to make me turn out my pockets, they are sorely mistaken.'

'But Birdie looked so frightened . . .' Mary interrupted.

'I'm sure she knows and understands the way I will deal with this matter. At the end of the day, Birdie is a Sederburg too.'

Julius returned to his office. Mary and Jim were left looking at each other. After a while, Jim shook his head and went back to his own desk.

Chipper Dooley was taking an altogether more pro-active stance towards the disappearance of her best friend. It had been a rough few days for Birdie, PR-wise. Chipper hoped that wherever she was, Birdie didn't know about the press she had been getting. Someone on the police investigation team had let it slip to someone else that the first suspects in Birdie's kidnap were people she had actually *paid* to whisk her away to make Dean Stevenson return her affection.

The response from Ohmygahd was typical of the caustic reaction the news inspired. Ohmygahd ran a huge piece on Birdie's fashion faux pas to accompany this latest juicy snippet of gossip. Chipper was distraught on her friend's behalf as she clicked through the shots of Birdie looking a fool.

'Why do they have to be so nasty?'

'She sort of brought it upon herself,' said Clemency.

'Oooh,' said Chipper, momentarily distracted by something online. 'I forgot about the time we wore matching dungarees.'

'Everyone makes mistakes,' said Clemency.

'But now we know that Birdie wasn't kidnapped by Mr G, people should be taking the situation more seriously.'

Then the video of Birdie filmed to accompany the ransom demand surfaced on YouTube.

'Enough already,' said Ohmygahd. 'Why doesn't somebody tell Sederburg that she's been rumbled? On second thoughts, this clip has to be the funniest thing we've seen all year. Maybe we should wait for another one.'

'It's not funny,' said Chipper. 'She really is in trouble. I know that look. She's not pretending. She's really afraid.'

Clemency nodded.

'We've got to counter all this nasty stuff on the Internet and make sure the investigation stays right at the top of everyone's agenda. I'm hiring an agent,' was Chipper's bright idea.

But the only agent Chipper had ever heard of was Justin, who managed Dean Stevenson. Following the revelation that Birdie had tried to fake her own kidnap to reignite her relationship with Dean, Justin had been kept very busy, sending Dean to interviews in which he talked about how sad he felt for the unfortunate heiress.

'I feel very bad about it,' was Dean's line. 'I'm an ordinary guy. I never expected to inspire quite such a big reaction in any girl.'

Every female interviewer hearing that line would respond in the same way: 'Oh, I don't know . . .' Then they'd cast their eyes down and up, Princess Diana coy. Just as Birdie had done when she'd 'accidentally' driven into Dean's car all those weeks ago.

When Justin got Chipper Dooley's call he was surprised but pleased.

'We have to turn this bad press around,' she said. 'I know Birdie was stupid expecting to win Dean back like that, but now it's obvious that she really is in trouble. We need to remind people of that and keep her face in the news for the right reasons. She could be anywhere. We need to make sure that the entire population of the United States is looking out for her.'

'But why are you calling me?'

'Because you know how to make headlines. I need your help.'

Justin thought about it. But not for long.

'OK,' he said. 'I'll help you.'

Though he represented Dean, there was nothing in the Hollywood agents' code of ethics that said he couldn't work for the mad ex-girlfriend too. In fact, let's face it, there was no agents' code of ethics, full stop. What's more, Justin had seen in Chipper's dedication to her lunatic friend the perfect character for a new reality show.

'I'll talk to my contacts at MTV. I think the search for Birdie Sederburg is something they should be covering. In the mean-time, we need to think about getting some good stories out there. And some merchandising. What was the name of the designer whose show Birdie was kidnapped outside?'

'Morrie Ray,' said Chipper.

Justin had his assistant get Morrie Ray on the phone and it was a matter of minutes before the hot designer had agreed to produce a limited edition T-shirt (just a mere 150,000) for the cause. He sent a sketch over for Justin's approval an hour later.

Chipper loved the design that Morrie had come up with. It

featured Birdie's shocked face (a still from the kidnappers' video) behind the bars of an old-fashioned birdcage. The kind that miners used to use to cart hapless canaries down into the coal mines.

'It's perfect,' said Chipper. She had the design faxed to DD, who also approved. And Clemency.

'But is this what Julius Sederburg would want?' Clemency asked.

'It doesn't matter,' said Chipper. 'He doesn't have the monopoly on love for Birdie Sederburg! Besides, Birdie would just love these T-shirts.'

That afternoon, Justin did what he was paid hundreds of thousands a year to do. He fixed things. The 'Free as Birdie' T-shirt was just the start of it. There would be matching bumper-stickers and baseball caps. And even a batch of Birdie Sederburg golf balls with the young heiress's face printed on the side.

'We can have them delivered to all the Sederburg resorts by the end of the week,' said the guy from Titleist.

'Can you do any better than that?' Justin asked. 'I can't guarantee that she won't have been found by Friday.'

Justin needn't have worried about the balls being obsolete and unsaleable before they were available to the general public. As soon as news of them broke on Ohmygahd, a waiting list to get hold of them had formed.

But the most important part of the whole campaign was going to be the benefit. Because there had to be a benefit. What was a good campaign without one?

'You're telling me,' said Dean, 'that you want me to headline at a show for my insane ex-girlfriend?'

'You're going to do it,' said Justin.

'Who else is in the line-up?'

Justin cleared his throat, then reeled off the names of a number of former *American Idol* contestants (none of whom had made it past the third round) in a manner that was supposed to make them sound exciting.

'They're all nobodies!' Dean protested.

'Look,' said Justin. 'Have you any idea what an achievement it was to put even that line-up together at short notice? We can use the theatre in the conference centre at the Sederburg resort in Denver. It was booked for a Mormon family reunion to celebrate some guy's eightieth birthday, but three of his wives got together and left him last week.'

'Oh God.' Dean clutched his forehead.

'Hey, if I had another week this thing would be happening in LA and I'd have signed Mariah Carey. But I don't have the time. I can't take the risk that Birdie will be rescued before this benefit happens.'

Chipper was very pleased with Justin's work.

'At last I feel like someone is taking this seriously,' she said.

Justin nodded in an understanding sort of way. Chipper didn't need to know that he had billed the whole campaign to his friend at MTV as your 'classic car-crash reality show' full of uber-rich losers and misfits. 'You'll be syndicating these clips for years.'

40

'Let me out! Let me out!' Birdie hammered on the door to the cold store. She hammered and shouted until her fists were raw and her voice came out like a croak. 'Let me out,' she shouted one last time. 'I'm afraid of the dark.'

'I don't think they care about that,' said Nate.

'Don't you dare talk to me,' said Birdie. 'It's your fault I'm in here.'

Birdie stepped away from the door. But it was so dark in that tiny windowless room that, of course, she stumbled over Nate's outstretched legs and ended up on her knees on the concrete. It was a painful fall. The jolt of the impact went through her entire body and the rough surface of the floor grazed the heels of her hands.

'Ow.' She turned over onto her bottom and pulled her knees up to her chest, rocking like a little girl. She sucked at the painful grazes in the hope that might make them feel better.

'This is all your fault,' she said.

'My fault?' Nate's surprise was audible. 'How does that work?'

'You pissed them off so they stuck us in here. At least I had a bed before.'

'I see,' said Nate. 'Correct me by all means, but I do believe that you were the person who paid to have herself kidnapped, which is how this whole disaster started.'

'And then you tried to kidnap me instead.'

'And if it had worked, then trust me, we would have been treating you with far more care than these guys. As it is, it didn't work but I still think you're damn well lucky that I managed to get mixed up in this shit. You'd be in far bigger trouble if I weren't here.'

'How did you even know about the kidnap? Did Clemency tell you?'

'She didn't need to. You did.'

'Hey?'

'You weren't exactly discreet. You should have been more careful when discussing your plans in the garden.'

'My own garden. At my own private house! You shouldn't have been listening.'

'Well, I did, thank God. Since it means you have company in this godforsaken place.'

'Yeah? What exactly is it you're going to do to make my life easier right now? We're locked inside a room with no windows and no light-bulb. What do you propose we do next? Do you know about teleportation? Because if you can't break me down into particles and have me materialize back in my own lovely house then I really don't see what use you can be to me at all. Except as someone to kick.'

She delivered a neat little kick to Nate's shin. It was incredibly accurate considering she couldn't see anything.

'Ow. That was unnecessary.'

'No, it wasn't,' said Birdie. 'I feel much better already.'

'Sometimes it's very easy to see why everybody hates you.'

'What? Not everybody hates me . . .' Birdie took a gulp of air that Nate recognized only too well as the harbinger of a sob.

'Don't cry, please,' he said. 'I don't think I can stand it.'

'You made me.'

'I did not want to make you cry. I want to make your life easier. Both our lives.'

'So, what are you going to do?' asked Birdie, as though 'escape coordinator' were just another job she could contract out.

'I'll think of something,' said Nate.

'Let me guess. You'll blast our way out of here with a rocket launcher. You'll — '

'Ssssh.' Nate reached out in the dark and put his finger where he expected Birdie's lips to be. He got her in the ear.

'Ow. What the fuck . . .'

'Just be quiet for a minute. You know how to be quiet, don't you?'

Birdie gave an approximation of quiet that involved much snorting.

'What can you hear?' she said.

'Nothing,' Nate replied. 'I think perhaps they've gone out.'

'They wouldn't have left us alone.'

'Why not?' said Nate. 'What are we going to do? We're locked in a cold store.'

'Oh God. Let me out!' Birdie banged on the door again.

'You're just wasting energy,' Nate pointed out. 'And I want you to be able to run if we have to.'

'Run where? In circles? In the dark!'

'What have you got in your pockets?' Nate asked.

'Let me see.' Birdie pretended to search. 'Oh, hang on. What's this?! It's a key!'

'Birdie. Be serious. Tell me what you really have. Everything. Whatever you have may be useful.'

'I've got nothing,' said Birdie. 'They took my iPhone. All I have is my invitation to that stupid fashion show.'

'Perfect,' said Nate. 'Give it to me.'

'You going to make an origami spade and dig us out of here?'

'Do you have any hairpins?'

'What?'

'In your hair? You must do. I mean, that's not your real hair, is it? In the ponytail?'

Birdie gasped. 'What are you talking about?'

'Look, this is no time for vanity. Take it off and give me whatever pins it's being held on with.'

Birdie reluctantly unhooked her hair. She wasn't keen on the idea. Mostly because it meant letting go of the notion that this was all some elaborate *Punk'd* style set-up. At any minute, the door could open to reveal a film crew, there to record Birdie's panic. She didn't want to look like a wreck when that happened.

'This is not a set-up,' Nate assured her when she expressed her thought. 'Give me the pins. Now, let's see if these people are as lazy and stupid as I think they are.'

All Nate had to do now was find the door. He stood up and started feeling his way along the wall. Even in such a dark room, he would have expected to see something. A little chink of light beneath the door. But the rooms beyond the door must be getting dark as well.

Eventually, Nate came to the doorframe. He followed it down to the floor and there, sure enough, he felt a breeze creeping in beneath the door itself. He felt along the bottom of the door and confirmed that it was warped, so that while it was jammed tight at one corner, at the other there was a gap of perhaps six millimetres at its widest.

Nate explained the situation to Birdie. 'There's quite a big gap.'

'I'm thin but I'm not that thin. Maybe you should write 'help' on the back of my invitation and push it out there for a passing mouse to pick up and take to the local police.'

Nate was already looking for the keyhole. He found it with his fingers and then poked his little finger inside.

'Fantastic,' he said. 'They've left the key in the lock.'

'On the other side of the door, dummy!'

'Not for long.'

Nate put his ear to the door. 'Come over here,' he said to Birdie. 'I need you to listen with me. I think we're on our own here but I need to be certain. Let me know if you hear anything at all. The slightest thing. Someone taking a breath. A snore.'

As confused as Birdie was as to why it mattered, she joined Nate at the door and they listened. Hard.

'Nothing,' said Nate after a while. 'That's good. Now I need you to start praying.'

While Birdie prayed, Nate slipped the invitation beneath the gap in the doorframe. Luckily it was the shape of an elongated postcard, which meant it stuck out the other side while leaving Nate something to hold on to in the darkened room. With the card in place, Nate turned his attention to the key. Using the hairpin that Birdie had given him, he wriggled it out of the lock so that it fell to the floor.

'Are you still praying?' asked Nate.

'Oh Lord,' said Birdie. 'Preserve me from idiots.'

Meanwhile, Nate was pulling the card back beneath the door. Slowly, slowly, slowly. When it was through, he felt the card's surface with his fingers and was rewarded with triumph. The key had fallen onto the card and he had managed to get it through the gap.

'How much do you love me?' Nate asked.

41

'Birdie,' said Nate. 'I am about to get you out of here. Do you promise to do whatever I tell you from this moment until we are back in Los Angeles?'

'I'm not promising anything.'

'I'm serious. I need you to promise me, for example, that when I open this door, you will keep your mouth shut.'

Nate put the key in the lock and turned.

He needn't have worried about Birdie speaking. She was, momentarily at least, utterly speechless. Nate really had got them out.

But beyond the dark confines of the cold store was yet more darkness. Though there were no curtains or blinds on any of the windows, neither was there much light from outside. A thick layer of cloud covered the waning moon. Having spent a whole twelve hours in the cold store, Nate and Birdie proceeded through the house as though they were blind, taking small shuffling steps.

There was, as Nate had suspected, no one in the house. The kidnappers must have gone into the nearest town to sink a few beers, never suspecting for a moment that their captives would get out of a locked room. Though they had, at least, taken the precaution of locking the front door.

'Damn,' said Nate. 'I thought we might be able to walk right out. Let's try and find an unlocked window. You try the kitchen.'

Birdie set to work. But she was soon distracted by what was outside the window. Earlier, when the kidnappers dragged her out to make the ransom video, Birdie hadn't had a chance to see anything except the makeshift video studio.

'Where the hell do you think we are?' she asked Nate now.

Blindfolded and drugged on the journey from Los Angeles, neither Birdie nor Nate had been awake when the white van arrived at its destination. They had no idea how far they had travelled. They had no idea how *long* they had travelled for. They might only have driven for an hour and still be within spitting distance of Hollywood. Or they might have been drugged and asleep for days, and right now be in a different state altogether.

Wherever they were, it was pretty isolated. There was not a single other dwelling in view. The house was surrounded by trees, the type of which Birdie didn't recognize, which further darkened the tiny house.

'This place doesn't look as though it has been lived in for years,' Birdie observed, flicking on a light in the kitchen to reveal a Formica-topped table and two dusty chairs.

'What are you doing?' Nate sprang across the room and flicked the light off. They could come back at any moment.'

'I don't think they're going to come back,' said Birdie. 'Would you look around you? There's no sign that they were intending to stay here and wait for my grandfather to pay the ransom. There's no food. No beers. I don't suppose this fridge even works.' She opened the door. The fridge remained dark and silent. It was empty but for the smell of food long decayed. 'Ugh. You know what I think? I think they were just going to leave us here for dead. I bet the ransom demand went wrong. Ohmigod, Nate,' Birdie began to hyperventilate. 'We would have died in that cold store!' She began to flap her arms in an attempt to calm herself but it only made her feel worse and pretty soon she was actually shrieking at the horror of it all.

'Calm down.' Nate wrapped her in his arms. 'Calm down. There's no point thinking about what might have happened. We're not going to die locked in that cold store. We're out. And any minute now, we're going to find a way out of this house.'

But first Nate went back to the cold-store door and closed it. Then he stuck the key in the lock again.

'What did you do that for?'

'If they do come back, we want them to think that everything is exactly as they left it for as long as possible, right?'

'They're not coming back,' said Birdie. 'I know that much is true.'

She was wrong. Almost as soon as she uttered her pronouncement, they heard the sound of an approaching car and the kitchen was flooded with light from the headlamps. Nate quickly pulled Birdie back behind the giant refrigerator, which still worked as cover if not as a fridge.

'What now?' Birdie whispered.

'We need to hide, of course. Do you think you'll be OK in a cupboard again?'

'I'm not going back in there.'

'Not that one. The cupboard under the stairs. While they're at the door, we need to dash across the kitchen and get in there without being seen.'

'Can't we just overpower them?'

'You saw the fat one. You've got to run to the cupboard, Birdie. Can you do that for me?'

'What choice do I have?'

'Attagirl. As soon as you hear the key in the lock.'

The key went in the lock. Birdie and Nate skidded across the room as though they were on skateboards. The sound of the cupboard door shutting behind them was completely masked by the sound of the front door slamming shut behind their captors. Exactly as Nate had hoped it would be.

'Hi honeys, we're home!' Robin called out.

Inside the cupboard under the stairs, Birdie's heart was pounding so fast and loud she was sure her captors must be able to hear it.

Fatman belched.

'Excuse me,' said Robin.

'Sorry, Robin, I keep forgetting what a cultured man you are.'
Robin let out a fart. 'Indeed I am, James. Indeed I am.'

Robin and Fatman settled themselves at the kitchen table and
opened the beers they had brought home in a brown paper bag.

'What the fuck are we supposed to do now? It's been twenty-
four hours since we sent our ransom demand and what has her
old man done about it? Absolutely fuck all. Are you sure we sent
the demand to the right email address?'

'Are you saying I fucked up?' was Robin's response.

'Of course not, man. It's just that . . . Nothing? Nothing at
all? I tell you, that man is cold. Was one of my family had been
snatched, I would pay up in an instant.'

'Fatman,' said Robin. 'What you have to understand is that
the rich are not like us. They do not view their family members
as people they love and adore. They view them as assets, like a
plane or a yacht. Clearly, Monsieur Sederburg thinks that the
price we have set for his granddaughter is too high.'

'A million dollars? He's got a hundred times more than that
in his checking account.'

It was true. Birdie listened incredulously. A million dollars too
high a price for her? Her grandfather could spend that much on
ties at Charvet. But he had refused to hand it over for her? What
was he playing at?

'Well, that was what the girl said he'd pay without too much
trouble. But I'm beginning to think that perhaps . . .' said Robin.
'Perhaps he thinks we're amateurs because we only asked for a
million.'

Birdie pushed Nate out of the way so that she could put her
ear to the keyhole instead. She had to hear more.

'How we going to convince him otherwise?'

'If we don't hear from him tomorrow, we start sending his
granddaughter back to him in instalments,' said Robin. 'Just like
we said we would.'

Birdie gasped. Robin was cleaning his fingernails with a knife again. Now he paused in his manicure to examine the blade in his hand, turning it this way and that so that the light glinted off it. 'This week, an ear. Next week, a finger. The week after that, one of her toes. Then her *hair*. All by FedEx.'

'And what about the other guy?'

'We could offer Sederburg a two for one, but I don't think he'll be terribly interested. In fact, he'd probably pay us to dispose of him. He's an eco-warrior, for fuck's sake. I predict that pretty-boy Nate Hathaway is going to end his days up here in the mountains.'

'You mean we're really going to kill him?'

'Of course we're going to kill him. He's seen us both without our masks. If anyone is going to give an accurate description, it's him. He's just one more weak link.'

'Should we do it now? Save us feeding him.'

Fatman stood up, cracking his knuckles. Birdie's eyes widened in horror as she saw Fatman look off in the direction of the windowless cold store that had been her prison until so recently.

'Nah,' said Robin. 'Not tonight. Besides, someone's got to dig a couple of graves and it ain't going to be you or me.'

'Why a couple of graves?'

'In case the old man never pays up.'

Birdie gasped, causing Robin to turn suddenly in the direction of the stairs. 'What was that?'

'Probably rats,' said Fatman. 'I'll get some poison tomorrow. Should I give the girl her dinner now?'

'No,' said Robin. 'The prisoners won't be eating tonight. I find that a bit of hunger makes people work harder and tomorrow they start digging.'

Robin had no idea how relieved Nate and Birdie were that they would not be getting any dinner that night. The longer they had before the idiots realized they weren't in that cold room, the better. It was a lucky break.

Still Birdie couldn't help crying.

'Ssssh,' said Nate. 'You've got to stay absolutely silent.'

'I can't help it. My grandfather won't pay my ransom. He hasn't even responded to their demand.'

'I'm sure he has his reasons. Haven't you ever watched a cop show? No one ever pays up right away. Never. I'll bet the cops have told him it's the best strategy. Now, keep quiet until they go to bed.'

Birdie gave a sniff and nodded.

42

In Los Angeles, Julius Sederburg was finally ready to meet with Detective Bryden and his team. The meeting had been scheduled for four in the afternoon but it was six o'clock before Julius finished a meeting with the architect who was planning some new buildings for the resort in Atlanta.

Julius didn't feel bad about being late. After all, as he pointed out to Detective Bryden right away, it wasn't as though they had anything new to tell him with regard to Birdie's whereabouts. 'There's nothing to discuss,' he said. 'We just wait until they get fed up.'

'Mr Sederburg,' said Bryden. 'These people may be prepared to hold Birdie for months.'

'I'll save a fortune on her allowance.'

No one laughed at the joke.

'We need to enter into some sort of negotiation,' said Bryden. 'I want you to respond to their demand.'

'I'm not giving in to it.'

'I know. But if we can engage them in some kind of dialogue, it may be helpful. The more often we hear from them, the more likely they are to slip up and give us something to work on.'

'What do you want me to do?' Sederburg sighed.

An officer equipped with video equipment stepped forward. 'We thought it might be a good idea for you to record a video clip of your own. All you have to say is that you want to negotiate.'

'I don't want to negotiate.'

'I've written you a little script,' Bryden persisted.

'I have people of my own to do that.'

'Just read this script and then perhaps offer a few words of comfort to your granddaughter. There's a strong chance that she'll see the clip and it will be a big boost to her morale. The more hopeful Birdie remains, the easier it will be for her to get through this.'

Sederburg looked at his watch. 'I'm supposed to be at dinner with the head of the golf professional association.'

'It will take five minutes,' Bryden promised.

Sederburg read through the script in an impossibly flat tone and delivered his 'words of comfort' for his granddaughter in pretty much the same voice.

'Hang in there, Birdie. Remember you're a Sederburg.'

'Poor girl,' said one of the female officers present.

'That's great,' said Bryden. 'Thank you, Mr Sederburg. You've given us everything we need.'

'Now,' Sederburg addressed the police team, 'I appreciate that this is probably the way you've always worked when it comes to kidnappings, but I have to tell you I don't have time to mess about. And it seems to me that we already know who we should be looking for, in any case. Why don't you go back to shaking down those hippies in Santa Monica till they tell you where Nate Hathaway has gone? I predict that when you find Nate Hathaway, that is when you'll find my granddaughter. Nate Hathaway is clearly the brains behind this. And I want his head on a stick.'

Waving his own walking-stick to underline his point, Sederburg set off for his dinner.

43

Robin and Fatman were night birds.

The cupboard under the stairs was not big enough to stand up in. Birdie and Nate were both beginning to suffer from having been curled up in there for so long. But Robin and Fatman showed no sign of slowing their drinking. They downed bottle after bottle but didn't seem to get any sleepier. Far from it. A couple of hours after returning from the bar, Robin and Fatman were singing songs and playing cards. They were planning to be up all night.

It wasn't until two in the morning that Robin finally started to yawn.

'You stay up,' he said to Fatman. 'I'm going to bed. But one of us has got to stay up and make sure the prisoners don't go anywhere.'

'How can they go anywhere? They're locked in the cold store.'

'You stay up anyway,' said Robin, as he swayed through the kitchen. 'I'll sleep better.' Birdie and Nate listened to his footsteps climb the stairs and cross the landing before they returned their attention to Fatman. He sat down in the seat that Robin had vacated (which was obviously the better of the two). He opened another bottle of beer but before he could drink it, his head was lolling back against the back of the armchair. And pretty soon he was open-mouthed and fast asleep too.

There was no time to lose. As Fatman's snoring settled into a rhythm, Nate slowly pushed open the cupboard door and started to climb out. There was a hairy moment when, standing straight for the first time in over five hours, Nate's legs were so overcome with pins and needles that he almost fell straight back down again.

Birdie felt the same pain. She clung on to Nate for support as the feeling came back to her extremities. Nate armed himself with a broom. Fatman didn't look as though he was planning to wake up anytime soon, but you never knew.

Fatman and Robin had left the door to the yard unlocked and propped ajar (to let some of the stink out. Fatman had been suffering prodigious gas that night). Nate nodded towards the door to make sure Birdie knew where they were headed. As if she had a better idea. Escape was so close. Just fifteen feet and a sleeping kidnapper were all that separated Nate and Birdie from the great outdoors.

They set off slowly. Nate went first, testing the floorboards with his toes and holding his breath with each step. But no tell-tale squeak announced his passing. Birdie walked in Nate's footsteps exactly, like a child playing a game. After each new step they paused for a moment, like statues. Progress was painfully slow but steady and soon they were within two feet of the door. Nate reached out for the handle. And that was when it happened. As the centre of Nate's body-weight shifted forward, the board beneath his front foot gave out the alarm. It was a teeny tiny squeak, but in the silence of the still house it sounded as loud as any siren. And it woke Fatman up.

'Hey!' Fatman sat up and looked behind him, seeing Nate and Birdie standing by the door. 'What the fuck?'

Nate yanked Birdie across the last two feet of floor and out through the door with such force and speed that she ended up on her knees again. But there was no time to apologize. He had to make sure that Fatman and Robin didn't get out of the house before he and Birdie could get out of the way. Moving as fast as he could and with more strength than he had ever imagined he might possess, Nate left Birdie to fend for herself while he blocked the door by putting the broom across the handle. Then he set to dragging the log box across the door. He got the box in place before Fatman got to the door. It held. But it wouldn't hold for long.

'Get the car started!' Nate shouted to Birdie as he piled a couple of garden chairs on top of the box.

'I can't,' she shouted back when she got that far. 'There's no key.'

'Then we're just going to have to run.'

Inside the house, Robin was quickly awake and shoving against the door with Fatman. With every shove the log box slid a little further across the verandah. The chairs had been no help at all. The broom handle snapped like a matchstick. Meanwhile, Birdie and Nate were running down the path towards the road. But Birdie was not wearing the kind of shoes that anyone was meant to run in. They were not making very fast progress. And soon Robin and Fatman were out of the house and close behind.

It wasn't long before the kidnappers were so close Birdie could almost smell their breath. She ran as fast as she could but her shoes were a practical handicap.

'Come on,' Nate shouted. 'Run faster!'

'It's no good.'

Birdie paused to catch her breath. Robin and Fatman were maybe a hundred metres away.

'Don't stop,' said Nate. He doubled back. 'Come on. Give me your belt.'

'What?'

'Your belt.' Nate pulled the red rope from her middle. 'Take one end and keep running. Keep close until I say, then we're going to run in opposite directions real fast.'

'Huh?'

'Just do it. And hang on to the rope.'

'We got you, you little fuckers,' Robin announced. He was so close he made a grab for Birdie's hair.

'Help!' she cried.

'Left!' Nate yelled back at her.

After a moment's hesitation (she had never been good at

directions) Birdie ran left. Nate ran right. The rope that had been Birdie's belt was suddenly stretched out between them at waist height. In the dark, Robin ran straight into the rope, was winded and fell over. Fatman ran straight into Robin, leaving them both on the ground in a heap.

'Keep running.' Nate grabbed Birdie by the hand.

He knew his stunt wouldn't give them much time, but it was just enough to get over the ridge and out of sight while Fatman and Robin struggled to upright themselves like a couple of upended bugs.

44

They ran on for another fifteen minutes, until Birdie said she had to stop or throw up. Looking behind him and seeing no sign of their pursuers, Nate agreed that they could stop. For now.

'But we need to climb up a tree,' he said. 'Keep out of sight until dawn. This one will do. Up you go.'

Birdie looked at Nate in disbelief. She had never climbed a tree in her life.

'I can't get up there. I don't know how to.'

'You never climbed a tree before?'

'Why would I?' she asked.

'Why not?'

'I can't do it,' she said firmly. But Nate had picked up the sound of voices drawing near again.

'You're going to have to.'

He kneeled down in front of her and made himself into a step. After much heaving and shoving, Birdie made it into the branches. And just in time.

Nate and Birdie froze as they heard the unmistakable sound of a rifle being clicked into readiness. Fatman and Robin were upon them.

'That was a gun!'

Nate put his finger to Birdie's lips.

'They won't kill you,' Nate assured Birdie. 'You're no use to them dead.'

That wasn't much comfort. Birdie clung to Nate as they

listened for the sound of Fatman and Robin's approach. They seemed so close. It wasn't possible that they could miss what they were looking for, was it? They stepped into the clearing, just feet from the occupied tree.

'Those fuckers,' said Fatman. 'I hurt my knee.'

'You're complaining?' said Robin. "How do you think I feel? I was crushed. Have you heard of the Atkins Diet? You are a fat fuck.'

'Man,' Fatman whined. 'We lost them. Why are we even bothering? Face it, they're miles away by now.'

Robin was unconvinced. 'I don't see how they could be. She was wearing those stupid shoes. She won't get far.'

'Is this even the way they went? I reckon they went back to the road.'

'No,' said Robin, stopping right beneath the tree that cradled his prey. 'It was definitely this direction.' He sniffed as though hunting for their scent in the air.

Birdie held her breath. She could count the hairs that lay over Robin's bald patch. He leaned against the tree trunk and lit a cigarette. He tossed the match into the leaf mould. Now it was Nate's turn to hold his breath as he prayed the glowing end wouldn't ignite the dry leaves beneath them. They were lucky. A wisp of smoke soon disappeared.

'If they carried on running in the same direction,' said Robin, 'I figure they would have gone right by here.'

Don't look up, don't look up, don't look up, Birdie prayed.

'But I can't see no more broken branches or shit like that in any direction.'

The conclusion of Robin's observation was obvious to Nate and Birdie. But not, it seemed, to him.

'Which means they could have gone in any fucking direction,' he said instead, looking every which way but skywards. 'But my guess is they'd eventually want to head back towards the road . . . In which case . . .' He crouched low like a Native American tracker examining a spoor.

Nate considered for a moment that Robin was messing with them. That he knew full well where they were hiding and, in a moment, he would fire the gun that was now resting barrel upwards against the tree trunk, right under Birdie's backside.

In the distance, some forest creature gave an eerie cry. Birdie pulled Nate closer still.

'What was that?' said Fatman. Birdie wasn't the only one who had been startled.

'It's just some coyote,' said Robin.

'No way, man,' said Fatman. 'That was way deeper than a coyote call. Which means that's way bigger than a coyote. I don't like it. You can look for them all you want but I ain't staying out here in the dark no longer. You heard what happened on that hiking trail last month. That was a cougar scream.'

'No it wasn't. In any case, we've got a gun,' said Robin.

'I'm telling you that was a cougar. You think you could hit something like that before it ripped your throat out?'

Birdie gave an involuntary gasp. Nate stuck his hand over her mouth.

'I ain't staying out here in the dark. That gun ain't no use to us if we can't see what we're trying to shoot. Let's go back.'

'What? There's a million dollars walking somewhere in this forest,' said Robin. 'You think I'm going to let that go so easy?'

'There's a man-eating mountain lion out here as well. You think I want to be breakfast?'

The eerie cough-bark came again. It sounded much closer.

Robin tutted. 'All right, all right. We'll go back to the house. But this is the most monumental fuck-up and I want you to know that I blame you.'

Grumbling all the way, Robin followed Fatman back to the house.

At last, Nate could risk taking his hand off Birdie's mouth.

'You're not going to scream?'

'I just want to breathe,' she said, when he took his hand away.

And breathe she did. Quick and shallow. 'Ohmigod, ohmigod, ohmigod.'

'Stop,' Nate commanded. 'You're going to give yourself a panic attack. Breathe deep. Slowly. Count while you're doing it.' He breathed in time with her, like a birthing partner. 'We're OK. They're gone.'

'You heard what the fat one said. They're going to come back out in the morning! They had a shotgun. We're going to get killed! And if not by those idiots then by a mountain lion! That's what they were talking about, isn't it? Don't try to tell me otherwise, Nate. You heard it too. That was a mountain lion! Oh God. It was getting closer. We're going to die! We're going to be dragged from this tree and pulled limb from limb. They can climb anything. I saw it on the Discovery Channel. We're being stalked by a mountain lion and it's going to eat me first! We're going to die!'

'No, we're not,' said Nate. 'We're going to be fine. Most of the creatures in this forest are more frightened of us than we are of them. Mountain lions included. We're going to stay here till daylight then we're going to get ourselves to the nearest town and call your grandfather. I'm going to get you home.'

'Let's go now,' said Birdie. 'While Fatman and Robin are gone.'

'We can't keep walking in the dark. You don't have proper shoes on and you could go down a pothole and break your ankle. Plus, if you really want to make yourself cougar bait, wandering blind is a good way to do it. We're going to wait here until the morning, then walk back to the road.'

'But the kidnappers said they're going to come back for us!'

'We'll be on our way long before they wake up. They don't seem like early risers.'

'They will be tomorrow . . .'

'Birdie, we can't go now. We'll make far better progress as soon as we have some light. You should try to get some rest. You can lean on me if you like.'

Birdie leaned back against the tree instead. 'I can't sleep like this. I might fall out.'

'Fine,' said Nate. 'Then you keep watch. Those tranquillizers must still be in my system. I can hardly keep my eyes open.'

45

How could Birdie possibly sleep? Stuck up a tree with her gardener. The gardener who had been just as intent on kidnapping her as Robin and Fatman had. He was just less competent. How could she trust him? When describing the disastrous MNA kidnap attempt, he had told Birdie that he hated everything her family stood for. Why should he have changed his mind? Though he had got Birdie out of the house, surely the most likely scenario was that he was just going to take her straight to some other set of hoods, who would make their own demands of her grandfather . . . All that talk of rescuing her when he was really just setting her up again.

Still, it didn't look like Nate's conscience was bothering him unduly. He seemed to have found a comfortable position. He leaned back against a fork in the branches and closed his eyes. His face took on a relaxed sort of expression. Birdie waited until she heard his breath fall into the tell-tale pattern that said he had fallen asleep.

She wasn't going to wait. Contrary to Nate's opinion, Birdie was sure that Fatman and Robin would not give up their search for her so easily. She was worth a million dollars, after all. They would be back as soon as dawn broke. Why should she be sitting there like a big pink duck when they arrived? Birdie decided she had to get down the tree and start to make her own way out of the forest. She didn't trust Nate and she didn't need him.

While Nate twitched and snored, Birdie carefully started to edge away from him, disentangling their legs slowly so that he wouldn't wake. It took a long while. A couple of times, she had to stop because she thought he might be entering a more shallow sleep phase, one that could be easily broken. But eventually, she was on her way down the trunk, scraping her knees as she descended, but free.

Which way to go? Darkness stretched on all sides. Birdie decided that her best bet was to head back in the rough direction of the house but aim a little further south so that she would come out on the road but safe from being spotted by Robin and Fatman. It shouldn't take long to get there. An hour or so. It was just a matter of reversing the route that had brought her this far. Soon it would start to get light.

With one last glance back at Nate, sleeping on in his man-sized nest, Birdie started walking. She looked straight ahead. Neither to the left nor the right, afraid of what she might see there. She hummed to herself to block out the noises: the cracking of branches that weren't breaking beneath her own feet, the primeval shrieks of birds she didn't recognize, the anguished yips of a coyote.

Her steps got quicker and quicker. It was cold and she was tired. She pulled the housecoat more closely around her but it really didn't offer much warmth. Her heart hadn't thumped so hard since she was a six-year-old on a ghost train. But she comforted herself with the thought that she was walking towards safety and freedom and Dean Stevenson's loving arms.

Three hours later she was still walking.

'What was that?'

Birdie jumped. In the forest to the left of her, a branch snapped loudly. She strained her eyes in the darkness to get some clue as to what might have caused the break. There was no sign of torchlight, which meant it probably wasn't Fatman or Robin. That was a good thing. But there wasn't much joy in the alternative. Since she had no real idea where she was, Birdie had little clue what she might expect to be foraging in that forest at night. Was this bear country? Her heart picked up the pace again as she made out an outline on the move. The shadowy creature looked too small to be a bear or a mountain lion, but perhaps that was just because it was a baby bear, with a mother the size of a truck following close behind. Mother bears were the most dangerous, liable to freak out if they considered their cubs in danger. Birdie pressed herself against a tree. Perhaps she should climb it? But bears could climb, couldn't they? Or at the very least, shake a tree so violently that anyone hiding up it would be flung out onto the ground!

'Shooo! Shoo!' Birdie half whispered to the 'little bear'. 'I don't want to get into trouble with your mom.'

There was a pause in the rootling. Birdie thought she could hear sniffing. Perhaps the little bear was checking her out? Whatever it smelled, it decided it wasn't hanging around. Birdie listened gratefully to the sound of her small forest companion scuttling away through the leaf mould.

She needed to distract herself. She tried to sing herself back to calmness. She sang quietly, hoping that her voice was too low to be heard by an approaching human, but loud enough to ward away anything else that might chance upon her. She reminded herself of Nate's assertion that most of the animals that lived in these woods were more afraid of bumping into a human than she should be of bumping into them. But then, when she was halfway through singing 'My Humps', Birdie heard another noise that sounded like a coyote bark. Or was it a mountain lion's cough? They were often mistaken for coyotes. She sang a little louder, to cover up the sound.

But the singing wasn't helping. She tried to think of something cheerful instead. She tried to think of her homecoming, telling herself that if she could imagine it clearly enough, it would definitely happen. And soon. She imagined walking into a packed ballroom at the Sederburg resort in Long Beach. Everyone she knew would be there, applauding as she crossed the room. Her grandfather would be waiting at the front, on the podium. He would envelop her in his arms before he told the whole room how much he loved her. Dean would be there too. When her grandfather had finished speaking, Dean would take the mike and propose marriage to Birdie right then and there, witnessed by everyone who had ever been important to her. And Emily B, who would run out of the ballroom in floods of bitter tears.

But the fantasy didn't seem to be working. Instead, Birdie found herself imagining a far more sombre gathering. She heard her grandfather giving a very different speech. Choking back tears, he informed the crowd:

'My darling granddaughter Birdie was the most important person in the world to me. I cannot tell you how deep my pain goes on this dreadful day. When I heard that the mountain lion shot after mauling two hikers was found to have my dear Birdie's Tiffany charm bracelet among the contents of its stomach . . .'

Birdie could hold the tears back no longer. They began to make hot tracks down her cheeks. Though she tried to sing her way out of it, her voice cracked on every wavering word.

She was going to die in that forest and it was all Dean Stevenson's fault. If he hadn't dumped her then she wouldn't be in this predicament. Or maybe it was Emily B's fault. If she hadn't made a play for Dean then maybe he wouldn't have dumped Birdie. Or maybe it was Clemency's fault. If she had been more careful about whom she talked to about the kidnap. Or if Chipper had been less of a wimp and expressed her reservations more firmly. Or if her grandfather had provided proper security for her like she was always asking him to do. Or if Nate's stupid green Avengers had been better prepared and kidnapped her first . . . Birdie went through practically everyone she knew and found a reason to blame them all. At one point, she even went so far as to decide that her first task upon returning to Los Angeles (if she ever saw her beloved city again) would be to sue the magazine in which she had first learned you could be kidnapped to order for propagating such a dangerous idea.

But after another hour with still no road in sight, the reality was setting in. If she hadn't paid Mr G to kidnap her, she could be spending that evening sitting out by her pool. Nate would be pruning some bush or other and everything would be all right. Instead she was alone in the wilderness, beset by wild beasts and doubtless being tracked by a couple of lunatics with guns. It was all her own fault.

Birdie sank down into the leaf mould on the forest floor and began to cry. The forest ahead of her seemed denser than ever. She was lost. Had she been heading in the right direction, she would definitely have come across the road by now.

'Oh God.'

She was tired and she was hungry. Slumped against the base of a tree, she knew that if she was going to stop, she should climb up the tree for extra safety, but she didn't have the energy. Besides, she felt as though she were in some kind of fantasy movie, wherein the trees were alive and every time she felt she was making some progress, they would somehow conspire to confuse her, crowding closer together and spinning around. It was impossible to tell which way was left, right, east, west, up down. These trees were definitely not kindly wood sprites, wanting to help her out.

Birdie looked up into the branches and was sure they moved to block out the weak morning light. She felt the gaze of a thousand eyes upon her, looking out at her from faces unseen; the ancient trees laughing at her pitiful situation. Small animals considered using her hair extensions as nesting material, bigger animals considered having her for lunch.

There had been moments in Birdie's life before when she had considered herself properly frightened. Waiting for the results of a math test, waiting for Chipper's mother to come home and see the carnage left behind by a teenage party, waiting to tell her grandfather that she had been arrested for driving under the influence . . . But in this moment, she experienced an altogether more visceral fear. It was something she had simply not allowed herself to feel for a very long time.

46

Contrary to Nate's prediction, Robin and Fatman were up very early the next day. Robin was in a vile mood, which wasn't improved by the correspondence received from Julius Sederburg.

'He's not going to fucking well pay.'

'We don't have anything for him to pay for,' Fatman pointed out.

'He doesn't know that yet.'

Robin put in a call to a Los Angeles cellphone number. 'Yes, I know you're an hour behind us. This is urgent. What's going on there? I thought you said he would pay up, no trouble. Yes, of course she's all right. I said we wouldn't hurt her and we won't . . . You *have* seen her. We sent the video, didn't we? All right, you'll get another one. Just get us the fucking money.'

Fatman had listened to the call. 'You think they believe we've still got her?'

'Why wouldn't they? We're professionals. It's not like we would have let her escape from a locked room. Come on, Fatman.' Robin picked up his gun. 'We've got some hunting to do.'

Nate slept remarkably well for someone who was trying to get his head down in the fork of a tree. It must have been the residual effects of the tranquillizers. They still had him disoriented and it was a moment or two before he realized that Birdie was gone.

'Birdie?' he called quietly.

He assumed she must have got down the tree to take a leak. Probably couldn't get back up again.

'Birdie?' She couldn't be far away.

There was no response.

'Birdie?'

Nate stood up in the fork of the tree and looked out for her. In that bright pink housecoat, she shouldn't be so difficult to spot. But the forest was quiet all around him and the green-brown vista was undisturbed by any man-made colours.

'Birdie?'

Still nothing.

Shit.

It finally dawned on Nate that Birdie must have decided to make a break for it alone. With a rising sense of annoyance, he climbed down the tree. Now that he was on the ground again, he peered hard into the forest for the slightest glimpse of her. The previous night she had been scared stiff of mountain lions and bears. It hadn't seemed likely that she would strike off on her own in the darkness. But she must have done.

Nate shook his head. He hoped that Birdie had taken note of their conversation of the night before and incorporated his plan for a successful way out of the forest into her own escape attempt. Had she retraced their steps back to the road? Would she be keeping a low enough profile to avoid those goons from the house? To the casual onlooker, it might have seemed that Nate was just staring into space as he tried to work out what Birdie might have decided. He concentrated on the way they had run to the tree the night before. But eventually he turned around and noted a trodden-down patch of vegetation with a sigh.

'Birdie,' he said in exasperation, as he took the path that led further into the forest. 'You idiot girl.'

Nate could soon see how Birdie must have found herself disoriented. The forest around the tree where he'd spent the night was uniformly dense in all directions. They had no time to look for landmarks as they ran from Fatman and Robin. Now it seemed to Nate that there were no natural landmarks anyway. It was hard even to tell in which direction the trees cast their shadows, which is how Nate would ordinarily have taken his bearing.

Fatman and Robin were far better equipped. They were dressed in the kind of gear that meant poison ivy or even more poisonous snakes held little fear for them. They didn't have to pick their way carefully through the undergrowth as Nate did. What couldn't be trampled beneath their boots, they hacked at with machetes. It wasn't long before they were back at the base of Nate and Birdie's tree. Nate, just five minutes ahead of them, heard their voices clearly.

'Why the fuck did they go this way?' asked Robin. Nate realized with a sinking heart that the kidnappers must have spotted Birdie's trail. And they were following it. Nate did his best to baffle them. He took a zig-zag line himself, hoping that they would follow him instead.

Fatman and Robin kept close behind Nate all day. He tracked in circles in an effort to keep them away from Birdie for as long as possible, hoping they might even give up. Maybe Birdie had already made it to the road. But though Fatman and Robin weren't particularly talented trackers (they passed within six feet of Nate several times) they were persistent and growing angrier all the time. Eventually, frustrated by their lack of progress, Fatman fired his rifle into a tree trunk.

It didn't help flush Nate and Birdie out, but the shot certainly sent the forest's permanent residents into a panic. The forest canopy, which had appeared empty of life, was suddenly full of the chatter of agitated birds, setting out from their homes like office workers responding to a fire alarm.

'What the fuck did you do that for?' asked Robin when the clatter died down.

'I was angry,' said Fatman. 'I'm fed up.'

'Well, good thinking, idiot. If they didn't already know we're on their trail, they certainly do know now. You didn't do us any favours.'

Unwittingly, Fatman had done Nate a far better favour than

confirming his position in the forest. The shot had scared more than the birds. As Nate pressed on through the forest, he came across the body of a large rabbit, freshly killed. Nate knelt and touched the little body. It was still warm. The predator that had taken its life had dropped it and run.

Finding such a fresh kill gave Nate a primeval feeling of unease but it also gave him an idea. Perhaps the best way to get Fatman and Robin off his trail was to convince them that there was no one to follow . . .

Nate took off his jacket. Working quickly, he pulled off one of the sleeves, then set about tearing up the sleeve. Once it looked suitably ragged, he dipped the ends in the blood of the unfortunate rabbit before draping the sleeve from a dead log. Then, with a grimace, he picked up the rabbit's body and, closing his eyes to block out the horror, squeezed it so that great gouts of blood fell from the gash in its neck. Soon it looked as though Nate had come off badly in a terrible struggle, which was exactly how he wanted it to seem.

Scene set, Nate carried the body of the rabbit with him into the undergrowth and waited.

It was getting dark by the time Robin and Fatman crossed Nate's path again.

Fatman was the first to notice the carnage.

'Oh man!' He held his hand across his mouth. 'I got blood on my shoes. There's blood everywhere!'

Robin was less squeamish. He pulled Fatman out of the way. 'Let me look,' he said.

'It . . . it's . . .' Fatman pointed at the sleeve hanging from the log.

Robin picked the sleeve up and examined it. Briefly. He couldn't hide his shudder as he dropped it to the ground.

'It got the guy,' said Fatman. 'It probably got her first.'

'Not necessarily,' said Robin.

'You want me to hang around here and find out? I'm telling you, man, there's a killer on the loose and it ain't one of us. I'm going back. I don't care if we lost Birdie Sederburg. Once one of those things has got a taste for human flesh they keep coming after it. They are unstoppable. I bet it's watching us right now. That blood is still wet. I'm getting the fuck out of here.'

Fatman turned and started to retrace his steps.

'Wait!' Robin called after him. 'She might still be alive.'

'I don't care,' said Fatman. 'I'm not getting eaten by a cougar.'

He kept walking. Then came the sound of that cough-bark. Even Nate shivered.

Fatman picked up the pace and soon he and Robin were running.

47

Birdie had not moved all day. She had given up. Exhausted and close to fainting from hunger, she could take not one step further. But as the night started to fall, she found herself somewhere else. She was back in the Alps. The weak evening light filtering through the trees in the forest had exactly the same quality as the light in the ski resort. She remembered looking out of the chalet window, watching the quiet street for her parents' return. The nanny had already left, reasoning that she was booked until five o'clock in the evening and the Sederburgs would doubtless be on their way.

'You're seven years old,' she'd said to Birdie. 'You're a big girl. You just stay in here and watch the TV and don't open the door to any strangers. Tell your mum and dad I had an emergency at home.'

'Have you got an emergency?' Birdie had asked.

'No. But I'm supposed to be meeting my boyfriend at seven. I need to get ready. Don't tell them that, though. It doesn't sound good. I'll give you this,' she pulled out a ten-franc piece, 'if you promise to keep quiet.'

Birdie took the coin and worried it between her fingers as she watched her favourite cartoon show. For a while, she was quite happy that her parents were taking their time coming home. She knew that the moment her father walked through the door, the television would have to be turned off. But eventually, even seven-year-old Birdie had decided that she'd had enough of *The Simpsons* (a totally forbidden cartoon back at the Sederburgs' home in the US). She was starting to get hungry. There was food in the refrigerator, but nothing a small girl raised with servants in Beverly Hills knew how to prepare.

She took up a position at the window, wrapped herself in the long curtain against the chill of the cold glass and watched the dark creep in.

Cowering at the bottom of that tree in the forest, Birdie relived that moment for the first time in a long while.

'Don't answer the door to strangers,' the nanny had said. So when the lady police officer came to find her later that night, Birdie refused to open the door. She felt the policewoman's cold slim hand grasping hers. It was as though she were an angel, come to help Birdie step over the threshold and into a world that would be very different from the one she had always known.

It took a long time for the mountain rescue people to retrieve her parents' bodies. Birdie wondered if her own body would ever be found.

'Mom. Dad. If you're out there, please give me a sign that there's nothing to be afraid of. I made a terrible mistake and now I think I'm close to dying.'

Would someone come from the other side to help her make this transition?

'Birdie,' she heard a soft, familiar voice calling her from her sleep. Was it her father? Was this how he sounded? 'Birdie, are you OK?'

She mumbled. 'I'm OK, Daddy. Take me home.'

'Birdie.'

The soft voice was close now. He had come for her. She felt her father's hands take her by the shoulders and gently shake her into wakefulness, but even as she opened her eyes, she was fearful of what she might see.

'Daddy?'

'I'm afraid not.'

'Nate?' Her voice was small and frightened but grateful. 'Nate. Am I dead?'

'I don't think so. Can you feel this?' He squeezed her hand.

* * *

'How did you find me?' Birdie asked.

'I followed the clues you left behind.'

'But I didn't leave any clues. I couldn't find my way back to you.'

Nate drew Birdie's attention to a broken branch. 'You didn't know what to look for. Why did you run off like that? I thought we had a plan.'

'I didn't think I could trust you. I thought you were going to set me up and take me back to your gang.'

'I promise that is the last thing on my mind. I just want to get us both out of this mess we're in. You have to trust me on that. Are you going to stick with me now?'

'What about Fatman and Robin?'

'I think they've given up,' said Nate. He would explain why they had given up later.

'OK,' Birdie said, rubbing her eyes and stretching. 'I'll come with you. Take me back to the road.'

'I'm afraid you've brought us too far in the wrong direction. The best thing is to push forward from here. But it's too dark now.'

'Have you got anything to eat?' Birdie asked.

Nate had set the dead rabbit down a few feet off.

'I've got something,' he said.

'Right now I could eat my own arm. Hey . . .' Birdie peered at him. 'What happened to your jacket?'

'Mountain lion,' said Nate, with a smile.

Birdie's eyes grew wild.

'It got torn on a branch. You know what would have been a good idea?' he added. 'If you had unravelled that housecoat like the ball of twine in the legend of the Minotaur.'

'The what?'

'Minotaur. I could have found you sooner. Never mind,' said Nate.

'I'm very cold.'

Nate regarded Birdie seriously. She was dressed only in that stupid housecoat. Her feet were bare. Exposure was a real problem. Even though the days were warm, the temperature during the nights could still drop into single figures.

'I'll light a fire,' said Nate.

'Have you got matches?'

'No. But I have a plan. And then I'll make dinner.'

'Where are we going to sleep tonight?'

'Here. I'll make us a shelter.'

'What if a bear or a mountain lion comes along?'

'That's why we're going to light a small fire. To keep us warm and to keep the bears away.'

'How do you know all this stuff?' Birdie asked.

Nate thought it probably wasn't a great idea to tell her he was making it up as he went along.

It took a long time to start the fire. Nate cursed the films he had watched as a child that made rubbing a couple of sticks together look so easy. Then Birdie wasn't happy when she learned they would be eating rabbit.

'I'm a vegetarian!' she protested.

'Birdie,' said Nate. 'It's already dead.'

'You killed it.'

'Actually, I think a mountain lion did.'

That was definitely the wrong thing to say.

'Ohmigod, ohmigod, ohmigod.' Birdie was wide awake and hyperventilating. 'It's probably followed the smell of the blood. It's waiting in the bushes right now.'

'Relax,' said Nate. 'I'll chase it off with a flaming stick. Just like a caveman.'

Still, he had to worry about a creature that was enough to send a guy like Fatman running. Just what had the reports concerning the attack on the hikers said about this animal? Nate wondered.

'I am in a nightmare,' said Birdie.

'And the only way out is through. Eat some rabbit.'

'I'd rather starve.'

'Which you will.'

It wasn't long before Nate was wondering exactly why he had kept searching for Birdie even after Fatman and Robin were scared off and he could have followed them back to the road.

48

Back in Los Angeles, the campaign to Find Birdie Sederburg was entering its third day. Dean had already appeared on several late-night shows and *Oprah* to explain the importance of keeping Birdie in the public eye.

'I'm not happy with this,' he told Justin.

'It's doing you a lot of good,' his agent replied. 'This caring image is going to translate into a lot of nice advertising work. You are the housewives' favourite.'

Meanwhile, Chipper was working tirelessly, getting her friends and acquaintances to buy tickets for the benefit in Denver.

'But it's in Denver,' they whined for the most part. 'That's miles away.'

To help overcome their objections, Chipper used her own credit card to charter a plane to take people there and back.

'You have no excuse,' she told everybody now. Still they wavered.

Justin soon explained the principle behind getting people to turn up for anything.

'You have to imply that they're really going to miss out if they don't come. Hint that the coolest person in your set has already bought five tickets. Or tell them that we've secured an exclusive set with a huge rock star.'

'Have we?' Chipper asked hopefully.

'No. We're arranging a benefit in Denver for an heiress who got *herself* kidnapped. This isn't Live Aid, my dear. But that doesn't mean you can't hint that it's going to be almost as good.'

After a crash course in spin from Justin, Chipper went back to her calls with renewed enthusiasm. Before long a rumour was circulating via Ohmygahd that the benefit line-up would include a mystery member of the Foo Fighters, who was a big fan of golf and a frequent visitor to the Sederburg resorts. Once that rumour was out, the tickets shifted as though they were anti-cellulite patches that actually worked.

Chipper was certain that her efforts to keep Birdie in the news were paying off. The hotline set up to take calls from people who thought they had sighted the heiress buzzed from dawn till dusk. The fact that Chipper had put up a reward of a hundred thousand dollars helped.

Chipper's team dutifully passed on all the information they heard to the police team, who eventually asked Julius Sederburg to call Chipper and tell her that while everyone appreciated her zeal, they felt that the information hotline was actually making their investigation *harder*.

Julius Sederburg didn't make the call. He had his assistant make it.

'The thing is,' said Mary, 'there doesn't seem to be much continuity in the information that's coming through. You've got people saying they've seen Birdie all over the place from Orange County to Ohio. Investigating each of these claims is taking up a lot of police time. You need to shut your hotline down and let the detectives handle it their own way.'

'Is that what Julius wants?' asked Chipper.

'It is,' said Mary. 'Though he thanks you for your help.'

What he had actually said was, 'For God's sake. Is it possible that Chipper Dooley is a bigger dimwit than my granddaughter? Can't we have her arrested for perverting the course of justice?'

'OK,' said Chipper. 'I'll do whatever he wants. But we're still having the benefit?'

'Oh yes,' said Mary. 'Mr Sederburg is looking forward to it.'

In fact he'd told Mary, 'I don't have to go to this. I've given them the theatre at the Denver resort and that is as far as it goes.

Remind them I'm a distraught grandfather. I should be left alone.'
Then he went into a meeting with some city planners from Kuala
Lumpur and the meeting overran, making him forty-five minutes
late for his daily briefing with the detectives who were doing their
best to bring Birdie back to Los Angeles unharmed.

Bryden and his team were no nearer to tracking Birdie down.
Since the video clip there had been another email saying that the
kidnappers were 'not pleased' with Sederburg's lack of response
to their demands. His disrespect would have 'grave consequences'
for Birdie. 'Watch out for the FedEx man,' the email ended.

Mary sobbed when the email popped into her inbox. She had
known Birdie since she was just a little girl and couldn't bear the
thought that anyone would touch a hair on her head. Let alone
send it to her grandfather by FedEx.

Julius grudgingly recorded a response.

'Tell Birdie we all love her,' Mary whispered from behind the
camera.

'Keep strong,' said Julius. 'Remember your family name.'

When the recording was over, Mary couldn't help voicing her
fears one more time.

'Mr Sederburg, I understand that you don't want to give in to
these kidnappers, but I can't help thinking that Birdie must be
scared.'

'Scared? Scared? If she is then she is no granddaughter of mine.
What is there to be scared of?'

'Er, the kidnappers. It seems like they mean business.'

'And so do I. I can tell you, Mary, that if my granddaughter
has learned anything from me in her life so far it is that Sederburgs
do not negotiate with bullies and that is what these kidnappers
are.'

Mary cast her eyes down at the word 'bullies'. Inwardly, she
said to herself, 'It takes one to know one.'

'I can assure you that Birdie will be taking this adversity like
a true Sederburg,' Julius continued. 'She will understand that

I am not going to pay the ransom. She will not be expecting me to buckle. She would not *want* that. She would want me to hold firm and refuse to cooperate with such ridiculousness. In any case, she brought this upon herself. Paying to be kidnapped to get her own back on a boy, for goodness' sake. Mary, what do I have this afternoon? I'd like you to arrange for me to play eighteen holes in Long Beach. See if Assise can play with me.'

'Of course, Mr Sederburg. I'll get onto it at once. But . . .'

'What?'

'Er . . . it's nothing.'

'No, Mary. You clearly have something to say. Spit it out.'

'I was wondering how it might look, if you, you know . . . If you are seen playing golf while your granddaughter is still missing.'

'It will look like I don't give a damn for the people who are holding her. It will look exactly as it is. I am not afraid. I will not give in. Nobody tells Julius Sederburg what to do.'

He underlined his little speech by thumping Mary's desk so hard that her pen pot made a suicide leap for the floor. He then left the room, leaving Mary to scrabble on the carpet for her biros.

49

It was hard to sleep in the wilderness. Nate warmed his hands on the embers of the previous night's fire as he watched the sun come up. Birdie dozed in his lap. She looked peaceful. Once he'd persuaded her to eat some rabbit, she had been considerably less cranky.

'I guess I'll have to look upon this as an adventure,' she'd said.

Nate wished he knew how long an adventure lay ahead. Birdie's attempt to make it home alone had brought them a lot deeper into the forest than Nate expected. He took a gamble that they would find civilization more quickly by pressing forward than going back. But Birdie wasn't going anywhere fast in those stupid shoes.

Nate pulled off his own sneakers and placed them beside her. She could wear them. Thrice-weekly pedicures had left Birdie's feet as soft and vulnerable as a baby's. Barefoot life on the beach had left Nate with hard, callused soles. He would manage.

'Ugh,' said Birdie when Nate offered her the shoes.

'Just put them on,' he said. 'It'll take us a year to get out of here if you insist on pretending to be Princess Mimosa.'

Birdie did so grudgingly. 'Let's walk. Down there?' She chose a random path.

Nate rolled his eyes. 'Now I'm in charge, we're taking compass bearings. Watch and learn.'

'Why do I need to learn how to do this?'

'For when I get to the end of my tether and leave you to fend for yourself.'

'OK.'

Birdie watched as Nate stuck a short stick into the ground and placed another stick at the end of the first stick's shadow.

'The tip of the shadow is always west,' he explained. 'The end is always east. We're going to head west in as straight a line as possible.'

Birdie gave a salute and they set off.

Nate's shoes were a pretty bad fit. They were easier to walk in than the Japanese wooden clogs but after half a day, Birdie had blisters the diameter of a dime.

Nate did his best to help her out. He pulled off the empty patch pockets from the housecoat and used them to make bandages.

'You look like something out of *Mad Max*,' he said when he had finished. 'What on earth were you thinking when you put that housecoat on to go to a fashion show?'

'This is designer vintage,' said Birdie, though there was no doubt that she wished she had decided to fling on some jeans that fateful morning instead. 'Can we stop yet?'

'Not quite yet,' said Nate. 'We're going uphill here.'

'I know. I can feel it.'

'And if we get to some higher ground we'll have a better idea of what lies ahead of us.'

'Please, God, let it be a house. I can't spend another night outdoors.'

'Didn't you ever go camping when you were a child?' Nate asked.

'Once,' said Birdie. 'Chipper had a nanny from Australia who was big into outdoor pursuits and she took me and Chipper camping in the school vacation. But we only lasted one night. Chipper's pet dog was snatched by a coyote.'

'Oh,' said Nate. 'I can see how that would be offputting.'

'The nanny was fired for upsetting us.'

'And that's really it?'

'I never spent another night outdoors. Until last night. Who was going to take me camping? My grandfather was too busy.'

'And even when you became an adult you didn't want to take a trip on your own? Just you and the wilderness? Getting away from the bright lights and the noise of the city. Enjoying nature in the raw.'

'No,' said Birdie. 'My grandfather owns one of the biggest luxury hotel chains in the world. I can holiday wherever I want for nothing. Why on earth would I go camping rather than take a suite with its own pool?'

'Camping isn't just about vacationing on the cheap,' said Nate.

'I'm afraid of snakes and I hate mud,' Birdie admitted.

'I love being out here. There is nothing so calming as the stillness of the world away from other human beings. I envy the people who were here first, who made their whole lives like this, who didn't have to worry about getting back to the office on Monday to spend sixteen hours in front of a computer screen.'

'I miss my iPhone,' said Birdie. 'You know it has a satellite tracking function? Now that would be useful.'

The crest of the hill rewarded them with nothing but a view of more hills. Though Birdie had been relatively cheerful all day, it was hard to maintain that now.

'We're going to die here, aren't we?'

'Come on,' said Nate. 'If you stop now then you definitely will die here. But if you can just keep walking . . . One more day, I promise. I know that we'll come across another human being.'

'The only people we're likely to come across are Robin and Fatman!' said Birdie in despair.

'They gave up long ago. There'll be a town within a day's walk. There are people everywhere.'

Nate tried not to think of the view from an aeroplane window, which told the real story.

'I'm so hungry,' said Birdie.

'Well, we're going to set up camp and I'm going to find you something to eat,' said Nate in a cheery fashion.

'I won't eat rabbit again,' said Birdie quickly. 'No way. If you're thinking about bringing me a dead rabbit then you can just forget it right now. Or a squirrel.'

'This is no time to be a vegetarian.'

'I'm not so hungry that I could ever eat a rodent.'

'OK,' said Nate. 'Rodents are off the menu. The forest is full of food. You've just got to keep your eyes open.'

'Hey! What about that?'

Birdie pointed out a fungus that was growing on the side of an old dead tree. She pulled a chunk of the bright orange spongy thing off. 'You can eat mushrooms raw,' she said.

Nate slapped it out of her hand before she could get it anywhere near her mouth.

'Never eat wild fungus. It's more often poison than not.'

Birdie was crying now. Nate's slap, though he had meant well, had shocked her.

'Then what can we eat?' she said. 'I am dying. I can't go any further without food.'

'Sit here,' said Nate. 'It's coming.'

50

Nate returned an hour later.

'I got supper.'

He was carrying something inside his sweater.

Birdie closed her eyes.

'You got a squirrel.'

'What with?' asked Nate. 'You're OK. I didn't get squirrel. But I found these.'

Birdie peeped through her fingers.

'Fish?' she asked hopefully. 'A bird that had already died?'

'You've got to be careful about eating stuff that's dead when you find it,' said Nate. 'You don't know what might have finished it off. The only time I would eat anything like that is if I saw a predator make a kill and it ran off when I approached. Like yesterday.'

'Fine, Nature Boy. What did you bring me?'

Birdie leaned forward as Nate opened the folds of his sweater for the big reveal. Upon which, part of dinner escaped and flew right into Birdie's face.

She stumbled backwards, flapping her hands in front of her.

'Get it off me! Get it off me!'

'Sorry,' Nate couldn't help laughing. 'I thought I'd killed them all.'

Nate laid his sweater on the ground. Birdie was silent with horror as she got a proper look at his bounty.

'Bugs,' she said eventually.

'Crickets,' he corrected her. 'Delicious and nutritious.'

'You think I'm going to put a bug anywhere near my mouth?'

'I know you're going to.'

Birdie sat down by the fire and crossed her arms.

'I'm not doing it.'

'Then go hungry,' said Nate.

'How do you know they're not poisonous?'

'The Native Americans ate crickets all the time. All over the world, people eat bugs. It's no different from eating shrimp.'

'I hate shrimp,' said Birdie.

'Well, you might hate these too, but I refuse to accept that until you've actually tried one.'

'You cannot make me eat an insect!' Birdie was starting to get angry.

'Birdie, we eat insects all the time. I read a study that said the average person unknowingly eats five or six bugs a day. They're hidden in flour. In sugar. I'm pretty sure there's a government quota for how many insect body parts can be contained in the average bag of flour and, trust me, it isn't zero. Get used to the idea. And that's not even mentioning the number of creatures that crawl into your mouth while you're asleep.'

Birdie covered her mouth with her hand. She dry-retched.

'This is a joke. This is all a big fucking joke. I want to go home. Call whoever it is put you up to this and tell them to send the helicopter now.'

'Birdie,' Nate said quietly. 'This isn't reality TV.'

Her face crumpled. 'I just want to get out of here.'

What Nate didn't tell Birdie was that he had never eaten a cricket either. He knew that they were edible because every time he'd taken a hike with his father and heard the chirrup of crickets by the side of the trail, his old man would rub his stomach and murmur, 'Tasty'. Then, if young Nate were particularly unlucky, his father would manage to catch one of the crickets and offer it to him for lunch.

'The Paiute Indians considered this a delicacy. You just pull the legs off and pop it in your mouth. Crunch it up. Go on, son.'

And then he would wave the cricket right in front of Nate's face and Nate would invariably run off screaming down the trail, leaving his dad convulsed with laughter, and the cricket was set free to become lunch for something less squeamish.

The joke continued into Nate's adolescence and adulthood, long after he realized that his dad had never eaten a cricket himself.

But it could be done. And that night it would have to be done. Despite the rabbit dinner of the night before, his stomach had been singing loudly all day long and he was starting to hallucinate the smell of baking. He didn't know how much longer he could keep going.

Though he thought it would probably be safe enough, Nate drew the line at eating the things raw. Instead he threaded the unfortunate critters onto a stick to make a cricket kebab. He hoped that the scary bits, the legs, the wings and the eyeballs, would all fall off into the fire, leaving only the body. That he thought he could handle.

'Dad,' he raised his eyes to the sky. 'I hope you're up there looking down on this.'

It wasn't a particularly rewarding cooking experience. No delicious smells filled the air as the crickets began to roast. The only thing Nate could smell was wood-smoke.

Birdie had given up complaining about the ingredients for that night's supper. She had resigned herself to another night without eating and simply lay down by the fire, drawing her knees up so that she was better covered by the housecoat.

Eventually, Nate decided that the crickets must be done. He pulled the kebab out of the fire and waved it in the air so that it would start to cool down. Alerted by Nate's movement that supper was about to start, for him at least, Birdie sat up.

'Mmmm, looks delicious, huh?' Nate said unconvincingly. Birdie shook her head.

'Bon appetit,' she said. She rested her head on her knees and watched him closely. Nate pulled the first of the crickets off the stick. The outer carapace was crunchy but still intact. The legs had not burned off. Nate tugged at them and tried to think about pulling the leaves off an artichoke. The image that came to mind, however, was of his cousin pulling the wings off a daddy-long-legs.

'I can do this,' Nate told himself.

But he found his mouth had gone dry. He had to force a smile onto his face as he brought the cricket to his lips. He opened his mouth and tossed the thing inside. Three crunches and a very difficult swallow.

'Oh God.' He leaned forward as the cricket went down. He held his fist against his lips to stop it from coming back up again.

'You never ate one of those before, did you?'

Nate shook his head.

'Then that was brave,' said Birdie.

'Or stupid.'

'What did it taste like?'

Nate grimaced. The taste was still very much in his mouth.

'Mostly it just tasted burnt,' he admitted. 'But beneath that, a little bit of nuttiness. Not great but not totally unpleasant.'

What was unpleasant were the tiny hard bits of cricket exoskeleton that remained in his mouth.

'Are you going to eat another one?'

'It would be a lot easier if I had a vodka shot to go with it, but yes, I am going to eat another one.'

Horrible though it had been, the cricket snack had set off a chain reaction. Nate's stomach had sprung into action and wanted more to work with. He finished another four. The fifth he couldn't face.

'Nate,' Birdie piped up. 'Don't throw that away. I guess I ought to have one.'

'Are you serious?'

'Since the steak's off . . .'

'I'm very impressed,' said Nate.

'I'm just desperate,' said Birdie.

He passed her the last of the crickets. As she reached for it, he abruptly jerked his hand away.

'My God!' he yelled. 'It moved.'

Birdie jumped to her feet and went squealing into the darkness. She didn't see the joke.

51

Another day, another long hike with no clear destination.

'I've been wondering,' said Nate. 'About Dean Stevenson. Since he's the reason we're both here, I'd like to know why you thought he was so special.'

Birdie could only blush in response. She'd been asking herself the question pretty much constantly over the past forty-eight hours. Dean Stevenson. For him she had faced death at the barrel of a gun, walked what seemed like hundreds of miles in a pair of outsized tennis shoes and, to cap it all, she'd eaten bugs. Had she known that was likely to happen, would she have bothered? Was he really worth getting cricket legs stuck in her molars?

What was Dean doing now? she wondered. Was he thinking about her? Had her plan worked? Was he going nuts with worry? Was he somewhere in that forest trying to find her? She doubted it.

And if she was honest, Birdie was starting to be a little ashamed that Nate was having to eat bugs for Dean Stevenson too. She glanced down at Nate's bare feet. He was right when he said that he had the feet of a hobbit, so rough and scaly from running around without shoes that they were practically hooves, but Birdie knew he must wish he had his own shoes on. She tried to imagine Dean doing the same thing: giving up his shoes for her. She couldn't. He wouldn't. That much she'd always known.

'Come on,' said Nate. 'I need a list of Dean Stevenson's redeeming features. I know he has good hair. My roommate told me that much. And super-fine abs.'

Birdie managed a smile.

'You don't want to hear about him,' she said. 'Tell me about you. How did you get into this whole eco-warrior thing anyway? You went to Stanford. You did law. You could have been anything. You could have been earning a million dollars a year by now.'

'Yes, and working a million hours a day. Almost certainly for something I didn't believe in. In fact, that was a defining moment for me. When I got an offer to be in-house lawyer for your grand-father's company.'

'Grandaddy offered you a job?'

'Well, not him personally. I don't suppose he has any idea who's working for him below director level.'

'I don't think he has any idea who's in his own family,' sniffed Birdie. 'I can't believe he wouldn't agree to the kidnappers' demands. I'm his only grandchild. His sole heir.'

'I wouldn't get too upset. It's usual practice. No one agrees to a kidnapper's demands up front. He's got to play the big guy. I'm sure if he really thought you were in danger, he would have agreed to what they asked right away.'

'But they said they would send me home piece by piece. You heard them.'

Nate grimaced slightly. 'That's true.'

'And he still wouldn't talk to them, to negotiate. It's not just that he's trying to psyche them out. He doesn't care about me. No one does. Never did. At least, not since Mom and Dad died.'

'I heard about that,' said Nate. 'They died young, right?'

'I was seven years old. We were in Gstaad for the holidays. Mom and Dad went off without me. I was in ski school on the baby slopes. They liked to do moguls together. They went off piste and got caught in an avalanche. They didn't find their bodies for three days. I was all on my own in the chalet for a night before anyone realized what had happened. Mary, my grand-father's assistant, had to fly over and pick me up.'

Birdie wiped a tear away with the back of her hand. Nate stopped and sat down. He pulled Birdie down to sit beside him.

'I think we need a rest,' he said.

Birdie nodded. She quickly pulled herself together.

'I have all these wonderful memories of them. They never got old. My mom never started to have surgery like Chipper's mom. Dad never made a fool of himself at anyone's Bar Mitzvah. It's not all bad.'

Nate gave a little snort.

'But sometimes I even envy Chipper's fights with her mom, do you know that? She's always saying she wishes her mom were dead because they've had some fall-out over an "It" bag, but I know she doesn't mean it.'

'I understand,' said Nate. 'I miss my father terribly. It was in his honour that I started getting involved with green issues.'

'You lost your father too?'

'A couple of years ago. Cancer. I was already a grown-up when it happened but that didn't stop it hurting like hell.'

'And your mother?'

'She's still around. You would like her. I'll introduce you to her when we get out of here. And you can introduce me to your grandfather. How about that?'

Birdie pulled a face to suggest that she thought the meeting might not go so well.

'He thinks eco-warriors are just a bunch of whacked-out potheads whose views are based more on envy of the rich than concern for the world.'

'Well, he'd be right about some of them. But not me. I hope that when I get you back to LA safe and sound, he might do me the courtesy of letting me finish the speech I began at the in-auguration of the Marshlands resort.'

'You're really serious about that, aren't you? Is that why you still came to find me after I ran away, when you could have just looked out for yourself? Is that the only reason you're so deter-mined to get me out of this place?'

'Not any more,' said Nate.

He offered her his hand to help her back onto her feet. Once she was up, he didn't let go.

Soon, something that was much more than a hill loomed above them. On the first morning of their flight from the kidnappers, Birdie and Nate had noticed the mountain range in the distance, of course, but neither of them had really expected to get so close to it. Full of optimism, Nate had assured Birdie that there would be civilization between here and there. It wasn't possible that such a wide expanse of land would be uncultivated. Birdie hadn't taken much notice either way. But three days later, here they were, standing at the foot of a veritable mountain.

'I can't make it up there,' Birdie said.

'We've got to,' said Nate.

'You can't make me.'

'The alternative is to leave you here to die. Birdie, we've been walking for three days. The kidnappers' house is maybe four days behind us. I figure we could be up this hill in a day and from the top, we'll be able to see more clearly where to go next.'

'This is not a hill,' said Birdie. 'It's a fricking mountain.'

'It's not so high,' Nate assured her. He looked up. It was a faintly giddying experience. The very highest rocks tore the clouds that crossed the sky. 'I have climbed higher in a day,' he said. He wasn't entirely sure he was lying. He thought he had climbed higher, but, of course, that was with all the right equipment: boots, ropes, day packs stuffed with water and protein bars to give him energy whenever he felt he was flagging. For the past three days he'd been drinking from puddles and eating insects. He wasn't even wearing shoes.

Birdie followed Nate's gaze up to the pinnacle and her eyes immediately filled with tears.

'I can't do it,' she said again.

'We'll take a view in the morning,' Nate told her. 'See what the weather's like.'

They built a shelter out of fallen branches and Birdie settled into Nate's arms. After three nights on the trail, she had lost the awkwardness of cuddling up to a man she barely knew without the aid of alcohol to dispel her inhibitions. At first she told herself that it was simply a matter of survival, a way to get through the night without freezing to death, but Nate's proximity gave her something more than warmth.

He must have thought she had fallen asleep. He stroked her hair. Birdie pretended not to notice and hoped that he in turn wouldn't notice the tear that escaped from her eye and ran down to the end of her nose.

52

The following morning, Birdie seemed different. She was quieter than usual. She didn't bitch about the chill in the air or whine about how in LA she didn't ever get up before ten o'clock. When Nate awoke, Birdie was already sitting up, warming her hands over the dying embers of the fire. Nate's sneakers were tightly laced on her feet.

'I'm ready when you are,' she said.

There was nothing to wait for. No breakfast to be eaten. Nowhere for Birdie to wash her hair.

They set off.

They didn't talk much as they began their ascent. It was chilly on that side of the mountain, bathed in shadow as it was. Nate led the way, picking out what he thought was the easiest path upwards. From time to time Birdie dropped behind a little. Nate waited patiently for her to catch up, extending his hand to help her over the worst bits.

By midday, they had made a surprising amount of progress. Birdie managed a smile when she saw how far they had come. Then she exhaled like a deflating balloon when she saw how far there still was to go. But she carried on. Up and up. At times they had to crawl on their hands and knees to cross a particularly tough patch. All the while the sun beat down relentlessly, turning even Birdie's carefully tanned cheeks pink.

In the sky above them, an eagle circled.

'Is he waiting for us to give up?' Birdie asked.

'He's going to be waiting a long time,' was Nate's answer. 'It's a bald eagle, by the way, in case you're interested.'

'Of course I'm interested.' Birdie paused to look.

It took them the whole day to reach the summit. And once they got there, the view from the top was beautiful but relentless. More wilderness, more trees. It was difficult to tell in the daylight whether there was anyone else out there. Nate and Birdie couldn't see a road, though at one point they saw a flash which was light reflected off either a car or water. Either one would be good. A car would be better.

They built a shelter and lit another fire. Supper was a few weedy wild onions and the nuts from a pine cone. It wasn't much of a meal, but the view from their open-air dining room was fabulous. They faced the west to catch the sunset. It was the perfect evening. Clear but for a few distant clouds that only served to make the change of colours more spectacular. The sky looked like the inside of a shell, radiating pinks and yellows as the sun dipped below the horizon.

At some point, Birdie reached across and squeezed Nate's hand. 'Thanks for getting me this far,' she said.

'Does this beat the Sederburg resort in Cabo?'

'You know what?' Birdie had to admit. 'It's not bad.'

And then, once the sun had gone down, there came an even more welcome sight. At first it seemed like a mirage. A hallucination. Neither Birdie nor Nate could dare to believe what they were seeing. A light. Not natural but man-made. And then another. And another.

'Are you thinking what I'm thinking?' asked Nate.

'People!' Birdie jumped up and down. 'Definitely. That's electric light out there. It's civilization! Hooray! We're going home. We've almost made it.'

She threw her arms around Nate's neck and kissed him on the cheek.

'Nate, I know exactly what I've got to do now. When I get back to Los Angeles, I'm going to tell my grandfather everything we've been talking about. He loves me. I'm the centre of his universe. I know that if I tell him what you've told me he'll listen to me properly and he'll be only too happy to reconsider his future plans. He'll stop work on the Marshlands resort. He won't start in New Mexico.'

'Would you really do that? You'll forget all about this when you get back to LA.'

'No I won't. How could I ever forget these past few days? It's true that I wouldn't have chosen to get kidnapped for real and find myself stuck out in the wilderness, but now that we've come through it, I feel that I've got much more from the experience than blisters. And not just an unusual canapé recipe. I can't wait to see Chipper's face when I serve crickets at my next party.'

Nate pulled a face.

'You will be the only guest allowed to pass.'

'Thank you,' said Nate, though he found it hard to imagine that he would ever really be invited to one of Birdie's parties.

Birdie jumped up again and climbed onto a flat-topped rock. She spread her arms wide.

'I, Birdie Sederburg, renounce my foolish consumerist ways and vow that from now on I will be a defender of Mother Earth.' She paused and looked at Nate. 'Do I have to wear patchouli oil?'

'God no,' said Nate.

'That is good to know. Anyway, where was I?'

She put her hand on her heart.

'You look very serious,' said Nate.

'It's a funny thing. I'm not really looking forward to getting back to civilization.'

Birdie took Nate's hands in hers.

'You saved my life. In more ways than one. Come on,' she said. 'Let's go and see if we can borrow a telephone.'

'Tomorrow morning?' Nate suggested.

Birdie grinned. 'That sounds like a very good idea.'

53

It was the day of the benefit. Chipper and Clemency had flown to Denver the night before, along with Justin, who anticipated that he would have to do much ego-stroking in order for the show to run smoothly. Dean arrived around lunchtime with his MTV crew in tow. They were kept very busy behind the scenes as wannabes by the dozen tried to muscle in on Dean's screen-time. One after another they addressed the camera, full of emotion, eyes glittering with tears as they talked about 'dear Birdie'.

'My thoughts are with her constantly,' said one girl who had been a novelty turn on *Pop Idol*. 'I can't stop thinking about her. She was so young, so kind and so beautiful. This is just so cruel.'

Chipper got a little angry. 'What's with the past tense? Will someone please tell that girl that Birdie isn't dead?'

Though the truth was that Chipper didn't know that for sure. The kidnappers continued to send their demands daily but there had been no more footage of Birdie. A lock of hair that the kidnappers sent to the Sederburg offices via FedEx was the right colour, but no DNA match. At best it was from Birdie's hair-piece. The detectives started to tell Julius that he should prepare to hear the worst. If the kidnappers weren't using Birdie in their ransom demands then it probably meant one of two things. They didn't have her because she had escaped. Or they didn't have her because she was already dead.

'In either case, there is no point negotiating with them any further,' said Sederburg simply. 'Mary, please schedule my afternoon so I have time for nine holes with the CEO of Supercorp.'

Chipper and her team would not give up. DD insisted on being involved as well. She said that she would dress all the female stars and Dean gratis.

'Don't let her anywhere near me,' Dean told Justin.

Chipper was only too happy to submit to DD's style expertise. And so she ended up wearing another creation by Makiko Clark, who was continuing with her bodysuit theme. DD chose a green all-in-one for Chipper. It was made from neoprene and the zip was cleverly hidden by a spine decoration that made Chipper look like a pre-schooler dressing as a lizard for Halloween.

Still, Chipper was excited. Especially when DD brought out the accessories to go with it.

'Now, Chipper, as you know Christian Louboutin does not ordinarily make shoes any larger than a size 42, but for you he has made an exception. The first ever pair of Louboutins in a 45.'

'But I take a 44,' said Chipper.

'They come up small.'

DD handed over the box. Chipper whipped the bright green platform sandals out of their tissue wrapping and cradled them as though they were puppies.

'Oh, DD,' she said, as she squeezed her feet into them. 'This is my dream come true. If only Birdie were here to see me. Real Louboutins.'

DD had a pair of shoes for Clemency, too. Clemency shook her head.

'I can't afford them.'

'They're a gift,' said DD. 'My contribution to the campaign.'

Clemency put them on and, despite herself, couldn't help but stand in front of a mirror and turn her feet this way and that, like a small girl in her mother's pumps.

*   *   *

The benefit began at seven sharp. First up were a girl band called Jailbait who sang their big(ish) hit 'Touch Me, Feel Me'. They were followed by a chanteuse who gave a rendition of Celine Dion's 'My Heart Will Go On' that was halfway between Whitney and Britney.

Dean's appearance was to be the climax. He treated the crowd to a rendition of 'I'll Never Forget You', which was to be his new single. It was an unashamedly schmaltzy song, and in the tradition of such songs, it inspired the crowd to bring out their cigarette lighters and hold flickering flames up to the ceiling. Which was all well and good until the manageress of the resort freaked out on the grounds of health and safety.

'Come on,' said Dean. 'We're not smoking. And this is for Birdie.'

The crowd cheered. The manageress relented.

Dean sang 'I'll Never Forget You' one more time. Then he held the microphone close to his mouth and addressed the main camera directly, as though he were looking straight into Birdie's eyes.

'Birdie,' he began. 'You and I, we've had our ups and downs. I didn't always treat you as well as you deserved.'

The crowd murmured their dissent.

'No,' said Dean. 'It's true. I didn't always listen to you like I should have done. I didn't see your pain. I closed my eyes to the hurt I caused inside of you. It breaks my heart to think that you put yourself in such danger because of me. You were a shining light in all our darkness. One good true heart in a world where so few are true. Your love was a rare and precious gift that I wanted to take back to the emotional department store. I never had such real love in my life. I didn't recognize it for the treasure that it was. I can only hope I get the chance to beg you to forgive me, because Birdie, if you don't come back to us, if something really bad has happened to you out there, then a piece of me will die with you.'

He ended the speech with a great, heaving sob. One of the female singers raced to comfort him.

'It's OK.' Dean struggled to regain his composure. 'I'm going to be all right. It's Birdie we should be saving our compassion for this wonderful evening. This evening is all about Birdie. It's not about me or my pain. Or about the song I wrote especially in her honour. Come on everybody,' he beckoned to the other performers who were filing onto the stage behind him. 'Let's raise the roof for Birdie one more time!'

Lighters flickered and yellow ribbons waved as Dean led his fellow musicians in a final rendition of 'I'll Never Forget You'. Having heard it three times in quick succession, the audience joined in, which especially pleased Justin since it proved for certain that Dean's song had the essential stickability of a potential top ten hit.

It was an emotional night. Chipper looked like a deranged panda when she joined the performers on stage to wish the crowd good-night.

'Should have worn waterproof mascara,' she said to Clemency as they headed for the after-party, which was being held in the resort's ballroom. Chipper had hired the caterers who did her parents' silver wedding anniversary party. They had decked the room out in yellow ribbons. Chipper was especially pleased with the cupcakes that had been decorated with edible decals of Morrie Ray's Birdie in a cage design, printed on ricepaper.

'You look great,' Clemency lied.

'Oh, Clemency,' said Chipper, enfolding her in a hug. 'I want you to know that since you and I have been working together on this campaign to bring Birdie home, I have come to think of you as a true friend.'

'Oh, Chipper.' Clemency tried to wriggle out of her grasp.

'It's true. I can't wait to tell Birdie how hard you worked to keep people on the case.'

'I don't understand why you even like her so much,' Clemency admitted at last. 'I mean, it seems to me that she's always picking on you. Making fun of you.'

'I don't feel like that,' said Chipper. 'Sure, sometimes she teases me but it cuts both ways and I get a lot out of being around her. And of course, I'll always remember the time she rescued me from the bullies at school. She became an outsider herself because she stuck up for me. That took a lot of guts. Plus, you know, when I found out what her life was really like, I felt like I had to look after her too.'

'You did?'

'Yes. The way she acts. It's bad sometimes but I know that a lot of that is her way of defending herself. She has adopted this hard exterior because that's the way she was raised. But ultimately, she is a good person. She's a three-o'clock-in-the-morning friend.'

It was hard for Clemency to believe that.

'But she was pretty nasty about me. I overheard her on the phone to you, referring to me as 'it'.'

Chipper shrugged her shoulders. 'She isn't perfect. You should have called her on it. She owes you an apology. I'm sure you'll get one.'

Clemency knew that she was about to cry, but it wasn't because of Chipper's touching speech.

'I'll see you later.'

'But the party has just started. Don't you want a Birdie cupcake?'

'I've got to make a phone call,' said Clemency.

Though Clemency would not admit it to Chipper, at last she too was beginning to be a little worried about the fate of her employer. As well she might. You see, Clemency knew exactly who had Birdie Sederburg and she knew that they were not people you would ordinarily trust to look out for anyone's best interests but their own. It had seemed like a great idea at the time. After that awful afternoon when she heard Birdie refer to her as 'it', Clemency had been beyond upset. She had quite literally seen red. It took enormous effort not to strangle Birdie as she slept. Clemency lay awake all night that night. She stared at the ceiling and ran through various plans for getting her revenge.

By the time morning came, Clemency had decided that she would hand in her notice and go straight to the tabloids. She would tell everything. From the truth about Birdie's nose job to the casual abuse she dished out to her staff. An exposé on real life behind the scenes with the Sederburgs would be worth six figures at the very least. Far more than the measly thousand she had asked Birdie to lend her. But then Clemency dug out her employment contract and read the small print. There was no doubt that if she went to the tabloids, the Sederburgs would come after her. She might end up losing twice as much in legal fees as she stood to gain.

Clemency's next idea was to redouble her old weight-gain campaign. She would put three spoonfuls of protein powder in every drink she handed to her boss. But though it would be satisfying to see Birdie hammering the treadmill in vain as her weight continued to edge slowly upwards, it really wasn't anywhere near enough to make up for Clemency's pain.

And then Birdie came up with her stupid kidnap idea and a lightbulb went on in Clemency's head. It was too easy after that. It was clear from the very first conversation Clemency had with 'Mr G' that he was a grade-one idiot. The meeting in the park only confirmed what Clemency thought. He was the kind of guy who couldn't get drunk in a brewery. There was no way that he would be able to pull off a kidnap outside one of the most secure venues in Los Angeles. He would be in handcuffs before he was out of his white van. It wasn't hard to track down an altogether more professional bunch who would step in and do the job properly.

Before she had her first op, Clemency had worked in security at a seedy hotel. That was where she first met Fatman. He had often boasted about the ways in which he supplemented his wages.

When Clemency called up, she pretended that she didn't know Fatman from Adam and he seemed happy enough with that. Even when they met face to face, he didn't recognize her.

It would be straightforward, he had promised. They would demand a ransom of half a million (an amount which Clemency was sure Julius Sederburg would cough up without quibbling), of which Clemency would take a hundred grand. She had set up a bank account for the express purpose. It would be quick. They promised that they would keep Birdie somewhere nice and safe and that she would be returned to Los Angeles in one piece. Not a hair on her head would be harmed. Now here it was, in an envelope, the hair from Birdie's head. And the ransom demand was so much higher. Almost two weeks had passed and Julius wasn't budging.

Clemency knew what she had to do.

'I see,' said Detective Bryden, when Clemency told him what she'd done. 'Of course, this means I will have to place you under arrest.'

54

Almost six hundred miles away, unaware of the drama unfolding in Denver as Bryden and his team prepared to swoop on Fatman and Robin, Birdie and Nate slept in each other's arms beneath a blanket of stars. The night was peaceful. Warm and still. Nothing stirred.

Then, stepping out into the clearing, as proud as any of its distant cousins on the African plains, came a mountain lion, the cougar that had haunted their dreams since they first heard its call. It was a female. Maybe six feet long from nose to tail. Her tawny coat was almost silver in the moonlight. Her enormous eyes were lined like those of an Egyptian princess. At the end of her tail was the black tip that had earned her the nickname of 'the painter'.

Nate woke first. He gently shook Birdie awake too, pressing his finger to her lips in anticipation of her fear.

But Birdie didn't shriek. Without saying a word, she sat up and joined Nate in watching their magnificent visitor.

Light-footed as any dancer, the cougar stepped up onto the flat rock that Birdie had used as her pulpit earlier that day. With a graceful dip of her head, she surveyed the valley spread out ahead of her. A veritable wild queen. All around was silent. The small animals that had chattered their alarm at her approach now fell quiet and prayed for her departure.

Birdie's heart beat within her chest as though it were a small animal with a mind all of its own. But she did not feel the fear she had expected. Instead she felt privileged. Slowly her heart resumed its normal pace and she found herself breathing in time with the cougar, still posed like a statue on that rock.

Without ever turning to look at Birdie and Nate, the cougar stepped down from her vantage point and continued on her way. Within moments, she was gone. As completely and silently as a ghost.

55

As soon as it was light enough, Birdie and Nate set off on the very last part of their journey. This day's walk was unlike those that had preceded it. No longer were they somber and fearful. Birdie actually sang and eventually persuaded Nate to overcome his shyness about his voice to join in on a rendition of Joni Mitchell's 'Big Yellow Taxi'. It seemed appropriate for Birdie's new-found eco-zeal.

Still, they were wary when they finally arrived at the first human habitation. The place was little more than a hut made of old railway sleepers and corrugated metal. While Birdie stayed out of sight, awaiting Nate's signal, he peered in through the dirty windows. It was lived in. There was bread on the kitchen counter and, most unexpectedly, a single wild flower poked its cheery head from a bottle that had once contained Jim Beam.

'Someone's been here recently,' Nate called, just as Birdie was surprised from behind by the resident on his return from the hills.

It looked bad for a moment. The guy was carrying a gun and looked as though he wouldn't be afraid to use it. He had a dirty patch over one eye. His clothes were ragged. Nate could smell him from twelve feet away. But his fierce grimace melted away when Birdie raised her hands in surrender and he saw that she was just as ragged as he.

'Please help us,' said Birdie.

'I got nothing,' said the man.

'We don't want anything,' said Nate. 'Except directions?'

The tracker had no phone but with the promise of a thousand dollars for his trouble, he agreed to drive Birdie and Nate to the nearest gas station. From there Birdie could call her grandfather's office.

'Where are we?' Birdie asked as they bounced along the dirt track towards the road.

'You're in Utah,' said the tracker. 'How'd you kids even get out here without knowing which state you're in?'

'Long story,' said Birdie. 'I expect you'll read all about it in the papers tomorrow.'

'I expect I won't,' said the tracker.

It was Mary who answered Birdie's telephone call.

'Oh, my darling!' she cried. 'Are you OK?'

'I'm better than I've ever been,' Birdie assured her. 'Can I speak to Grandaddy?'

'I'm afraid he's not here right now . . . He's, er . . . He's in a meeting.'

Julius Sederburg was unable to be the first to welcome his granddaughter back to civilization, because when the news that she had been found came through, he was on the sixteenth hole at the Sederburg resort in Long Beach. He claimed he was too overcome by emotion to make it back to the clubhouse in time.

'And you must send a helicopter for her right away,' he said to Jim Smith. 'Take her to St Marguerite's to be looked over. I will be there as soon as I can.'

Birdie waited for the helicopter in the car park of the nearest hospital to the gas station, where she and Nate had been given primary treatment for the cuts and bruises they'd sustained on their long hike back to civilization. Birdie was disappointed that her grandfather wasn't the first man out of the chopper, or even the last. But she was glad to see Jim Smith, who had known her since childhood (and administered her accounts). After so many years, she considered him almost an uncle. Indeed, he gathered her into a hug as though he were. Like Mary, Jim Smith was very fond of Birdie. Memories of her as a tiny girl still outweighed in his mind the vacuous nightmare she had become in her late teens.

'Jim! I'm so glad to see you,' she told him.

'Thank goodness we've got you back,' Jim said. 'We have been working so hard to track you down. The police have been on the case day and night. They found the house where you were held at three a.m. this morning. Those bastards who were holding you had cleared out, but we'll get them. Don't you worry.'

'I'm just glad to be going home. Jim,' said Birdie. 'I want you to meet the man who saved my life, Nate Hathaway . . . Nate, this is Jim Smith. He has been looking after my personal accounts since I was a little girl.'

Nate stepped forward, hand extended to shake, but Jim Smith did not return the gesture. Instead, his brow wrinkled with concern.

'Nate Hathaway, you say?'

'That's right,' said Nate.

'Birdie.' Jim took her by the arm and pulled her aside. 'Do you have any idea who this man is?'

'He's the kindest, most fabulous man I ever met . . . '

'He is a dangerous criminal. He's part of a notorious gang of eco-terrorists and he assaulted your grandfather at the inauguration of the Marshlands resort. There is a warrant out for his arrest.'

'Oh, it's OK, Jim. I know all about Marshlands. That was a mistake, but . . . '

'I hope to have a chance to apologize to Mr Sederburg in person,' said Nate.

'No chance.' Jim Smith gave a signal to his security men, who were already moving forward. Within seconds they had Nate in an arm-lock.

'What? Stop that! Stop that!' Birdie kicked and slapped the security guys ineffectually. 'You can't do this! Jim, you've got to tell them to let Nate go. He saved my life!'

'Birdie.' Jim put his hands on her shoulders and pulled her

out of the way. 'This is a serious situation. Come on, girl. Let the guys do their job.'

They were doing their job very effectively. Nate seemed to have gone limp in their grip. After so long with hardly any food, he had no fight in him.

'They're hurting him. Nate!' Birdie called after him.

'It's OK,' he said. 'It's OK. I'll sort this out. I'll see you soon.'

'Nate!' Birdie tried to run after him. 'Nate, I think I love you.'

'I know,' he said. 'I think I love you too. We're going to be together again. Be strong.'

Jim gripped her tighter. 'Birdie, you need to calm down. You've had a terrible ordeal these past few weeks. You're not thinking straight as a result. We need to get you back to Los Angeles and into hospital. The team at St Marguerite's is already waiting for you. Come on.'

And with that, together with the assistance of one of the security guys, he bundled her into the back of the helicopter.

'Thank you for all your help,' Jim told the staff who were waiting to see her off.

'Give the nursing staff a wave,' he instructed Birdie.

Birdie didn't wave. She was too busy trying to catch one last glimpse of Nate, who was being loaded into a police car.

'He's not a criminal. He saved my life,' she told Jim Smith one more time.

'Yes, I'm sure he did. You can tell me all about it later.' Smith brought out a little bottle of pills. 'But why don't you take one of these and have a little rest for now?'

In the back of the squad car, Nate pondered his predicament.

'You're in a lot of trouble,' said the officer who was cuffed to him. 'Why'd ya do it? You were a law student, weren't you? You had a bright future ahead of you.'

'None of us have got a bright future if men like Julius Sederburg can't be stopped.'

56

By the time Birdie got to the private hospital in Los Angeles, where her grandfather's favoured physicians awaited her, the entire world had been alerted about her miraculous return from the dead. The hospital lobby was thronged with reporters, eager to get an exclusive on her condition. And there, too, was Dean, with an enormous bouquet of yellow roses wrapped with a big yellow ribbon.

'Because I never forgot about you, babe. Not for one second. I have been going out of my mind.'

Birdie took the roses from Dean and submitted to a kiss on her cheek.

'Who are all these people?' Birdie asked.

'Oh. Them. Don't take any notice. They're just the crew from MTV. I've been doing this show about my life. *Dean's World*, they called it. They follow me around. On the set of *PCH*. When I'm at home. Primarily I just agreed to do it so that I could keep your name in the front of everyone's minds, sweetheart.'

'Send them away,' said Birdie firmly.

'They won't get in the way. Just act like they're not there, Birdie darling.'

'How am I supposed to do that?'

'I did a benefit for you in Denver last night. It was incredible, Birdie. All your closest friends were there. The girls from Jailbait . . . '

'I don't know the girls from Jailbait.'

'I sang my new single. I wrote it just for you.'

One of the crew handed Dean a guitar. He sang a verse.

'Isn't that the song you sing to Shannon in the series finale of *PCH*?'

'Sort of,' said Dean. 'But the lyrics have been changed.'

'Please just leave me alone, Dean.'

'Birdie, act like it's just you and me on our own in here. Reunited after a terrible trauma. Two people desperately in love.'

'But we're not.'

'Eh?'

'We're not on our own and we're definitely not desperately in love.'

'Come on, darling . . . She's just feeling a bit tired after everything she's been through,' Dean said to the camera crew at the door.

'No. I'm not. I'm just stating the truth. You never loved me, Dean. You dumped me on national television. I have no doubt you realized I was 'the love of your life' when your agent told you it would be a good career move. Well, over the past couple of weeks, I have had plenty of time to think about what we had and really, it was nothing. Because you're not capable of anything else. You're a big fat nothing too.'

Now it was Dean who wanted to stop the cameras rolling.

'Don't film this,' he said. 'She doesn't know what she's talking about.'

'Oh, for heaven's sake,' said Birdie. 'Just go.'

'Cut! Cut!' Dean was waving his arms at the cameraman. 'Will you stop filming?'

As Dean moved towards the cameraman in an increasingly threatening stance, the cameraman stepped backwards into the corridor. Dean followed. As did the production crew, all eager to see a fight. Birdie took advantage of the moment to shut the door firmly behind them. Though moments later they were back, hammering on her door and begging entry again, she refused to let them in. She pressed the panic button that connected directly to the nurse's station and sat on the bed with her hands over her ears until a bunch of orderlies arrived to escort her visitors away. With great pleasure.

'I have more important things to deal with,' she told them.

Birdie put in a call to her grandfather.

'I need to know what has happened to Nate Hathaway. At once. Tell Grandaddy he has to sort it out.'

'I'm sure he will, dear,' said Mary. 'He's just a little tied up right now.'

Post-game analysis in the clubhouse.

Chipper was Birdie's next visitor.

'Ohmigod, ohmigod, ohmigod!' She stood in the doorway and squealed.

'Is that MTV crew gone?' Birdie asked her.

'They're still in the lobby. But they're OK really. Did you hear about the benefit? That was my idea. I called Dean's manager Justin and he totally got on the case. We had T-shirts done.' She opened her jacket to flash one. 'And every Sederburg resort has been selling golf balls with your face on them.' She handed Birdie one of the balls. It was slightly battered. Birdie looked horrified.

'Thank you. I think. Where is Clemency?'

Chipper bit her lip. 'She's in police custody. Don't worry about her, Birdie. She's going to get what she deserves.'

'I don't understand.'

'She set you up! Her and the gardener.'

'You mean Nate?'

'Yes, him. Can you believe he's a drugs baron?'

'No. No, I can't.'

'Your grandfather is going to make sure Nate goes to jail for like a million years. Oh, I can't believe I forgot. Birdie, look at these.' Chipper indicated her feet. 'They're Louboutins! Now, when are they going to check you out of here? You look fine to me. Super-skinny,' she added admiringly. 'And now Dean wants you back, Emily B is going to be *sick* with envy. Sick as a dog.

We need to have a party. Your house? I'm sure I could get some more Birdie cupcakes from the guys who catered the benefit after-party.'

'Chipper, this is all wrong. I don't know what Clemency did, but Nate should not go to prison. He got me out of some serious trouble. He's a good person. He made me realize that I'd been living in some kind of dream world. You and I, Chipper, we've never worried about anything more than getting hold of the latest 'It' bag. Spending some time out there without my iPhone and my car and all those other things I thought I couldn't live without really made me think about what's important. I'll tell you something, it isn't Louboutins.'

Chipper looked down at her shoes. Her face betrayed her disappointment.

'Nate and his friends aren't troublemakers. They're trying to safeguard everybody's future. Can you believe that here in our country there are people who live in poverty because they can't get enough water to irrigate their crops, because some luxury development just up the road diverted all the water?'

Chipper seemed to be trying to follow Birdie's point.

'My family fortune is built on exactly that kind of development. Sederburg golf resorts have been developing sites all over the world without any concern for the local wildlife or the local communities.'

'But, Birdie, I just don't get it. I mean, your grandfather is a nice guy. Remember that charity ball he hosted for the dogs' home last year?'

'A tax dodge.'

'Really?'

'Oh, Chipper. You're so naive! You really think my grandfather cares about stray animals? He saved money by hosting that party. He knew there isn't an actress in Hollywood who won't go gooey-eyed over a puppy. And the coverage in *InStyle* was free advertising for the resort. My grandfather never did anything for anyone else in his life.'

'I can't believe you're saying that! You're all the family he's got.'

'And he's all the family I've got. But did he cut short a meeting to come visit me? Did he hell!'

Chipper's world view was being seriously challenged. She sat down on the chair next to Birdie's bed and tossed the Birdie golf ball from hand to hand. Seeing Chipper's worried frown, Birdie tried to soften the moment.

'I saw a mountain lion last night.'

'Ohmigod!' Chipper leaned forward to hear more.

Birdie recounted her last twenty-four hours in the wilderness, from the mountain, to the lion, to singing 'Big Yellow Taxi' with the man she really loved.

57

It was seven in the evening before Birdie's grandfather arrived. He asked Chipper for a few moments alone with his granddaughter.

'I'm sorry, sweetheart,' he said, placing a perfunctory kiss on her forehead. 'There was business to be attended to.'

'Of course,' said Birdie.

'But now I'm all yours.' Julius smiled and for a moment Birdie felt like she was a little girl again. Then Julius glanced at his watch and the moment was over. 'Though I have a dinner at eight,' he said predictably. 'Now, I need to know everything about your kidnapping and how you got out of there. Obviously, we know now that you were kept in Utah. The detectives have found the house, but there was no sign of the kidnappers. Do you think you could recognize them?'

'No,' said Birdie. 'They wore masks.'

'I see. We'll still find them. I'll have the police show you photos of every felon in the state to see if you can pick out the kidnappers from their eyes. Starting tomorrow. I know you need some rest.'

'I'm fine.'

'Or maybe Nate Hathaway will just give up the pretence that he doesn't know exactly who they are . . . '

'He doesn't. Grandaddy, we need to talk about Nate. Where is he?'

'He's safely out of the way, my love. You don't have to worry any more.'

'But you don't understand. You've got to talk to the police and get Nate out of custody. He saved my life.'

'He kidnapped you. And he humiliated me. I will not be humiliated.'

'If he hadn't got me out of that house, I believe I would be dead. I love him.'

'What?' Julius snorted. 'Sounds to me like having messed up the chance to get his hands on a ransom, Nate Hathaway thought he might marry his way into my fortune.'

'It's not like that. He doesn't want money. The ransom he planned to demand for me was that you stopped developing the Marshlands site. And the plot in New Mexico. Do you have any idea of the effect both those resorts will have on the neighbouring land?'

'It's business, sweetheart. Don't let it worry your little head.'

'I am worried. We don't need the money, Grandaddy.'

'Have you got any idea how much your lifestyle costs?'

'Not any more. I know what's important now. I want to go to college and study ecology. We can sell the house in Beverly Hills to fund it. I don't need to live in an eight-bedroom house on my own.'

'Let's see how you feel about that in the morning. Now, I've got to go to this dinner. Don't want to be late. You need to get some rest, so make sure it's lights out before nine. I don't want you to think about anything except getting better until tomorrow, and then we can start working on nailing Nate Hathaway and catching those other bastards. Now, do you think you could do something about your hair before Friday afternoon? It's looking kinda ratty.'

'What's happening on Friday?'

'You are going to open the newest Sederburg family golf course. We will show those people once and for all that the Sederburg family are not to be trifled with.'

'Grandaddy?'

'Yes, my love.'

'Do you mean the course in Orange County?'

He nodded.

'It's an ecological nightmare. I can't put my name to it.'

On the television, which had been running in the background throughout their tender reunion, a grave-faced reporter stood on a hill while the landscape burned behind her.

'Environmentalists believe that this will become a more and more common sight as the world heats up and pressure on valuable water resources increases as more and more luxury developments are built on what was once hallowed land. But is it worth it? After all . . .' The camera panned around. ' . . . these executive homes are in peril of being engulfed by the fires they may have helped to cause. Is it time to say no to the increasing encroachment of the city on the countryside?'

'You see?' Birdie drew her grandfather's attention to the television. 'Sederburg Golf Resorts are part of the problem!'

Julius ruffled Birdie's hair.

'I'm serious, Grandaddy. Will you think about what I've said?'

Julius Sederburg nodded and was gone. Having not seen his only living relative for more than six weeks, he had spent just over five minutes at her hospital bedside.

But he didn't leave the hospital right away. He paused in the corridor for a brief chat to her psychiatrist, Dr Friend.

'I don't understand why she doesn't seem to be more angry at these people who held her.'

'It could be Stockholm syndrome,' said Dr Friend. 'We see it happen often with kidnap victims. They start out agreeing with what their captors are saying in order to appease them and before you know it, they think that those beliefs are for real.'

'Hmmm. Birdie certainly doesn't seem to be herself. What can be done about this?'

'We're keeping her under close observation.'

'Good,' said Julius. 'I give my permission for you to keep her here as long as you need to. I don't want her back until she stops spouting her stupid nonsense. In fact, I don't want to see her before the weekend.'

Dr Friend looked a little perturbed. 'We can't just keep her in like that. We have to have a real reason. If my evaluation shows no areas for concern then . . .'

Julius Sederburg reached into his jacket and brought out his wallet. As he counted off a number of bills, he asked the doctor, 'Exactly how good a reason do you need? Whether my grand-daughter is mentally ill or not, I am disturbed by the things that are coming out of her mouth and I would like you to keep her out of my way until I tell you otherwise. Sedate her if that's what it takes.'

Dr Friend protested. 'Mr Sederburg. This goes against every code of ethics I have ever been a party to. I cannot take your money. My career is worth more to me than this.'

'How much more?' said Sederburg, getting out his wallet again.

Dr Friend's eyes bugged out as he stared at the wad of notes Sederburg pressed into his hand.

'There. I think that's helping your conscience already, isn't it?'

Julius Sederburg patted the doctor on the shoulder.

'What kind of a grandfather would I be if I didn't make sure that my granddaughter was properly cared for?'

Chipper Dooley flattened herself against the corridor wall as Julius Sederburg strode on by. Her heart was skittering. She could not believe what she had just heard. She knew that Julius Sederburg had a reputation as being a hard man when it came to business, but she never would have believed that he could be so cold about a member of his own family. The only remaining member of his family, as it happened. Had he really just demanded that his granddaughter be sedated?

It was like something out of one of those costume movies, where a girl gets sent to the asylum because she kissed a boy she wasn't engaged to.

Chipper had plenty of friends who had ended up in places like this. It had seemed so cool at the time. But when they came out, they often seemed slightly altered in a bad way. Addicted to prescription drugs rather than the ones they used to buy on the street.

Something had to be done. Chipper knew that there was nothing wrong with Birdie. Nothing at all. And she understood, for the first time in her life, that Julius Sederburg was an unscrupulous man. He didn't want to have Birdie locked up for her own good. He wanted to have her locked up because it wouldn't look right. His own granddaughter protesting against the opening of another golf resort. But how would Chipper help her?

Birdie was watching the news report on a forest fire in Utah when Dr Friend returned with his clipboard.

'Hello, Dr Fiend,' said Birdie.

'Ha ha, very funny,' said Dr Friend. All his patients ended up calling him Dr Fiend at some point. He had even begun to consider it a crucial part of their recovery. Or the beginning of a really steep slope into mental oblivion. One of the two.

He picked up the remote control and turned off the television.

'Now, I don't think we really need to be watching this right now, do you? It's just a little bit depressing.'

'Actually,' said Birdie, 'I do want to watch that. I want to know what's going on out there.'

'Well, of course you do.' All the same, Dr Friend refused to let her have the remote control back. 'And it's good that you're getting angry. You're hoping those bastards who locked you up got caught in the fire, huh?'

'No,' said Birdie. 'Why would I want that? I'm concerned for the environment.'

Friend laughed and made a note on his clipboard.

'What are you writing?' Birdie asked. She leapt from the bed, surprising Friend into dropping the clipboard on the floor. Snatching it up, Birdie saw that he had written 'Stockholm syndrome'.

'What does that mean?'

'It means you've been brainwashed. You're not concerned about the environment, Birdie. You're a party girl. A socialite. You're confusing your opinions with Nate Hathaway's, but don't worry. I can help you out with that.'

'I am not nuts,' said Birdie. 'I have not been brainwashed. But my time with my so-called kidnapper Nate showed me what I have been ignoring. What we've all been ignoring. Somebody has to take responsibility for the future of the earth. We can't go on building golf courses everywhere and pretending that it doesn't make a difference. In a bad way.'

Though Birdie thought she was talking relatively calmly, Dr Friend was straightening up from picking his clipboard from the floor like someone who found themselves picnicking in the presence of a bear. He held his hands out in front of him as if to ward her off. He moved slowly, stealthily. Birdie continued to express her concern for Mother Nature without taking much notice of where Dr Friend's left foot was going. It was going for the panic button hidden beneath the bed.

Seconds later, the orderlies were there. They whirled around Birdie like the ribbons on a maypole, quickly securing her arms and legs. A hand over her mouth muffled her protests as Dr Friend emptied a syringe into her arm.

'Now you will get some sleep,' said Dr Friend. 'And in the morning we will talk about this a little more sensibly.'

It was happening already. Birdie was under sedation. Watching the commotion from her place in the corridor, Chipper started to be afraid. She dared not go in there. Instead she made a run for the car park.

58

Chipper didn't know who to turn to. Clemency, who had seemed so wise in so many situations, was in jail. Chipper's mother was on a week-long spa break in Arizona. Chipper would have called Mary, Sederburg's assistant, but that didn't seem appropriate right then. The only other person she could think of who might have an idea how to get Birdie out of her fix was Justin.

Justin had just spent half an hour calming Dean Stevenson, who was mortified that his reunion with Birdie had turned into such a mess. He was racking his brains for a way to make lemonade out of that particular pile of lemons when Chipper called and gabbled out her tale.

'Justin,' said Chipper. 'We have to do something. We have to get her out of there.'

'How are we going to do that?'

'You're supposed to be smart.'

'Doctors don't just lock someone up because their grand-father says so.'

'I saw Julius Sederburg give Birdie's physician a bribe.'

Justin sighed. 'That's what you think you saw. Maybe he was giving him a donation for the hospital. Even if he wasn't, how can we prove otherwise? Were there any other witnesses?'

'I don't think so,' Chipper admitted.

'Then I think you should just let the doctors do what they do best.'

'Julius Sederburg had Birdie locked up because he doesn't want her to spoil the opening of his golf course.'

'Do you have any idea how powerful that man is? You start

throwing around accusations like that, you're going to find yourself in very deep water. Probably literally.'

'Justin,' Chipper put on her most serious voice. 'You made money out of all the stuff we did for the Free Birdie campaign, didn't you?'

'Well,' Justin hemmed and hawed. 'I made my usual percentage, yes.'

'Then you owe her your assistance. I'm not asking you to accuse Julius Sederburg of anything. I just want help getting Birdie out of hospital so that she can say her piece at the opening of the course. If we get to her and she doesn't want to be sprung, we'll leave her there.'

After a while, Justin began to think that Chipper's idea might not be quite so crazy after all.

The publicity team at *PCH* had been fielding a lot of difficult questions about the environment lately. They had got a lot of bad press for promoting the use of gas-guzzling cars. Though the heroes of the show were supposed to be surf bums – a group of people usually known for their concern for the environment, the sponsors of the show, a huge Japanese car firm, had insisted that the surfers always jumped into a huge SUV at the end of each episode. Dean in particular had been singled out as a hypocrite. While several of his co-stars had seen the light and bought hybrid cars, Dean insisted on hanging on to his own SUV. In Chipper's plan, Justin saw an easy way to resurrect Dean's eco credentials.

'You guys can't do this on your own,' he said. 'You're way too recognizable. The minute Dean turns up at the hospital he will be swamped by people wanting his autograph or to take pictures. And you, Chipper, your face is also too well known. Have you got an agent, by the way?'

'I don't,' Chipper told him.

'Then perhaps you and I should have lunch one day soon.' Justin's mind whirred as he mentally cast Chipper as the lead in a new series of *The Simple Life*.

'Well,' said Dean, 'if we're both too recognizable, who can we get to help us?'

Justin steepled his fingers in the gesture that Dean knew always preceded a zinger.

'I have a plan.'

59

There wasn't much time. Later that afternoon, Dean and Chipper climbed into Dean's Lexus along with a cameraman and a sound guy from Dean's MTV show. The production crew in another enormous car followed them to the hospital.

Meanwhile, Justin asked his assistant to clear his diary for the afternoon. He too was going to the hospital, but he had a couple of errands to run on the way. First he stopped off at the office of his good friend Eric. Eric was a cosmetic surgeon and he and Justin had been friends forever. Justin sent many of his clients to Eric to have subtle work done and in return for a discounted rate on nose jobs and ear pinning, Justin also kept Eric supplied with a string of lovely young dinner dates.

Eric was in a consultation when Justin arrived, but he soon wound up the conversation with the paranoid starlet he was trying to talk out of nose job number three to see what his best buddy wanted.

'Hey, my man! You come to take me for lunch?' Eric asked.

'Not today. I need a favour,' said Justin.

'You persuaded Dean to get that 'deviated septum' fixed?' Eric made air quotes around the words 'deviated septum', which were the perfect excuse for a nose job that people would have to know about.

Justin shook his head. 'Give me time. But right now I just need to borrow a couple of things? Do you have a spare coat?'

'Hey,' Eric held his hands up. 'What do you want my coat for? You're not going to spend the afternoon playing doctors and nurses with that foxy little waitress from Matsuhisa?'

'If only,' said Justin, wondering if Eric would ever notice that, despite his prowess as a flirt, Justin had never, ever actually gone home with any of the girls they met on their expeditions. 'Do you have a spare coat? And a stethoscope?'

'Hey, if you're intending to impersonate a member of the medical profession, I need to know what you're planning to achieve.'

'I'll tell you later,' said Justin. 'And I promise never to blow your cover when you're pretending to be a shit-hot Hollywood agent.'

Eric conceded defeat. There were definitely occasions when pretending to be an agent worked better with the ladies than the truth about his profession. Eric opened a cupboard in his private bathroom and pulled out a white coat. Then he unhooked his stethoscope from around his neck and handed it to Justin.

'Don't you need this?' Justin asked.

'Nah,' said Eric. 'All the rest of this afternoon's appointments are guys.'

Justin shook his head, remembering how Eric had told him that he often used the ruse of checking a girl's heartbeat to cop a feel of her tits.

'I'll get it back to you tomorrow.' He paused. 'Assuming I'm not in jail.'

'May the force be with you,' said Eric, as he always did.

'I love you, Eric,' said Justin. Which was actually completely true. Justin had been in unrequited love with his uber-hetero best friend for years.

In the Lexus on the way to the hospital, Dean and Chipper kept up a running commentary for the MTV cameras. Sitting in the passenger seat, Chipper was largely obscured by an enormous bouquet of flowers and a teddy bear that should have had a seat belt of its own.

'I realize that I treated Birdie badly,' Dean explained to the camera. 'I'm on my way to the hospital to ask her forgiveness. Her best friend Chipper here thinks I have a chance.'

'Oh yes,' said Chipper, parting the roses so that the camera could see her face. 'I think he has every chance. I've known Birdie Sederburg since we were children and I know that she is a very kind and forgiving person. She won't hold a grudge.'

'All the same, I'm feeling very nervous,' said Dean.

He turned to give the camera his very best smile, causing him to take his eyes off the road for slightly too long.

'Look out!' screamed Chipper as they narrowly avoided going under the tailgate of a truck.

'Sorry,' said Dean, regaining his composure.

'Can we turn the camera off for a while? I want to get there in one piece,' said the sound guy.

Meanwhile, Justin was also taking enormous risks with his driving. Of course, Eric had managed to get the full story out of him before he could leave the office. When Eric looked at him with those big brown eyes, there wasn't a secret in the world that Justin wanted to keep from him. Well, he just about managed to keep his biggest secret again but he spilled the beans about that afternoon's mission right away and when he did, Eric ran straight back to the bathroom cupboard.

'You need this too.'

He gave Justin the flashing red light he sometimes put on top of his car.

Justin didn't think he would find the guts to use that flashing light. As he left Eric's office, his heart was already pounding with the thought that he was about to put on a white coat and stethoscope and try to pass himself off as a shrink. But half an hour later, sitting in absolutely stationary traffic on the 405, with sixty miles between him and St Marguerite's hospital in La Jolla and time running out, Justin decided that something had to be done. The traffic-pool lane was empty. He didn't have enough passengers in his car but he did have a red light and Eric's ID.

Winding down the window of his BMW, Justin reached out and stuck the light to the car roof.

'Here goes.'

Justin set the light flashing. As if by magic, the traffic parted. He was in the traffic-pool lane and away.

Dean and Chipper got to the hospital first. The girl on the front desk was weak at the knees with delight to see Dean in person but her boss, a rather more matronly woman who would only have rolled over for George Clooney, in his underpants, stood firm by her instructions.

'We are not allowed to admit anyone to see Miss Birdie Sederburg,' she said. 'Dr Friend has left instructions that she is not to be disturbed without his permission.'

'But I've brought flowers,' said Dean.

'I can take them for you,' said the matron. She reached for them but Dean kept them firmly out of her reach.

'I want to give them to her myself.'

'That will not be possible.'

'Look, I know that Birdie has every reason to be mad at me, but if you just give me a chance to see her I'm sure I can explain. Her best friend Chipper here thinks she'd like to see me.'

'I do,' said Chipper.

'It's not up to her. Dr Friend has ordered that Miss Sederburg will have no visitors except medical staff.'

'That's outrageous!' said Dean. Though in fact, everything was going exactly according to plan. 'Birdie Sederburg is being kept prisoner against her will.'

'You'll have to turn that camera off,' the chief nurse told the cameraman. 'This is a private hospital.'

'Make me,' said the cameraman.

The nurse pressed a button beneath the desk and, as though they had been summoned there like genies, two security guards were instantly in attendance.

'You ready to run?' Dean asked Chipper.

'Is it time? Do you think Justin's here yet?'

There wasn't a moment to find out. Dean and Chipper and

the attendant camera crew had to set the next part of the plan in action regardless. They set off into the hospital gardens with the security guards in hot pursuit.

Dean and Chipper didn't get far.

'Stop!' said, Dean putting his hands up. 'And mind the face. We'll go. We'll leave the premises peacefully. But just let me do one thing first.'

The security guard loosened his grip just a little.

'I want to be able to sing a song for the woman I love.'

'A song?' The guard was nonplussed.

'Yeah. You know. Serenade her. Do you know which one is her window?'

60

Up in her room, Birdie heard the commotion as Dean and Chipper were chased around the grounds. Now she looked out of the window and saw him setting up speakers and tuning his guitar. Unbelievable. What that man wouldn't do for publicity! And what was Chipper doing, getting mixed up with Dean Stevenson's self-promotion plans? Birdie was angry. She shouted from her window, 'Go away! I don't want to see you or hear you.' Then she sat down on her bed with her arms crossed over her chest. If she looked out of the window, it would only make it look as though she had forgiven that idiot down in the grounds.

It took a while before Dean was ready to sing. In that time, the entire population of the hospital got wind of what was going on. Those patients who were allowed to roam the hospital grounds freely, gathered around Dean in a semicircle. Staff on their breaks joined them. Other patients and staff crowded the hospital windows to watch from inside.

Soon, only Birdie was feigning disinterest.

'Ladies and gentlemen,' Dean addressed the crowd. 'I'm sorry to disturb your peaceful afternoon, but there's someone inside that building that I really want to reach out to. Someone I didn't fully appreciate when I had her in my life.'

Hearing every word, Birdie tutted.

'As they say, you don't know what you've got till it's gone. And that's the name of the first song I'd like to play for Birdie Sederburg. It contains a very special message! A VERY SPECIAL MESSAGE INDEED,' he shouted. 'About the things

that really matter in life. About the person who's really important to you.'

Birdie sat up a little straighter on her bed. This really was too
much. Now he was singing 'Big Yellow Taxi'! That was her song.
Hers and Nate's. Birdie looked around the room for something
to throw at him. How dare he sing that song? He didn't even
know the title. He had no idea!

Birdie pulled a bunch of flowers out of a vase and was ready
to pour the water out of the window onto her one-time par-
amour. But before she could, the door to her room burst open.
A doctor she didn't recognize stepped inside.

'Who are you?' she asked the man in the white coat. 'You're
not Doctor Fiend.'

'No, I'm Doctor Nut-job.'

'What?'

'I mean, I must be a nut-job to be doing this.'

'Hang on,' said Birdie, 'I recognize you. You're not a doctor
at all! You're Dean Stevenson's agent. Get out!'

Birdie started to shove Justin back towards the door.

'Hold on!'

'Where's your hidden camera? Give it to me now or I'll call
for security!'

'Wait,' Justin pleaded. 'Give me a chance to explain. I'm here
to help you.'

'By filming me in my hospital bed?'

'I'm not filming anything. Look.' He held his hands up.

Birdie had the emergency cord in her hand.

'Don't pull that,' Justin begged her. 'I'm here to get you out
of here. Dean doesn't want you back.'

'I knew it,' said Birdie. 'Another publicity stunt.'

'He's trying to help you too. He's out there with Chipper
causing a distraction with his singing so that I can sneak you out
of this place into my car. We're going to the golf course so you
can confront your grandfather about Nate.'

'Nate! Have you seen him?'

'I haven't seen anyone and as soon as I get you to the golf course, I'm going to pretend I never saw any of you in my life. Now come on.'

Outside, Dean was getting to the final bars of his song.

'If the audience don't ask for an encore, we're stuffed,' said Justin. 'Come on.'

'OK.' Birdie started to put on her shoes. As he watched her lacing up her sneakers, Justin spotted the ankle strap of Birdie's monitor.

'Shit. We've got to get rid of that.'

'You got a knife?'

Justin patted his pockets. 'No. Have you?'

'I'm in a top-security room in a mental health unit. What do you think?'

'Goddamn,' Justin cursed. He stuck his head out of the window. Dean had stopped singing and was accepting his audience's applause. It all looked pretty friendly but Justin, who was more observant than most, spotted the two security guards in conversation with a man in a white coat. He sensed that as soon as the clapping stopped, Dean and Chipper were in trouble. But no one was asking for an encore. Justin decided to take a risk. He opened Birdie's window as far as it would go (which was not far enough for anyone to wriggle through) and shouted out through the gap, in a high-pitched voice, 'Bravo! Keep on singing, my love!'

'Was that supposed to be me?' Birdie asked when Justin slammed the window shut and turned his attention back to the ankle tag.

'It worked,' said Justin, as Dean launched into a unique rendition of the 'The Girl From Ipanema'.

'What are we going to do about this?' Birdie asked, as she waggled her ankle.

'I'll call my dealer.'

'How's that going to help?'

'He has one of these things. Never wears it. Clipped it onto one of his dog's collars so that it looks as though he's always in the house or the yard. I'll ask him how he got it off.'

'With a big knife?'

'We don't have a big fricking knife!' Justin was getting agitated. He looked out of the window again. The two security guards and the doctor were looking up at him. He jumped back out of sight.

'Hey! Ricky, my man.' Justin looked a little embarrassed as he slipped into street speak. 'I got me a little problem.'

The secret, apparently, was lots of butter. And being double-jointed . . .

'Shit!' said Justin when he heard. He banged his cellphone against his forehead. 'Shit! Shit! Shit!'

'But I *am* double-jointed,' said Birdie. 'And I have some Jo Malone body lotion. That should work like butter, right?'

Justin tried not to barf as he watched Birdie practically fold her foot so that the tag slid off.

'That was disgusting,' he concluded.

But it had worked. Now all they had to do was get out of the building.

Dean and Chipper knew that they had to keep the rest of the staff occupied until they got the call from Justin saying that he and Birdie were safely on the road. Dean had assured Justin that it would be 'no sweat'. After all, wasn't he the hottest thing on TV? But Justin knew that Dean's gift for enchanting the public had never been tested in anything but thirty-second shots. He wasn't Robbie Williams. He only knew two songs. And now he was playing 'Parking Lot' again.

'Come on,' said Justin.

'I don't think I can do this.'

'Of course you can. Before you got kidnapped, you were a world-class ligger. You walked into parties you weren't invited to all over Hollywood. You were legendary, Birdie Sederburg. All it takes is a bit of chutzpah. You've just got to look like you're meant to be there. Well, all we're going to do now is apply the same principle in reverse.'

Justin handed the white coat and glasses to Birdie.

'Now, you put these on. You're the doctor and I'm the concerned visitor. You're just going to walk me out to my car.'

'I can't do it!'

'You can, you can.' Justin was already helping Birdie into the coat. 'You have to.'

When Birdie was dressed in the coat, the stethoscope and Justin's glasses, he grabbed her by the arm.

'I have to hold onto your arm,' he explained. 'I'm practically blind without my glasses.'

'So am I with them on! How strong is your prescription?'

'We'll make it between us.'

Justin took the clipboard containing Birdie's notes from the end of the bed. 'Hold this in front of your face if you think anyone is looking at you.'

It was a big hospital and not every member of staff knew everybody else who worked there but, unfortunately, Birdie Sederburg's face was familiar to everyone. As she and Justin began their escape, they passed several people who looked twice, doubtless responding to the familiarity of Birdie's features. But as Justin had found when he walked into the hospital, the white coat was like an 'access all areas' pass. Nobody seemed to need to know who was inside it.

They'd made it. Justin was sure he was going to have a coronary as he strapped himself into the driver's seat.

But at that very same moment, upstairs in what had been Birdie's room, Dr Friend was just discovering the empty bed and the discarded tag. And within seconds he had pressed the button on the string around his neck that alerted the entire hospital staff that a patient was on the loose.

'This is a code red,' he yelled into the intercom. 'Patient 654 is not in her room. I have reason to believe she may be absconding. I need a lock-down on the entire hospital. Close the main gates at once. No one is to be allowed in or out until the patient has been recovered.'

The message to lock down reached the gatehouse thirty seconds later, just as Justin was negotiating the last dangerous curve in the drive at rather more than the prescribed ten miles an hour.

'Come on, baby,' he was talking to his car. 'We're home free. We're home free.'

But the nearer they got to the gates, the smaller the gap between them became, until it was obvious that the great iron gates were swinging slowly shut.

'Shit!' said Justin and Birdie as they realized the same thing at exactly the same time.

'We're never going to make it,' said Birdie.

'We've got to,' said Justin. He put his foot to the floor, praying that the sales patter he had fallen for when he bought the car didn't turn out to be just that. 'This baby is supposed to go from nought to sixty in point four of a second. I can damn well get through that gate before it closes another inch!'

He was almost right. But not quite, as the sickening sound of iron gates on extremely expensive paintwork attested. But though scratched, the car was through. They were outside the hospital. And soon the apocalyptic shriek of the hospital siren was a memory. They were on the 405 and heading south to the brand new Sederburg resort.

'Well, that was exciting,' said Justin.

'Thank you,' said Birdie. 'I know this car means a lot to you. Though instead of getting it fixed up, you might want to consider something more ecologically sound . . .'

'Don't start,' said Justin.

61

Back at the hospital, chaos reigned. Dr Friend called the police to warn them that Birdie had absconded in a dark red BMW. The California Highway Patrol promised to look out for the car, but in truth, they would not be making their very best effort. There was a big match on that afternoon and most of the patrol cars were more interested in the results of that than tracking down an absconding heiress.

'Where are we going?'

'We're going straight to the golf course, but . . .' Justin looked Birdie up and down. 'I think perhaps you should change before you make the speech of your life. Presentation is so important.'

'I know,' said Birdie. 'Shall we stop off at a mall?'

They pulled into a tiny mall just off the highway, which had no clothes stores but a branch of T.J. Maxx. The old Birdie, the girl who would blow the equivalent of the average person's monthly wage on a dress she would wear once, would not have been seen dead in T.J. Maxx. Not even if going there was supposed to be the latest ironically hip thing to do, as espoused by the likes of Chloe Sevigny.

'How about this?' Birdie picked up a navy blue suit.

'Makes you look like Jodie Foster playing a detective.'

'Perfect. I think when you sell rights to the movie of this story, you should ask Jodie Foster to play me.'

Back at the hospital, Dean had definitely finished singing. Along with Chipper, he sat in the hospital director's office, flanked by the two enormous security guards. They had been told that the police were on their way and that they were likely to be charged with all manner of offences from breaking into the hospital to singing out of tune. But Dean and Chipper didn't care. Chipper's eyes glittered with glee as she heard Dr Friend in the corridor confirming that Birdie had made it out of the hospital grounds and was on her way to God knows where.

'You have to tell us where she's going,' said Dr Grohl, the hospital director.

Dean and Chipper both mimed zippers across their lips and then giggled at their unconscious choreography.

'This is no laughing matter. Birdie Sederburg is a patient in this hospital because she is in need of round-the-clock medical and psychological supervision due to the trauma of her kidnap.'

Chipper snorted. 'That's bullshit. She's here because her grandfather bribed that man over there.' Chipper pointed straight at Dr Friend. 'I heard it all. I was standing in the corridor when Julius Sederburg left Birdie's room after his only visit here. Dr Friend told him not to worry about Birdie's condition. He said that he could see no reason whatsoever why she should be in the hospital a moment longer. He was ready to discharge her but Julius Sederburg said he didn't want that. He offered Dr Friend thousands of dollars to keep Birdie in here until he could be sure that she wouldn't disrupt the opening of his latest golf resort.'

'Is this true?' Dr Grohl turned to Dr Friend.

'Of course not . . .'

'I heard everything!' Chipper persisted. 'Birdie went from being fine to being sectioned right after Julius Sederburg left. Check her notes. Is that a coincidence? And check Dr Friend's locker. He's probably still got the cash.'

Dr Friend blushed deep red.

'Miss Dooley.' Dr Grohl fixed Chipper with his most avuncular look. 'Do you have any idea what you're asking me to believe here? You are making a very serious accusation.'

'I know. And I'm prepared to stand by it.'

'It will be your word against Dr Friend's.'

'And mine.' One of the nurses who had been standing at the back of the room suddenly raised his hand. 'I heard the whole thing too. I was in the utility cupboard next to Birdie Sederburg's room. I heard Dr Friend's conversation with Mr Sederburg and later I saw him counting money in the staff changing-room.'

'Oh God!' Dr Friend went from bright red to horribly pale. He knew what this meant for his career. Everybody in the room knew.

'I need to know if these two young people are telling the truth,' said Dr Grohl.

Dr Friend broke down. 'I needed the money! My daughter wants to go to Hawaii for a cheerleading contest.'

It was all Dr Grohl needed to hear.

'Well, this is all very different from what I thought was going on. Miss Dooley, Mr Stevenson, I'm sorry if you feel you've been handled badly. In future, if you suspect that something of this kind has occurred, you should report it to the relevant authorities right away. Dr Friend, as I'm sure you understand, I have no choice but to initiate disciplinary action. Nurse, I will need your written report. And I will need to talk to Julius Sederburg right away. In fact, I think I should have the police listen in on the conversation.'

Dean and Chipper squeezed hands.

'Should we call off the search for Miss Sederburg?'

'She needs to know what's going on.'

Birdie already knew the truth about her grandfather. When Justin told Birdie the whole story – about the conversation Chipper had overheard in the corridor – Birdie was disappointed but not surprised.

'Nothing gets between my grandfather and business,' Birdie confirmed grimly. 'Nothing at all. I must have been such a disappointment to him.'

'It doesn't reflect badly on you,' said Justin. 'You know that, don't you?'

'I know. And now he's going to find out exactly what kind of a granddaughter he raised.'

62

At the Sederburg Marshlands Resort, Julius Sederburg was circulating among his esteemed guests. It seemed that everyone wanted to ask him about his granddaughter. At least this time they weren't asking about her in that way that implied he had somehow failed in his familial duty by allowing her to grow up to be nothing more than a ditzy socialite. She had always been such an embarrassment to him. She'd never done a day's work in her life. The thought of leaving the empire he had worked so hard to create in her incapable hands made him feel quite ill. And now she had decided to become an eco-warrior . . .

'Yes,' he said. 'Birdie's still in hospital. Nothing sinister. She's just a little tired and weak after all the excitement of the past few weeks. It's understandable. I'm sure you'll see her back in the gossip columns before long.'

'Well, give her our regards,' said the guests. 'What happened to her was just terrible. May those hoodlums who kidnapped her be brought to justice at once.'

'Oh, they will be,' said Julius Sederburg. He would make sure of it. No one made a fool out of him.

Julius's guests happily drank vintage champagne while a live band played. But then it was time for the business of the ceremony to take place. Stepping up onto the stage, Julius quieted the band. Then, to ensure that he had everyone's attention, he nodded to Mary, who stepped a little closer to the mike and cleared her throat.

'A-hem.'

The crowd turned to face the stage.

'Thank you, Mary.'

Mary melted back into the crowd.

'Ladies and gentlemen,' Julius began. 'I am so glad that you could all make it here today. It's less than six months since we stood together on this spot and my golf pro here put that silver spade in the earth and made the first cut for the construction team. Well, what a few months it has been. There were people who thought that I would not be able to build this resort. There were people who thought that this piece of land would be better off left as it was. But I knew differently . . .'

Julius Sederburg was proud of what he had done with his life. As he looked out across his new golf course, his heart swelled. He wanted the entire world to see what he had done. He had tamed the wilderness once again. There was nothing that could stand in his way. He opened his arms to encompass the scene before him. Eighteen holes of golfing perfection. An adoring and grateful crowd. He'd brought employment and recreation to an area that had been nothing but mud and grass. Fit only for the birds.

This was what man was put on earth for, Julius told himself. To make it better for his fellow man. How could anyone not see the beauty of his vision?

'And now, ladies and gentlemen, I'd like to ask the lovely Miss Freda Lee to step up beside me and cut this ribbon.'

The elderly actress was helped onto the stage by a couple of bouncers. Even in her seventies, Freda Lee could be relied upon to make a few column inches. She had never been much of an actress but her personal life was legendary. She was on her seventh husband and could still fit in to some of the outfits she'd worn as a teenage starlet. That afternoon, in fact, she had squeezed herself into the glittering golf ensemble she'd worn for her part in a 1950s comedy called *Men Only*. It was quite impressive. Until she started moving and the discrepancy between the hot pants and the arthritic hip joints became clear.

'Thank you!' she addressed the crowd in a shaky voice. 'I'm so glad to be here today. Now, what do I cut this ribbon with?' She pulled out a pair of glasses and peered at the table in front of her, where a pair of shears trimmed with yet more ribbon lay waiting.

The crowd waited patiently for Freda to do her job. Julius tried not to get impatient, though truth be told, he was slightly regretting having booked the woman he'd worshipped when he was a teen. That pic on her website must be twenty years old, he decided.

Soon it wasn't just Julius who was getting impatient. The people at the back of the crowd were starting to shift. They were looking in the wrong direction: back towards the car park instead of at the stage.

'Well,' Julius attempted a joke, 'I didn't know we were paying you by the hour, Freda. Come along. These people want more champagne.'

It was no good. The joke hadn't restored their attention. Instead, more and more people were turning to face away. They were beginning to murmur. Julius was not happy at all.

'What is going on back there?' he hissed at Mary.

Mary pressed her earpiece into her ear to take a message from the security staff at the back.

'I think your granddaughter has just turned up.'

'What?'

63

The crowd parted to let Birdie through. Dean and Chipper, who had finally caught up with the other two in the car park of the golf course, joined Justin and followed her.

'Hey, Grandaddy!' she called out. 'Bet you didn't expect to see me here this afternoon.'

'No,' said Julius, plastering on a smile. 'I certainly did not. But I sure am happy to see you now, sweetie-pie. It's a lovely surprise. I'm real glad that the doctors decided you were well enough to join us this afternoon. Now why don't you and your young friends have a glass of champagne and I'll be right down to talk to you after we've got over the boring business of opening yet another golf course?'

Julius gestured to one of the waiters, who stepped forward with a tray full of glasses. But Birdie refused a drink. She just shook her head and continued to walk towards the stage. There was a murmur of surprise through the crowd. Largely because Birdie Sederburg was wearing what appeared to be a *normal* outfit.

'You don't mind if I say a few words, do you, Grandaddy? I know all these lovely people have been asking after me since the kidnap and I want to let them know exactly how I am.'

Julius nodded beneficently. 'Would you like to step up here?' he asked.

'I'd love to,' said Birdie.

She took the mike.

'Ladies and gentlemen, I'm so glad that I could join you here today at the opening of my grandfather's latest pet project. It was touch and go whether I would make it at all, I can tell you. The staff at St Marguerite's certainly are dedicated to their work.' She paused and turned to look Julius Sederburg in the eye. 'Grandaddy, standing up here together, you and I must look like the picture of a perfect family bond. The self-made millionaire and his socialite granddaughter. What could be a happier picture?'

Julius nodded. 'You make me look good,' he told her.

'Thank you. But what the people who are gathered here today don't know is that you and I have had our differences of opinion. You've often talked about cutting my inheritance because I've never done a day's work in my life and because you said I would amount to nothing. A *big fat nothing*, when you were being especially generous. And that was fair enough.'

There was a murmur through the crowd. Just where was Birdie going with this speech?

'It's true that I enjoyed the fruits of your labour without a second thought. I squandered your money on silly outfits and socializing with the similarly hopeless scions of other self-made tycoons. Like Chipper Dooley over there. I think you once said she wasn't intelligent enough to beat a chimpanzee in a game of tic-tac-toe. But she was smart enough to arrange a benefit in my honour while I was missing. I love you for that,' Birdie added, giving Chipper the thumbs up.

'Birdie,' said Julius. 'You can stop right there. I never said that Chipper wasn't clever. And I am proud of you, my darling. I always have been. Baby, please be reasonable. Cutting you off from your inheritance has never crossed my mind.'

'It doesn't matter any more,' said Birdie. 'Right now I'm telling you that I don't want my inheritance. When I quit this earth I want to leave it a better place and by that I do not mean somewhere where everyone in the first world has access to a golf course while children in the third world walk miles for clean water. This fabulous new golf resort – the only real 'baby' in your life – is an ecological disaster. It may look green and lush but that lushness comes at great expense to the surrounding countryside.

Already, local environmentalists are reporting an increase in pollution caused by the run-off from the resort hotel, the foundations of which have disturbed the water table, presenting an increased risk of landslip and collapse for established buildings further down the road. It's not just here. Other proposed Sederburg resorts here in California and in New Mexico present similar risks. You've seen the reports, Grandaddy. And you had your lawyers bury them.'

'Now look here,' said Julius. 'I won't have you upsetting my guests. We'll talk about this at home over dinner . . .'

'I don't think you and I will be sitting across a table from one another for a long time,' said Birdie. 'Not since I found out that you paid a physician at St Marguerite's hospital ten thousand dollars to have me committed until Monday, specifically so I could not embarrass you here today.'

'Birdie, that is the most ridiculous thing I have ever heard. I'm your grandfather. I love you. Why on earth would I have had you confined to a mental institution against your will?'

'I don't know, Grandaddy. Why don't you tell the nice officers who've come to interview you?'

Detective Bryden and his colleagues were by the drinks table, looking longingly at the champagne they couldn't touch.

'Ladies and gentlemen,' said Julius Sederburg. 'I apologize for this interruption. I will be back with you in just a few moments, when I've sorted this misunderstanding out.'

EPILOGUE

Julius Sederburg did not return to the stage The accusation that he had bribed a doctor to have his granddaughter committed was not something he could talk his way out of as quickly as he hoped. Charges were brought and bail was set. He found the money, of course, but was surprised to feel considerably more impoverished when Birdie refused to take his call later that night.

Birdie was busy finding bail for Clemency. Chipper told her how hurt Clemency had been by their constant references to her sex change. Clemency got out of jail and she got the apology that would have kept Birdie out of Utah. She wasn't out of her own set of woods, though. She would still face charges. But Birdie promised to help find Clemency's legal fees and they expected a good result.

There was one more surprise in store for Clemency. Dean Stevenson with a bunch of roses.

'I always kind of liked you,' he said. 'That's why I kept asking you to wash my car.'

Having been a boy herself, Clemency kind of understood his reasoning.

Chipper was just happy to have her best friend back in Los Angeles, but that didn't mean a return to their old routine of party, shopping, party. Birdie's speech at the golf course had struck a chord with Chipper. Not so much about her duty of care for the environment, but about never having done a day's work in her life. She decided it was time to change that. She had rather enjoyed running the Free Birdie campaign. Justin agreed to take her on as an intern. She looked forward to one day buying a Birkin with her own credit card.

On his release from custody, Nate went back to the MNA house in Santa Monica, but only to tell them that he wouldn't be staying. He was going back to law school, determined that he would use his skills to change things from the inside. He'd never attempt a kidnapping again.

A week after she got back to Los Angeles, Birdie had a date. She had not been so excited about a first date since the day of her first date with Dean Stevenson. But that afternoon's date with Nate would not require a thousand-dollar shopping spree.

Nate arrived as Birdie was struggling to choose between two pairs of Louboutins and some Manolos. She invited him into her dressing-room.

'Forget shoes,' said Nate. 'Let's just have a picnic on the beach.'

'I don't have a picnic basket,' said Birdie.

'How about that?' asked Nate, pointing at the 1960s chiller bag, which had lain at the bottom of Birdie's wardrobe since her first big night with Dean. 'Isn't that a chiller bag?'

'Actually,' said Birdie, 'it's a valuable vintage design statement. But if I've got some ice-blocks in the freezer downstairs, it would probably just about work.'

CHRISSIE MANBY

The day Emily Brown opens her very own beauty salon, she couldn't be happier. This has been her dream since she was a little girl. And she's even more pleased when her business starts to take off, especially after a celebrity endorsement from reality TV star Carina Lees.

But even with the Z-list celeb's support, things start to go mysteriously wrong, and it soon becomes clear that someone's got it in for her.

Are Carina's favours as false as her hair extensions? The search for the truth will lead to all out Spa Wars.

Available in Hodder paperback

HODDER

CHRISSIE MANBY

Marrying for Money

Happy Ever After? Don't bank on it . . .

Have you ever dated someone distinguished but dull – who pays for your dinner and drinks?
Have you ever developed a taste for someone tasteless?
Have you ever lain back and thought of Tiffany?
In short . . . have you ever thought about marrying for money?

In Little Elbow, hunting ground of the rich and famous, size does count – the size of a man's bank balance, that is. And the Grosvenor sisters will do anything to get their hands on a big one. But when faced with the choice between a Wall Streeter addicted to his cell phone, a software tycoon with no social skills, and a poor but handsome handyman, Grace and Charity Grosvenor soon learn that if you want to marry for money, you have to work for every penny . . .

Available in Hodder paperback

HODDER